BAKED TO DEATH

BOOKS BY CATHERINE BRUNS

Cookies & Chance Mysteries:

Tastes Like Murder

Baked to Death

A Spot of Murder
(short story in the Killer Beach Reads collection)

Realtor for Hire Mysteries:

Killer Transaction

Priced to Kill (coming soon!)

BAKED TO DEATH

a Cookies & Chance mystery

Catherine Bruns

Acknowledgements:

I am so fortunate to have such a supportive group of people in my life. Special thanks to retired Troy Police Captain Terrance Buchanan who is always willing to answer my questions, no matter how numerous they might be! A debt of gratitude to critique partner Diane Bator and beta readers Constance Atwater, Krista Gardner, and Kathy Kennedy for taking another journey with me. Profound thanks to Frank and Patti Ricupero, Amy Reger, Sharon Hmielenski, and Karen Clickner-Douttiel for the use of their treasured family recipes. To my own family—sons Phillip, Jacob, and Jared, and especially my husband Frank for his love and immeasurable patience. And as always, deepest appreciation to publisher Gemma Halliday and her fabulous staff who make it so easy for me to do what I love.

CHAPTER ONE

———

The compressed sand burned my bare feet as I ran toward the crystal clear blue water with brilliant sunlight cascading down upon it. I dog-paddled in, just enough so that the water came up to my shoulders when I stood and let myself sink into the delicious coolness around me. Ah, this is living. *Only one thing missing.*

The well-built man who dove in and swam toward me was a nice touch. He drew closer and walked the last few steps. My mouth dropped open in surprise as recognition set in.

"Nice bikini, babe." He winked at me.

I stared at the smooth, muscular chest in front of me, skin golden in the sun, and the wet, black swim trunks that clung in all the right places. I fought to control my rapid breathing before I started panting like a dog. *It can't be.*

"Aren't you Bradley Cooper?"

Bradley smiled down at me with eyes the same color as the water. I turned around, sure this must be a mistake, looking for any other signs of life on the nearby shore. Nope. We were the only two around. Was he really talking to me?

"Sally Muccio, have you been drinking again?" He wrapped his arms around my waist. "I was wondering where you were. It was getting lonely out here."

Okay, so apparently he *was* talking to me. Had *I* been drinking? I couldn't remember. "Um—"

"Don't worry. I'll take care of everything." Bradley lowered his face, and just as his lips were about to brush against mine, his phone pinged. He grinned and held up a finger then reached down into the pocket of his swim trunks. "Gotta take this, babe. Could be my agent."

I stared at the phone, fascinated. "It works under water?"

He studied the screen then flashed me another smile. "Of course. I bought it in Hollywood."

Well, that explained everything.

Bradley put the phone back in his pocket and sighed. "Gotta go, babe. New part. I'm flying to Australia tonight." He blew me a kiss and started swimming further away from the shore and me.

"Wait!" I said. "Where are we?"

He yelled over his shoulder. "Bahamas. Don't you remember anything? And it might be a good idea to start laying off your granny's cheesecake, too."

"Hey, that's not nice!" I shouted after him.

Bradley kept swimming, but I could still hear his voice perfectly. "Later."

"You're going the wrong way!" His phone started ringing again, louder and more obnoxious than ever. "And could you please shut that thing off?"

The ringing continued to grow louder until I was forced to cover my ears. I took a step forward and stumbled. Preparing for the water to cover me, I shouted, "Wait!"

Thunk!

I opened my eyes to find myself lying facedown on brown shag carpeting. The shower was running in the adjoining bathroom, and I could smell coffee brewing. I hoisted myself up on my elbows and looked around. The ringing of the cell phone was still going strong, but at least I knew where I was now. At my boyfriend's. Relief washed over me. *Dang. What a dream.* I really had to stop eating Mexican food before bedtime.

The ringing finally came to an abrupt and merciful stop. I reached on top of the nightstand for my phone and stole a glance out the window. There was at least two feet of snow on the ground and another foot predicted for today. Lovely. No Bahamas here, but another *B* word came to mind. I was in the Buffalo region—Colwestern, New York, to be exact. In January, of all months. Yes, it didn't get much worse than this.

I sighed and looked down at the screen of my neglected phone for the first time since last night when I'd arrived to spend the evening. Three missed calls from a private number. There was a text from my mother, asking if we were still coming for dinner tonight, and another from my best friend and business partner, Josie Sullivan, reminding me she was opening the bakery this morning.

A third text was from my baby sister stating that she was about to have a nervous breakdown. She'd highlighted the word *breakdown* with about a dozen exclamation points. Gianna was a recent graduate of Harvard Law School and taking the bar exam next week. She'd already convinced herself she was going to choke. I knew it wouldn't happen. Gianna was the brains in my family. She'd ace it.

Gianna had been assisting Josie and me in my cookie shop when we needed an extra hand. We'd been swamped with patrons the past couple of months, especially over the holidays. Now that it was January, we were convinced that the surge in business wasn't letting up anytime soon. Because of this, we were interviewing a woman for part-time help today.

Last week Gianna had been waiting on customers when one asked her how the studying was going. She'd immediately burst into tears. Colwestern was a small town, and most people were aware she'd been going to prep classes and studying like a fiend since she'd graduated last year. Josie and I were starting to think it might be a good idea if Gianna stayed out of the shop for a while.

I sent Gianna a quick text reminding her it would all be over soon and that she would do great. The phone rang as soon as I finished, startling me, and I nearly dropped it. "Hey."

"Hey, yourself. I was wondering if you were planning on coming to work today," Josie said. "You know, that little bakery you own? The one that opened an hour ago?"

I reached for my pink satin robe—a Christmas gift from my boyfriend—at the bottom of the bed. "Very funny. I'll be there. You knew I'd be late today. And I'm covering for you on Monday, remember?"

My cookie shop had gotten off to a bit of a rocky start when I'd opened it last September, thanks to a patron dropping dead on my front porch. After Josie and I had discovered the murderer, business had returned to normal and now exceeded my expectations most days.

"Better give yourself a little extra time to get to work,"

Josie said. "The roads are pretty nasty. Oh, and I've got some news when you get here."

"What kind of news? Is everything okay?"

"It's all good," Josie said. "I've been so busy with customers that I haven't been able to do much baking though. But the storm is supposed to pick up, and I'm guessing that will keep people from coming out. I know you want to spend a few hours with your man, and it's rare that he finagles a morning off, but get here because I may burst something if I have to wait much longer to tell you."

I glanced at my watch. Ten o'clock. "Okay, I'll be there as soon as I can."

The shower had stopped, and I flopped back down on the bed for a minute. I was thrilled that things were going so well with my business, but sometimes wished my boyfriend and I could spend one uninterrupted day without real life crashing in around us. He'd hinted at that lately, too. He'd also brought up cohabitation as well, but I wasn't sure I was ready yet.

A painful divorce last August had left me bruised and scarred. I'd been determined to swear off men for a while, but my grandmother had convinced me to go forward with my life and follow my heart this time. And I had done just that.

Something I should have done ten years ago.

The door to the bathroom opened, and I smiled at the man who stood in the doorway. He was wearing a pair of faded blue jeans and nothing else. His dark hair was damp and curled below the nape of his neck, and his midnight-blue eyes were fixed on me. When he smiled, my heart constricted inside my chest.

Mike Donovan had always managed to have this effect on me ever since his family had moved to Colwestern when we'd both started high school. The first time those deep-set eyes found mine, I was lost. We'd dated for two years, and I'd been convinced he was the man I was destined to marry. Some unfortunate circumstances had torn us apart, and while on the rebound, I'd hooked up with the man who later became my husband, Colin Brown. Our shaky-from-the-start marriage ended abruptly when I found him in bed with someone else.

It had taken ten years, but Mike and I had found our way

back to each other.

He walked over and sat on the edge of my side of the bed and gathered me into him, planting a soft kiss on my lips. I stared at his handsome and rugged tanned face. He smelled of the spicy aftershave I loved to inhale. Filled with desire, I ran my hands over his powerful chest.

"Sleep well?" Mike said into my ear as his lips brushed across it.

I giggled. "I don't remember getting much sleep."

"You were out like a light when I went to make coffee," he murmured as his lips traveled downward to my neck. "Was it a good dream?"

It took me a minute to even remember the dream. "Eh, I've had better." Then I recalled the unflattering comment. "Do you think I have cheesecake thighs?"

Mike stopped kissing me and drew his eyebrows together in confusion. "Excuse me?"

I pushed the robe aside and pointed at the olive skin tone of my leg and thigh. "Nothing. Um, I mean, I'm getting fat, right? You can tell me the truth."

His eyes shone as he kissed me again and reached down to untie the belt of my robe. His hand skimmed against my bare leg, heating it until I was convinced it must be on fire. "Hmm. I don't see any cheesecake here. Only perfection."

And in a split second, Bradley Cooper faded into a distant memory.

* * *

A little over an hour later, we were in Mike's new Ram truck headed for my shop. He had insisted on taking me to work since the roads were slick. He put the truck in park in front of my bakery and turned to wrap his arms around me. "When was the last time I told you how much I loved you?"

"It's been at least twenty minutes," I teased. "And for the record, I love you, too."

He cradled my face in his hands. "If you really love me, you'll marry me."

I froze at the mention of the *M* word. For the record, it

wasn't the first time Mike had mentioned marriage. He had hinted at the subject before Christmas but only enough so that I knew he'd been looking at rings. I'd begged him to hold off for a while. The very mention of the word gave me heart palpitations. Despite how much I loved Mike, I knew I wasn't ready. Yet.

He brushed a strand of hair back from my face. "Sal, these have been the happiest four months of my life. Well, since we first dated, I mean. I'm sick and tired of spending a night at my place and then back to yours. Just move in with me, and then we'll fly off to Vegas and get married."

"I can't leave the shop right now."

"Josie can handle things for a few days. Gianna can help."

I shook my head vigorously. "Gianna is in no shape to help with anything. Her exam is coming up next week."

"Another reason for us to get married right away. You move in with me, and she can have your apartment over the shop. She needs to get away from your loony parents."

I couldn't argue with that logic. "By the way, Mom wants us to come for dinner tonight. She's been asking for over a week now, remember? Then we're meeting Josie and Rob at Ralph's for drinks to celebrate her birthday on Monday."

"Oh, I forgot." He looked unhappy. "We really need to get away. Have some time alone."

"I already spend so much time at your house people are starting to talk. Mrs. Gavelli came into the shop yesterday and called me a tramp."

Nicoletta Gavelli was my parents' next-door neighbor. She'd lived there since I was a baby and had been calling me similar names pretty much since I'd learned to walk. They'd escalated on the day that she'd found me playing doctor with her grandson—at his suggestion—when I was only six years old.

Mike grinned. "Ah, the old lady's jealous." He grew silent and ran a finger gently down the side of my face.

"What?"

"You're beautiful, that's what. And you've been avoiding my question for weeks now." He reached for my hand and kissed it. "I love you. And I want to marry you. I wanted to marry you years ago. If I hadn't screwed up that night—"

I put a finger to his lips. "You didn't screw up. I never gave you a chance to explain. I should have trusted you more."

Mike wove his fingers through my hair and observed me thoughtfully. "But you're not going to marry me, are you?"

I blew out a sigh. "It's way too soon after the divorce. What would people think?"

He gazed at me with a determined set to his jaw. "Who cares what they think? This is our life. No one is going to tell us what we can and can't do. I almost lost you a few months ago. If that had happened—" His eyes grew soft. "You're the only person on this earth who matters to me."

A lump as large as a mountain formed in my throat, and tears stung the backs of my eyes. Unlike me, Mike had had a rough childhood. Abandoned by his father at the age of five, he'd suffered years with an alcoholic mother and an abusive stepfather. When she was dying of cirrhosis, he'd been the one to take care of her. Another reason I loved him so.

"I just need some time," I said. "It will happen. I'm not going anywhere. Promise."

He sighed. "Okay, I'll try to be patient. But I'm going to promise you something, too."

"Oh, yeah? What's that?"

Mike glanced out into the street, watching the snowflakes whirling around in the white winter wonderland. Then he turned back and stroked my cheek with his fingertips. "Nothing will ever come between us again. I won't let it."

I kissed Mike softly and let myself out of the truck. He waited until I was by the front door of the bakery and had turned around to blow him a kiss. He smiled, waved, and the truck roared off.

"Someone's been busy." Josie's large blue eyes shone as I wiped my boots on the mat just inside the door. Her long, auburn hair was pulled into a bun on top of her head. We'd been best friends since third grade when her family had moved here from Maine. She was an expert baker and decorator, and my business would never survive without her talent.

Right now she had her hands full. There were three customers waiting in line, and I could smell her delicious spice cookies baking in the back room. I felt guilty. Even though this was my morning to come in late. I should have acted more responsibly.

"Grab the cookies out of the oven, will you?" She asked as she collected money from an elderly woman standing in front of the counter.

"Don't forget my free fortune cookie, girlie." The woman grunted as she waved her liver spotted hand at Josie.

Josie bit her lip and turned away from the counter to ring up the sale. This was one of the few bones of contention between us. With every purchase, customers got a free homemade fortune cookie. Josie thought they were a waste of money, but I enjoyed seeing people's reaction to them—especially children's.

"Sorry. The roads slowed us down a bit." I ran into the back room, grabbing some oven mitts to withdraw the trays of cookies from the oven. Even though the aroma was tempting, I fought the urge to snitch one, remembering the Bradley Cooper cheesecake comment again.

Josie appeared at my side a minute later. She transferred the spice cookies to a cooling rack. "Customers are all taken care of. I can multitask quite well when I have to."

I bit into my lower lip. "Jos. I didn't mean to be this late."

She waved her hand dismissively. "After everything you've been through, I couldn't be happier for you. And Mike, too." She put her hands on her hips and examined my face closely. "He asked you again, didn't he?"

"Yes," I sighed.

"Sal, just marry the guy. He loves you, and you love him. What's the problem?"

I tied on an apron and turned my face away. "I'm scared." It was a relief to finally say the words out loud.

"Okay, you had a bad marriage, but that wasn't your fault. The scumbag cheated on you. Mike's the best thing that ever happened to you. Well, besides me, that is."

I grinned. "Smart aleck. Now tell me what the good news is."

Josie's eyes gleamed. "This is *huge*."

"Well, I know you can't be pregnant again so—" Recognition dawned on me. "Oh my God. Is it what I think it is?"

She reached into her apron pocket and waved an envelope at me. "We've been selected as contestants for Cookie Crusades!"

I screamed and clamped a hand over my mouth. When I realized there was no one else in the building, I started screaming again, and we threw our arms around each other.

Cookie Crusades was a reality baking competition show that played on the Food Network. It was filmed in Orlando, Florida, about forty-five minutes from Tampa, where I'd lived for a time during my now defunct marriage. Four teams of bakers competed for a grand prize of twenty thousand dollars. The money and the prestige would both be terrific for my business.

Interestingly enough, each show featured bakers from either the same state or neighboring ones. More often than not, the people selected knew their competitors.

"Do we know anyone who's going?" I asked. "This is so incredible."

Josie shook her head. "I didn't see any names I recognized. After the letter came by priority mail this morning, I went to their website and checked. They posted the contestants' names yesterday. I wish I'd remembered to check then. Anyhow, one bakery is from Albany, another from Jersey, and the third from Vermont. No worries. We'll kick butt."

"Wow," I breathed. "So when do we have to be there?"

"Wednesday afternoon," Josie said. "Rob's mom is going to take care of the kids while he's working. The competition is Thursday, which means we can fly back on Friday."

As much as I was thrilled, I hated the idea of leaving Mike and doubted he'd be able to come with me. He had so much construction work waiting that he could barely keep up.

Josie folded her arms. "I know that look. Don't worry. Lover boy will be fine while you're gone."

"I was thinking how much we could both use a vacation. Gosh, Florida sounds good right about now."

"It'll be your first time back since the divorce," Josie said.

I shrugged. "No biggie. It's not like I'm going to run into

Colin. Tampa's at least a half-hour drive from there."

Josie's face was wistful. "I wish I could afford to take the kids to Disney World."

"When they're older, and you can stay longer," I assured her. "You want them all to remember the experience. The baby's too little anyhow."

"I'm so excited! We've got to think about what recipes to use. And that definitely means we have to hire someone today. I hope this woman works out. She was the only one to apply."

I frowned. "And leave a new employee in charge while we're gone? I'm not sure I'm comfortable with that, Jos."

"Maybe we'll have to close down for a couple of days. We can figure out something. There's no way we can afford to pass up this opportunity though."

There were some fortune cookies cooling on parchment paper that Josie had made earlier. She handed me the tray. "Put these in the case for me, will you?"

I grabbed the tray and placed it on top of the display case while I reached for a piece of waxed paper to move them into the case with. I placed the cookies in the case two at a time. The last one slipped and fell out of my hand, smashing open on the floor. "Shoot."

As I reached down to pick up the shattered cookie, the fortune stared me right in the face.

Beware of coming events that cast their shadows beforehand.

"Wow, these messages just get weirder and weirder."

"What'd you say?" Josie called out.

"Nothing," I yelled back and reached down to straighten the contents of the case. Although Josie made the cookies from scratch, we bought the fortunes by the bagful from a novelty shop.

The bells over the door announced that we had another customer. The storm was getting worse, and I was surprised people were still coming out in it.

"Be with you in a sec," I said without looking up.

"That's okay, Sal. I've got all day."

I froze at the sound of the familiar, deep voice. *No. It can't be.* The hairs rose on the back of my neck, and my stomach muscles contracted into a giant knot. Slowly I raised my head and found myself staring into dark, brooding eyes. Eyes that were cold and angry as they met mine.

Colin.

CHAPTER TWO

———

It had been over a year since I'd last seen my ex-husband. When I'd first filed for divorce, he'd tried to force his way into the apartment I'd been sharing with a coworker. Probably the smartest thing on my part would have been to leave the state entirely and go home after I'd discovered his infidelity, but I'd been too ashamed to share the story with my family at first.

The past year had not been kind to Colin. His dark eyes were too large in a gaunt face, and his once healthy, ruddy complexion was sallow. Brown hair that he'd always kept short and well-trimmed was now long and held back in a ratty ponytail. He'd probably lost at least fifteen pounds. For someone who'd never been overweight, the change was significant.

I swallowed hard and tried to calm the anxiety rising within me. It was ridiculous to experience fear when I'd once loved this man. We'd dated for five years and been married for an additional five. The first year or so of marriage had been happy, and then, like Jack and Jill, everything tumbled downhill. As I stared into eyes I had once known so well, one thing was for certain—this was not the same man anymore.

"What are you doing here?"

His eyes swept over my body, and he gave me a slight smirk. "Looking good, Sal. I was hoping I'd find you here. You never answer your damn phone anymore."

A light bulb clicked on in my head. "You were the one who kept calling me from the private number last night and then again this morning."

He smiled. "Correct. Good to find you here and not still at Donovan's. I wasn't in the mood to deal with him and his macho attitude today."

The thought that my ex-husband might be stalking me sent a tremor of fear through my body. Colin had gone to high school with both Mike and me. Back then, I'd always sensed that he'd had a bit of a crush on me, but Colin never acted on it until Mike and I broke up. Those two had never run in the same circle of friends. While both had been popular, especially with girls, Mike had always been somewhat of a loner, while Colin loved to lap up the attention.

I glanced into the back room. Josie was on the phone with her back to me, probably taking an order. I was on my own for the time being.

Colin seemed to guess my thoughts. "Don't worry. I'm not going to try anything. I'm not here to win your undying love back, either." He flicked snow off of his jacket and made a nice mess on my blue-and-white checkered vinyl floor. He turned around to survey the shop with its three little white table and chair sets situated by the front window, adorned with tablecloths my Grandma Rosa had crocheted—two white and one beige. He reached up to touch the silver-framed artwork on my cream-colored walls, leaving a lovely thumbprint next to the frame.

"Nice place. I heard you're doing well."

Uh-oh. The reason for his visit was becoming clear in my mind. Colin wasn't here because of me—it was my shop he was interested in or more specifically, the money it was making.

He tossed his jacket over the back of a chair as if planning to stay a while. "I was beginning to think you weren't coming in today. Thought you might stay at Donovan's for a nooner."

My lips curled back in distaste. "You're disgusting. I want you to leave. Now."

Colin ignored me and sauntered over to my Keurig, bypassing the new Espresso machine I had recently purchased in favor of a Breakfast Blend K-cup. "Not so fast. We have some unfinished business."

"Don't touch my stuff. And we have nothing that's unfinished. We've been divorced for almost five months. I'm done with you. Forever."

Colin removed his cup of coffee from underneath the

machine, took a sip, and walked toward me. My heart thumped wildly against the wall of my chest, but I was determined not to show him any fear.

I sniffed at the air. "You've been drinking."

He shrugged. "What if I have been? I don't see where it concerns you anymore. But this." He extended his arm toward the display case and then in the direction of the tables. "*This* concerns me."

"What the hell are you doing here?" Josie snapped from the doorway.

Colin took a long swallow of his coffee. "Ah, Mrs. Sullivan. The Wicked Bitch of the East. It's been a long time."

Josie placed her hands on her hips and thrust her chin forward. "Not long enough. Get out. We don't serve scumbags."

Colin laughed and threw his cup in the trash. A few drops of coffee splattered and hit the floor. "Just give me my money, and I'll be on my way."

I drew my eyebrows together in confusion. "What are you talking about? I don't owe you any money."

"Sure you do." Colin ran his hand over the edge of the counter. "Part of this business belongs to me. And I'm here to collect my share."

Josie drew her cell phone out of her pocket. "I swear to God—I'll call the police if you aren't out of here in thirty seconds."

Colin cut his eyes to her. "I'm simply having a conversation with my ex-wife. The same ex-wife I encouraged to open a bakery while we were married." He leered at me. "Don't you remember, doll face? You told me it was your dream to run a business someday. And I said you should open a bakery. Especially since your best wench is so good at baking cookies and stuff like that."

I clenched my fists as my sides. "I'm not giving you one dime. We aren't married anymore, and you don't have a claim to anything. So get out."

He wagged his finger in my face. "Not so fast. I have a lawyer who thinks I stand a good chance at getting half of this business."

I locked eyes with Josie, who stood frozen with her

mouth hanging wide open. "You're only trying to scare us," I said.

He reached into his trouser pocket and handed me a card that read *James Latham, attorney-at-law*. "Call him and ask if you don't believe me."

The bells over the door jingled, and Colin's younger brother, Kyle, walked in. While the two brothers were similar looking with their dark hair and piercing brown eyes, Kyle was quite a bit larger in size than his brother. He was also three years younger than Colin, making him the same age as my sister, Gianna. They'd been friends in high school.

He nodded to us curtly. "Hi, Sally. Josie."

"Hey," I said. "I hope you've come to escort him out."

Kyle looked faintly embarrassed. "Sorry. I told him not to come here. He's freaking wasted. He got into town last night and is staying at some fleabag motel because no one wants him in their house."

Compared to his solid brother, Colin looked like a good stiff breeze might blow him away. He glared at Kyle. "Don't tell this bitch anything. It's none of her business what I do anymore. She ruined my life."

I sucked in a sharp breath. "I ruined *your* life? I worked almost sixty hours a week at Starbucks while you couldn't hold a job and screwed around with other women. So please explain how I ruined *your* life?" Tears stung my eyes as they always did when I got emotional or angry. This situation involved a little of both.

Josie put her arm around me. "Who the hell do you think you are to talk to her like that? She was the best thing that ever happened to you."

"Wait for me in the car," Colin barked at his brother. "I'm almost finished here."

Kyle looked from him to us with a question in his eyes.

"It's okay," I said. "We'll be fine."

Kyle shrugged and turned on his heel. He pushed the door open with great force as a gust of blinding wind and snow spiraled into the shop.

I squared my shoulders against Colin. I was tired of this man trying to manipulate my life. He was sinking into a bottomless black pit, and I'd be darned if I would let him drag me down with him. I'd been down that road before while we were married and was never taking that detour again.

"You need to leave." I folded my arms across my chest. "I have nothing to say to you anymore."

"All right. I'm going to cut you a deal. You give me twenty grand, and I'll sign my rights away to your business."

"You have no rights," Josie snapped. "You're nothing but a loser."

Colin narrowed his eyes at her. "This is none of your concern. It's between me and my wife."

"Ex-wife," I shot back.

"Whatever. The fact remains that Latham says I have a case. We were married when you thought of the business, and I was the one who gave you the idea. And now that you've recently bought the building, I might have a claim to that, too."

I was thunderstruck. I'd been renting the place with an option to buy but last month had gone ahead and taken out a mortgage on the building. How in the world did my ex-husband find out?

Colin went on. "I'll be back tomorrow. Unless you want me taking you to court, I suggest you come up with twenty Gs and fast." He reached for his jacket and then turned around, sizing me up again. "I should have known you'd go running back to that jerk Donovan first chance you got. He always did have some kind of magical hold on you. Maybe, for all I know, you were cheating on me with him during our marriage. That could put a whole different spin on my case."

The bells jingled merrily in the wind as he departed. I continued to stare after him in silence, wondering what I ever saw in that man.

I had no time to even attempt to digest the situation. Josie and I had just retreated to the back room to discuss my ex's antics when the bells were set in motion again. We peered out of the doorway to see a woman of about forty standing there, stomping snow off her boots, and shedding her coat and gloves.

Josie whispered in my ear. "This must be our prospective employee. Are you still up to interviewing her?"

"Of course," I lied and grabbed a notepad and pen off the

block table. I tried to shove the unpleasant meeting with my ex to the back of my head and focus on the task at hand. My hands were shaking, and Josie noticed.

"Sal—"

I shook my head. "This will be a good diversion."

We walked out of the back room together.

"Hi." I smiled at the woman. "Can we help you?"

"I'm Sarah Fredericks. I have an appointment with Sally about the job."

"That would be me." I extended my hand. Despite the gloves she'd worn, her hands were cold and frail to the touch. "Please sit down."

Sarah had shoulder-length, blonde hair with some premature gray mixed in. Somber, brown eyes were set in a pale, well-lined face that suggested her life may not have been an easy one. She sat down at the middle table by the front window.

This was awkward for me. I had never attempted to hire anyone before and didn't have a clue as to what I was doing. I was also afraid I might ask something that was not deemed permissible.

"Can I get you a cup of coffee?" I sat across from her, with Josie in the chair between us.

"No, thank you." Sarah looked uneasily out the window at the snow that was now descending from the sky at a heavier rate.

"Something wrong?" Josie asked.

Sarah shifted in her seat. "I'm a little worried my daughter's school might call and say they're being let out early because of the storm. I may have to leave if that happens." Her face colored slightly. "I'm a single mom, and I don't have anyone else to take care of her."

My heart went out to her. "Don't worry. We'll talk fast."

I couldn't help but wonder how she planned to take a new job if she had no one to rely on for babysitting. Josie and I were searching for someone to work alternate shifts so that we didn't have to stay until seven o'clock every night and could perhaps come in late one or two mornings a week. I wasn't sure how this situation was going to pan out and tried to decide how to casually broach the subject.

Josie seemed to have no trouble. "Sarah, how would you manage the job during school and summer vacations? We need someone we can depend on."

Sarah's eyes darted from Josie's face to mine. "Julie goes to camp during the summer for a few weeks. I was hoping maybe I could bring her with me sometimes. She's such a good child. You wouldn't even know she was here."

"Uh-huh." Josie narrowed her eyes. I knew that look well. My best friend had four boys—all under the age of ten. The words *good child* did not exist in her vocabulary.

I cleared my throat. "How old is she, Sarah?"

She smiled and produced a picture from her wallet. "Julie's eight. Isn't she beautiful?"

I took the picture between my hands and examined the photo of the lovely little girl with curly, blonde hair and dark-blue eyes that reminded me of Mike's. I sighed. Children were something I had always longed for. My ex-husband had made it clear from the beginning that kids were out of the question. I should have known then that it was a mistake to marry him, but I had been young and foolish and convinced I could get him to change his mind eventually. After seeing him earlier, the memories kept flooding back.

Ever the opposite of Colin, Mike couldn't wait to start a family, and we'd had several discussions about the topic as of late. Given how old-school my father was, my head told me to wait until we were married. My heart was another matter though.

Focus, Sal, focus. "She's absolutely beautiful." I handed the photo to Josie.

Smiling, Sarah leaned forward eagerly. "Do you two have any kids?"

I shook my head. "Not yet. Josie does though."

Sarah seemed to feel this was a topic that might win Josie over. "How many do you have?"

"Too many," Josie replied as she handed the photo back.

Sarah lowered her eyes to the table.

"Ha, she's such a kidder." I kicked Josie under the table. "I'd love to have a little girl like her someday."

"Thank you." Sarah beamed.

I picked up my pen. "What kind of experience do you

have?"

Sarah put the picture back in her wallet. "I love to bake in my spare time at home. Everyone raves about my oatmeal raisin cookies. I previously worked as a cashier for Wellington's Delicatessen up until last week. They had to downsize, and you know what that means. Last hired, first fired."

"I'm sorry." I made a note on my pad to call Larry Wellington. Mike had recently installed a floor for them, so I knew he had the number. "How long were you there?"

"About six months." Sarah twisted her knitted hat between her hands. "Before that, I did some babysitting out of my home."

"So you've never actually worked in a bakery?" Josie asked.

Sarah's face turned crimson. "No, but I'm a quick learner." She gave me a pleading look. "I really need the job."

I bit into my lower lip. I wanted to help the woman, but this wasn't sounding ideal for us. I worried about having the little girl in my bakery. Not that she wasn't welcome, but what if she got hurt somehow? The word "lawsuit" danced before my eyes in bright lights. It was too much of a risk for me to take.

Sarah's phone buzzed, and she glanced down at the screen. "Shoot. The kids are on their way home. I'm going to have to leave." She stared at us nervously. "I'm really sorry."

"It's fine," I assured her. "I think we're done here anyway."

The three of us got to our feet, and I extended my hand to Sarah. "I'll let you know our decision by tomorrow."

"Okay." Her face was optimistic. "I really enjoyed meeting both of you. I hope you'll give me a chance. I won't let you down."

The bells over the door chimed as she departed, her body hunched over to protect herself from the wind of the storm.

Josie put her hands on her hips. "I know what you're thinking, Sal, and you might as well forget it. There's no way this is going to work."

I sighed. "But I really want to help her."

Before Josie could respond, the front door was pushed open, and a young woman in her early twenties blew in along with a large gust of snow.

"Whew!" the girl said. "That wind out there is totally wild!" She glanced at me. "Let's see. You're Sally, and this must be Josie."

Josie looked her up and down. "Can we help you, Miss—?"

She laughed and held out her hand to us. "Mitzi Graber. I saw your ad in the window as I was driving by and was wondering if I could fill out an application."

"Uh, sure." Josie nodded to the chair vacated by Sarah. "Please have a seat."

Mitzi draped her coat across the back of the chair and crossed her legs. She was smartly dressed in a black woolen skirt with a white angora sweater and black boots. Her short, dark hair was cut into a bob, and a sprinkle of freckles covered a tiny upturned nose. Blue eyes that were both inquisitive and sharp roamed around my shop, observing everything at once.

She sniffed. "You're baking spice cookies. Maybe some chocolate ones, too."

My mouth opened in surprise. "You either have baking experience or a great sense of smell."

Mitzi laughed. "My parents used to own a bakery. I practically grew up there."

Josie looked intrigued. "Did you do much baking or decorating?"

Mitzi nodded. "I've done it all. I make birthday cakes when I have spare time. Mostly for kids' parties."

"Do you have any children?" Josie asked.

I kicked her under the table again. I knew this was one question we were not allowed to ask.

"Err, what I mean is," Josie said, "I have four kids and was wondering if yours might want some playmates."

I rolled my eyes at her with the sudden urge to smack my head against something hard.

Mitzi laughed. "Nope. No kids, and I'm not married. Just a boyfriend who works too hard."

I smiled. "I know something about that, too."

"I saw you and your guy picking up takeout last night at the Mexican restaurant around the corner," Mitzi said. "Isn't he a construction worker?"

Surprised, I nodded.

She grinned. "He's totally hot."

Heat warmed my face. I knew Mike was hot, too. Heck, the whole town knew it. Still, her comment made me slightly uneasy. And extremely possessive.

Mitzi's smile disappeared. "I'm sorry. I guess that wasn't an appropriate thing to say."

"It's fine, really," I lied. "So would you be okay with rotating hours to accommodate both of our schedules?"

"No problem whatsoever," Mitzi said. "I can bake, run the register, and wait on customers. A little bit of everything. And I love trying out new recipes."

"What happened to your parents' bakery?" Josie asked.

Mitzi lowered her eyes to the floor. "Business died off, so they only have an online bakery now. No actual storefront, but they're working on it."

"That's great to hear." I made another note on my pad. "Do you have any references?"

Mitzi looked at me in surprise. "Well, just my parents. I can give you their home phone number if you want to speak with them."

"Probably not necessary," Josie said.

I extended my foot under the table again. Josie's leg was probably black and blue by now.

Mitzi handed me back the application that she had been completing while we were talking, and I glanced at it. "We'll be making a decision later today. You'll hear back from us by tomorrow, either way."

She grinned as she shook our hands. "It was great to meet you both. I hope you'll consider hiring me. I think it would be a blast to work here."

Mitzi put her coat on and walked out into the swirling snow. She turned around to wave at us gaily through the window.

"I like her," Josie said. "And she's got experience. As far as I'm concerned, she's hired."

"I don't know," I said. "There's something about her that bugs me. I can't put my finger on it. Maybe it's because she's so forward."

* * *

The storm finally stopped in late afternoon, resulting in another foot of fresh fallen snow. I hated January in New York. Darkness fell so early in the evening that by 6:45 the sky was pitch-black with only a sliver of the moon showing.

The rest of the afternoon was slow after Colin's departure. We'd already figured people wouldn't be braving the storm if they didn't have to, so it was a good time for Josie and me to catch up on some baking, discuss recipes for Cookie Crusades, and reach a decision about our hired help.

I'd called Wellington's Delicatessen and been told that while Sarah had been a good and honest employee, there were a few occasions when she'd called in sick or had to leave early because of her daughter. I'd tried to phone Mitzi's parents but had only gotten voice mail. I didn't leave a message. Would they really give their own daughter a bad reference? Highly unlikely.

"Well? Should I call Mitzi and ask her if she can start on Monday?" Josie asked.

I sighed and stared out the window into the darkness. "Yeah, I guess. I feel like such a creep. I know Sarah really needs this job. More so than Mitzi, I'm betting."

"Do you want me to call Sarah, too?" Josie asked.

"No, I should do it." My phone pinged, and I glanced down at a message from Mike. *Running late. Should have known I wouldn't get out on time. Can you get a ride? Meet you at your parents.*

I texted back. *No problem. Be careful. Love you.*

I got an instant *Love you more* back.

Josie glanced over my shoulder at the screen and grinned. "Aw. How cute."

"Shut up." I smiled and then dialed my parents' house. My grandmother answered on the first ring. "Hey. Could Dad swing over to pick me up?"

"Yes. I will tell him," Grandma Rosa replied. "What about your young man? Will he not be coming?"

"Mike will be there," I assured her. "He got stuck at a

job and is running late."

"He works too hard. Your father is leaving now. He has a surprise he wants to show you as well." Grandma Rosa snorted into the phone. "The man is not right in the head."

My father, Domenic Muccio, was sixty-five years old and in perfect health. Ever since he'd retired from the railroad a year ago, he'd developed an obsession with funerals and death. *His* death, to be precise. I didn't know of anyone else who had an annual subscription to *Coffins Are Us.* He and my mother had been married for thirty years and, as long as I could remember, had always been very much in love. Their relationship was a bit of an oddity since my mother behaved like a teenager most days, and he acted like he was on his last leg. But, hey, since it seemed to work for them, who was I to judge?

I disconnected and turned to my best friend. "I wish there was something I could do to help Sarah."

"You can't save the world, Sal. Speaking of which, what are you going to do about that dirtbag ex-husband of yours?" Josie didn't exactly mince words when it came to Colin.

I grabbed a broom and started to sweep the floor. "I don't know. I guess I'll have to go see Colin's lawyer on Monday and find out if he's telling the truth."

"If this guy's representing Colin, he won't tell you anything," Josie pointed out. "What about Gianna? Does she know anyone who specializes in matrimonial law?"

"Probably." I blew out a long breath. Where was he getting the money for representation? Maybe he was convinced he'd win and had arranged to pay the lawyer out of his winnings. A flicker of doubt crept into my head. Was it possible that Colin could really take the shop I worked so hard for—away from me? I'd definitely have to talk with Gianna.

A horn tooted from outside. We went to the window, but it was too dark to see anything. At that moment, my father bustled in, his round face bright red from the cold. He was dressed all in black—thermal jacket, slacks, and gloves. His balding head was topped off by a layer of snowflakes.

"Is it snowing again?" Josie groaned.

"Only some flurries. No big deal." He pointed at the display case. "I need a fortune cookie, Sal. It's important to know what kind of day I'm going to have tomorrow."

Josie put her coat on. "Domenic, what's the big fascination with those things?"

My father stared at her in amazement. "What's not to be fascinated about? There's a lot of truth in those little messages, let me tell you."

I handed him two fortune cookies, but he shook his head and handed one back to me. "No, no. You have to open one, too, my sweet girl."

Not again. I groaned. "Dad, I'm really not in the mood right now."

He gave me a wistful, almost pleading expression. My father knew well how to guilt me into things I didn't want to do.

I gave in. "Oh, all right."

Dad glanced at my best friend. "How about you, Josie?"

She gave a slight shake of her head. "Um, no, thanks. I'll enjoy hearing about yours."

We waited until my father cracked his cookie open and watched his lips move silently as he read the message. "*Savor your new adventure while it lasts.*"

I drew my eyebrows together. I really hoped this was not a veiled reference to a coffin. "Guess that one missed the mark, Dad."

"No way. It makes perfect sense. Step out onto the front porch and tell me what you see," my father instructed.

We followed him out into the darkened night and stood on my lighted porch. He pointed to the vehicle parked at the side of the curb.

"Did you get a new car?" I squinted for a closer look and then thought my eyes might fall out of my head.

Josie let out a little squeak resembling a mouse.

My father was driving a shiny black hearse.

"Dear Lord!" Josie exploded. "Where did you get that thing from?"

My father grinned with pride. "It's part of my new job. I'm now employed as a part-time driver for Phibbins Mortuary. They said I could bring it home tonight since I have an assignment early tomorrow morning. Hurry up, Sal. Wait till you see how smooth this baby rides. Josie, do you need a lift, too?"

"No thanks. I'm good." Josie whispered in my ear, "I'm so good, but it looks like you just ran out of luck."

I slumped against the front door. "I can't believe I have to ride in that thing."

"Better check that fortune cookie," Josie teased. "It probably says, 'Get ready for the wildest journey of your lifetime.'"

"Hurry up, Sal!" My father got behind the wheel and started to honk the horn.

Wincing, I held up a finger, and he nodded with impatience. Josie and I went back into the shop and switched the lights off.

"I'll lock the back door since I'm parked in the alley." Josie glanced at me. "Still feel like going out tonight?"

"Of course. I wouldn't dream of not going out—we're celebrating my best friend's birthday! Let's make it for ten since Mike's running late."

Josie hesitated. "But Colin—"

I shook my head. "I'm not going to let Colin ruin my life anymore. He tried that once, and I'll be damned if he gets another chance."

Josie gave me a hug. "That's my girl. I'll see you guys in a couple of hours." She winked. "Drive safely."

I went to the front door and changed the sign over to *Closed*. I waited until she had slammed the back door then locked and shut the front door behind me. I stared down at the fortune cookie still in my hand. With a bit of trepidation, I removed the strip of paper then held it up against the porch light to see.

It never pays to kick a skunk.

I looked at the message again and immediately burst into laughter. Well, there was nothing to fear from this message. As I had suspected all along, I'd been fretting over these sayings for no reason. I put the strip of paper in my pocket and got into the passenger side of the hearse. I scolded myself for even entertaining the notion that these fortunes might actually mean something. The whole idea was just so ridiculous.

CHAPTER THREE

I glanced at my watch—after 9:00 and still no Mike. My family was gathered around the cherrywood dining room table. My father sat at the head, the obituary section of today's paper spread out in front of him and a wine glass to his left. This was his daily dinnertime routine. My mother stood behind him, concentrating on giving him a neck massage.

Gianna sat across from me. She'd already polished off three glasses of wine and hummed away to herself under her breath. Occasionally, she'd stop for a beat to rest her head down on the table.

Gianna had everything going for her. She was intelligent and beautiful. People always said we resembled twins. We both had large brown eyes the color of milk chocolate, but her hair was a shade lighter than mine, a rich chestnut color that flowed around her shoulders in perfect waves. I, on the other hand, spent a small fortune on defrizzing products that never seemed to help.

My grandmother watched Gianna in disgust. "I cannot wait until this test is over with. Your sister is crashed."

"I think you mean smashed," I corrected, glancing at the clock on the wall.

"Yes, that is what I said." She patted my hand. "He will be here. Do not worry. He is a good boy, and he loves you."

My father snorted. "Sal, when's he going to make an honest woman out of you?"

"Domenic!" My mother gave him a light smack on the top of his head. At age fifty-two, Maria Muccio looked better than me most days. She had a perfect, size-four figure and an angelic face that consisted of soft brown eyes, a tiny nose, and teeth she whitened religiously. Her shapely legs modeled a black, sleeveless mini dress that was paired with four-inch platform heels. Mom had had a face lift last year and had recently been talking about entering the local Hotties Over Fifty beauty pageant. Another reason Gianna was consuming alcohol at a rapid rate tonight.

"All I ever wanted was a normal mother," Gianna had confided to me recently. "You know, one who went to PTA meetings, baked cookies for my class—stuff like that." She'd cocked her head to one side. "*You* bake cookies. You'll make a really good mother."

I was concerned my sister might crack up before her actual exam. Perhaps Mike was right. Maybe I should move in with him temporarily and let Gianna stay at my place for at least a few days. She needed a quiet, stress-free environment. Heck, right now the zoo would be a better choice than my parents' home.

"Well?" my father asked again.

Before I could respond, the doorbell rang, and I heard Mike's voice. "Hello?"

"We're all in the dining room, dear," my mother called.

I pushed my chair back. Literally saved by the bell. I crossed the hallway and walked through the living room into the foyer where Mike was hanging up his jacket.

His mouth was cold and rough as he kissed me. "Sorry I'm late."

"It's okay." I studied his face. He looked tired, and I knew first hand that he hadn't had much sleep last night. "How's the kitchen coming along?"

"Don't even ask," he said grimly. "This woman is a friggin' nightmare to work for." He drew my hand to his lips. "I just want to forget about her and this crappy business for a while. Right now, all I care about is spending tonight and all day tomorrow with my girl."

I thought of the episode with Colin earlier. Ten years of my life wasted on the wrong man when they should have been spent with this one. A tear leaked out of my eye before I could stop it.

He frowned and brushed his thumb lightly across my cheek. "Hey. What's wrong?"

I shook my head. "It's nothing. We can talk about it later. Come on. Everyone's waiting."

"Sal—"

"You heard her." Grandma Rosa appeared behind me. She observed Mike closely and then shook her head. "You look like you need a good meal. My Sally is a wonderful girl, but she does not know how to cook that well. Only dessert. And you cannot live on dessert."

I wasn't so sure about that. I'd tried dessert once for breakfast, lunch, and dinner and really had no complaints.

"Now you go in there and rough your face good," Grandma Rosa ordered.

I bit into my lower lip to keep from laughing. "It's stuff your face, Grandma."

"Whatever." Grandma Rosa nodded at Mike. "You go. I would like to talk to Sally alone for a minute."

Mike gave her a kiss on the cheek, and she patted his in return. When he had left the room, she turned to me with a pleased look upon her face. "It makes my heart sing to see you two together as it always should have been. He loves you so much."

"And I love him." My lower lip trembled.

She watched me in concern. "There is something wrong, and I think I know what it is. Your clown of an ex-husband."

Grandma Rosa always seemed to have an uncanny sense of foreboding and events to come. But this prediction was downright eerie. "Are you psychic or something?"

She laughed and smoothed the hair back from my face. "No, *cara mia*. He called here last night looking for you. He did not give his name when I asked, but I knew who it was. I remembered the voice." Her tone was cautionary. "He wants money, doesn't he?"

My stomach convulsed as I nodded. "He's going to try to sue me for the business. I don't think he has any rights, but what should I do?"

She put her arms around me. "You will go back into the dining room and have some cheesecake."

It was an awesome yet strange suggestion. Still, I could never resist my grandmother's cheesecake. Then I thought of my dream last night and hesitated. "My thighs can't stand it."

She frowned. "I do not understand. But you should never argue with an old lady. Now go in, and sit down with your young man before your father grills him to death. Then you go out with Josie and Robbie to celebrate her birthday. Life is not all hard work. You both need to have some fun, too."

I sighed. "Maybe I'm stressing over nothing."

She nodded. "That is what I think. Do not worry. These things have a way of working themselves out. Something tells me that Colin and his threats will not amount to anything. Trust your grandmother."

* * *

Mike grinned as we approached the front door of the bar. "Every time I walk through these doors, I think about that night when I kissed you for the very first time. Right in this spot." He gestured at the snow-covered wooden porch and then leaned down to brush his lips across mine as if reenacting the scene. "Just like that."

"Well," I teased, "it's good that I've taught you a few things since then."

Mike let out a roar of laughter as he held the door open for me. The place was packed, typical for a Saturday night. Since there wasn't much going on in the Buffalo region during the month of January, Ralph's served as the perfect diversion when you were bored with television on a wintry Saturday evening.

Ralph's was more than a bar—it was a staple in our hometown of Colwestern. The building had been here for as long as I could remember. When we had first started dating, Mike had been too ashamed to bring me inside his house. With an alcoholic mother and an abusive stepfather, Mike was never sure what might be happening on the home front. So on our first date, we'd wandered down the street from his mother's house to Ralph's where he'd convinced him to give us a couple of sodas. We'd sat on the porch and talked. For hours. And then he had kissed me. I'm quite certain that was the moment I fell in love with him.

There was a rustic feel to the place. Large beams

covered the ceiling, and there was a television set up behind the bar that was tuned to an NFL playoff game. Mike liked sports and was a very athletic runner, but he didn't even glance at the screen as he held my hand tightly, and we crossed the crowded floor.

We caught sight of Josie and Rob at a table near the wall, and I waved as we made our way over to them.

Rob stood up to give me a hug and pumped Mike's hand. "Glad you guys could make it."

Rob Sullivan was over six feet tall with brown hair in a buzz cut and a matching, well-trimmed beard. He was two years older than the rest of us, and Josie had started dating him on the sly when we were both in the tenth grade. Shortly after we'd graduated, she'd discovered she was pregnant. They'd married a few months later, and she'd quit culinary school just before the baby was born.

Rob was the total opposite of his wife—quiet and reserved. Although their relationship had started off a bit tumultuously, they loved each other deeply and had now been married for ten years with four beautiful boys to show for it.

A waitress approached our table with a round of beers.

"We went ahead and ordered for you guys," Josie said as she grabbed one.

Mike reached into his wallet and produced a couple of bills that he gave the waitress, despite Rob's protests. "Our treat. For Josie's birthday." He reached for my hand.

Josie grinned and raised her beer in salute. "Thanks, dude." She took a long sip and then wiped her mouth with the back of her hand as her eyes searched my face. "Did you tell Mike about our little visitor today?"

I nodded as Mike's hand tightened around mine. "We— uh, talked about it on the way over here."

Talking was a bit of an understatement. Mike had muttered a few choice curse words while he'd gripped the steering wheel so tightly that his knuckles had turned white. He had then declared that if Colin ever came near me again, he'd have to answer to him.

"Let's talk about something else. First things first, your birthday present." I reached into my purse and produced an envelope that included an e-ticket I had printed earlier in addition to two hundred dollars in cash. "An airline ticket for Florida this week and some spending money. Happy birthday."

Josie clamped a hand over her mouth. "No way, Sal. I can't let you do that."

I leaned my head against Mike's shoulder as he wrapped his arm around me. "It's already done. If it wasn't for you, we never would have gotten this far. I couldn't enter a competition like this by myself."

Josie reached over to hug me. "I don't know how to thank you."

Mike took a long swig of his beer and watched us with a bemused look upon his face. "What's this about Florida?"

Shoot. With everything else going on, I'd forgotten to tell him. "Josie and I have been selected to be on Cookie Crusades this week. It's the baking competition I told you about. Remember? They film in Florida, so we need to fly down there."

His arm tightened around me, and he kissed the top of my head. "That's great, baby. How long will you be gone?"

"Only a couple of days." I watched his face for a reaction, but he didn't seem to have one. He acted genuinely happy for us. The insecure Mike I'd dated in high school would have been busy suggesting reasons why I shouldn't go. "Any chance you can come, too?"

He shook his head sadly. "I wish. Laura Embree wants her kitchen done by the end of next week." He tweaked my nose. "That's going to mean a lot of late nights until then."

"It's Laura Embree's kitchen you're remodeling?" My jaw dropped. Laura was the owner of the Paradise Motel and Bar. She was an extremely wealthy woman in her early forties and very attractive as well.

He shrugged. "Yeah. I thought I told you."

Josie and I exchanged glances. We'd heard of Laura's reputation with men before. She was like a queen spider that trapped unsuspecting flies in her web. She had a healthy appetite for young, good-looking men, and my boyfriend definitely fit the bill.

Rob laughed. "I heard that chick has quite the reputation." He reached for his beer, but Josie nudged him so hard in the elbow that he almost dropped it.

Mike caught my deer-in-the-headlights look and kissed my cheek. "It's a job. That's all. I have no interest in her. Besides the money she's throwing my way, that is."

I knew I could trust Mike, but the thought of that woman trying to tempt him annoyed me to no end. "I can't wait till you're finished there."

"Believe me, neither can I," he sighed.

I pushed my chair back. "I need to use the ladies room. Be right back."

I walked by the small dance floor where two couples were swaying to a song by Maroon Five blasting from the jukebox. I continued past the pool table in the dimly lit corner to the restrooms located directly across. Ralph had draped a sign across the table indicating it was out of order. There were a few cracks in the turf he obviously wanted repaired before anyone used it again.

There was no one else in the small two-stall bathroom, so I took an extra minute to fix my hair and adjust the gold choker that had become entangled in my hair. I was looking forward to spending the entire day with Mike tomorrow. He'd mentioned that maybe we could go for a ride on his snowmobile, but I thought spending the day in bed sounded so much better. I didn't think it would be difficult to convince him of that as well.

I reached for the brass knob and pulled the door open. I had taken one step out of the room when someone grabbed my wrist and pushed me back inside the bathroom. My head hit the side of the hand dryer on the wall, and I let out a low moan. In shock, I stared at the face in front of me.

Colin. His jacket was gone, and he stood there before me in a disheveled dress shirt rolled up at the sleeves. His eyes were red rimmed, and I could detect rage brimming beneath them. He reeked of alcohol so badly that I briefly wondered if he'd been asleep behind Ralph's bar all evening.

He pinned both of my arms over my head with one hand and grabbed the chain around my neck with his other. He looked pleased as it constricted around my throat, and for the first time ever, I was genuinely terrified of what this man might do to me. Colin was a lot of things, but he'd never been physically abusive toward me while we were married.

"Let go of me," I managed to choke out.

"Who the hell do you think you are to belittle me like that in front of my brother? Huh?" He tightened his grip around the chain, and spots started to dance before my eyes.

"I can't breathe." My voice came out as a whisper. "Please let go."

Colin's face was right next to mine, and his sickening grin formed icicles between my shoulder blades. What had happened to the man I married? It was obvious he'd been replaced by a cold and calculating monster.

"You think you're better than me, don't you? Well, you're not. And I never really loved you. You didn't mean anything to me."

While the smell of him and the grip around my neck were more than enough to cause acute pain, it was his actual words that cut through me like a sharp-edged razor. The room was hot and close and starting to grow dark around me. "Don't—"

Someone banged on the door, and Mike's worried voice drifted through the air. "Sal, are you okay in there?"

Caught off guard, Colin turned his head for a split second and unconsciously relaxed his grip enough that I managed to get one hand free and promptly clawed him in the face with my nails.

"Bitch!" he shrieked.

The door burst open. Before I even knew what happened, Mike had picked Colin up like he was a rag doll and thrown him across the room where he landed in the center of the pool table. Colin lay there stunned in a temporary daze.

The chatter from the bar area stopped immediately as everyone turned to stare. Rob and Josie rose from their seats and started toward us.

"Call the police," Josie yelled to Ralph, who stood behind the bar.

Mike examined my neck with care and then gathered me in his arms. "Are you okay? Did he hurt you?"

From the corner of my eye, I saw Colin leap to his feet and run toward us with a pen knife in his hand. "Look out!" I screamed.

Mike turned around but wasn't quick enough as Colin thrust the knife at him. Mike drew his arm back, and his fist connected with my ex-husband's jaw. Colin fell back against the wall, stunned for a moment. He turned and ran through the bar area then disappeared from my line of vision.

Blood dripped from Mike's arm onto the wooden floor. For a moment, all I could do was stare, mesmerized. When I opened my mouth to speak, no sound came out.

Josie came running with a hand towel she'd snagged from the bar area. She wrapped it around Mike's arm, despite his protests.

"I'm okay." A muscle ticked in his jaw. "I'll be even better after I kill that son of a bitch."

Josie examined my face. "Are you all right?"

I glanced from her to Mike's arm and immediately burst into tears. "I should have given him some money. This is all my fault."

Josie hugged me tightly as I sobbed.

"Look at me," Mike said, the towel around his arm quickly changing to a deep shade of crimson. "This is *not* your fault. That guy is a loose cannon. Desperate people do desperate things. This is in no way or shape your fault. Understand?"

I blew out a sharp breath and put my hand out for Mike's keys. "We need to drive you to a hospital to be checked out."

"Let's see if we can stem the bleeding somewhat first." Rob walked over with Ralph's first aid kit. In a minute, he had Mike's arm bandaged, and the flow of blood had subsided. Josie grabbed another hand towel to wrap around the bandage.

"Sal's right. You're probably going to need stitches." Josie glanced around the room. "Where'd scum of the earth go? Did he crawl under a rock somewhere?"

Ralph, in his early sixties with silver hair and a large belly that slopped over his pants, hurried over to us. He'd been talking on the phone—to the cops, I hoped. "You kids okay?"

"Fine." Mike gestured to the pool table. "Sorry about that. I'll pay for it."

Ralph snorted. "You'll do nothing of the sort. I needed a new one anyhow. And when that loser turns up again, I'm holding him responsible."

"How did he get out of here?" Josie asked.

Ralph shrugged. "He ran out the front door like a madman. A couple of guys chased after him, but he had a good start and managed to lose them. No matter. The cops will find that lowlife eventually." He examined Mike's arm. "You better get over to the hospital and get that looked at, kiddo."

We started for the front door while Josie ran back to the table to grab our coats and my purse. Everyone who had gathered on the bar floor moved aside to let us pass. I thought I saw Mitzi waving to us through the crowd, but I couldn't be sure. Plus, I didn't want to deal with her right now.

"Sally?" I heard a voice call.

Puzzled, I turned around. Luke Zibro stood there. He'd been a friend of Colin's since high school but now lived in Florida. We'd relocated there as well when Luke had found a bartending job for Colin. He was a good-looking guy with short light-brown hair and warm hazel eyes. He stared at me in confusion now.

My mouth dropped open in surprise. "Luke, what are you doing here? Did you come with Colin?"

He nodded. "I drove up yesterday to see my folks. Colin asked if he could bum a ride with me. Said he had business to attend to."

The business meaning my bakery. "Was he stalking me tonight?"

Luke's face reddened. "We were parked down the street from your parents' house, waiting for you to come out. He said he needed to see you, but when he saw you leave with Mike, he changed his mind and made me follow you guys here. Honest, Sally, he said he just wanted to talk. I had no idea he was going to pull a stunt like this. Guess I should have known better."

"It's not your fault." I turned to Mike. "You remember Luke from high school, right?"

"Where's Colin staying?" Mike growled as he put his face next to Luke's. "With you? If so, you'd better advise him to pack up and head back to Florida because if he comes anywhere near my girlfriend again, I swear to God I'll kill him."

Luke's eyes widened. "Uh, I'm staying with my folks.

Colin's at a hotel. I guess his family didn't want him in their homes. He was pretty sore about it, too. He's at the Hotel Six on Stanley Street." He cursed under his breath. "The guy's out of control. I got tired of waiting for him and figured I'd come in to see what was going on. He ran right past me without a word. Two men were chasing him."

"Sorry. We really need to get Mike's arm checked out," I said. "Maybe we could talk tomorrow, okay?"

He nodded and watched us pass. "Sally, if there's anything I can do—"

"Thanks for the offer."

Josie and Rob were waiting outside for us. She held my purse out to me.

"It's not necessary for you guys to go to the hospital with us," I said. "Stay here and try to enjoy yourselves. We'll be fine."

"Nothing doing," Rob said. "He can't drive himself, and you're in no shape to. Get in our car, and leave Mike's truck here. Then Josie and I will drive it over to you guys later."

* * *

It was about two o'clock in the morning when Josie and Rob finally dropped us off at Mike's house. He had ten stitches in his arm but other than that, was fine. He'd lost some blood but not enough for a transfusion to be necessary. The doctor advised him to take a couple of days off work and rest. Mike had burst into laughter when he'd said that.

As we got out of the backseat, I hurried around the vehicle to hug Josie.

Mike shook Rob's hand then came up behind me to give Josie a peck on the cheek. "Sorry we ruined your birthday celebration. Sal and I will make it up to you."

She laughed. "It's fine, really. I'm just glad you're okay." She turned to me. "Call me tomorrow?"

"Sure," I smiled. "Thanks for everything. And please apologize to your sitter for us."

They waved and sped off as Mike unlocked the front door.

I watched my breath travel through the frigid air. "Are

you sure you're all right? How bad is your arm?"

"It hurts," he admitted, "but I've taken worse beatings."

Mike undoubtedly referred to the way his mother and stepfather had treated him when he was younger. He didn't comment any further. There was no need to. His unspoken words hung heavily in the night, similar to the crystals of ice that covered the naked tree branches.

Spike was at the front door to greet us. He was a black-and-white Shih Tzu that I had helped Mike pick out at the local shelter when we had first dated. Although Spike was almost twelve years old, he still acted like a puppy most of the time.

He wasn't happy about our late arrival and had made a special effort to show us his displeasure. A throw pillow from the couch was lying on the floor with all the stuffing ripped out of it. Fortunately, there were no other messes since Mike had installed a doggie door for Spike that led into a small fenced yard. The dog looked at Mike now and wagged his tail hopefully. He wanted to go for a walk.

"I'll take him." I reached for his red leash with the little black puppy paw design, which hung on the kitchen wall.

Mike grabbed it out of my hands. "No. I'll take him. I'm not letting you out of my sight. Not while that psycho is still on the loose."

"I don't think he'd come here," I said. "Especially after what happened tonight."

Mike stared. "The guy is on edge, Sal. He's obviously into drugs or booze and God knows what else. I've seen that crazed look before. My mother used to…" He stopped suddenly as a haunted expression permeated his handsome face.

My throat was tight with tears as I reached for him, but he only shook his head and attached the leash to Spike.

"I'll just take him around the block. You look beat, baby. Hop into bed, and I'll be there soon."

It was useless to argue. I cleaned up the stuffing on the floor and changed into a pair of cotton pajamas. I washed my face, brushed my teeth, and then flopped down onto Mike's comfortable double bed. The front door opened a minute later. Spike started to bark, and Mike immediately shushed him. As I began to drift off, I heard him in the bathroom brushing his teeth.

He entered the darkened bedroom, and I could make out his figure as he undressed.

When he lay down, he gathered me into his bare chest. "Sal."

"Hmm," I said, half asleep.

Mike brushed a light kiss across my lips. "He's never going to hurt you again. I promise." He started to say something else, but I went out like a light and never heard the rest of the sentence as I fell into a deep, dreamless sleep.

It seemed like only a minute later that I was awakened by Spike barking, and the front door slammed. Spike barked again as a vehicle drove off. Still in a subconscious state, I was unable to decipher if the vehicle was a figment of my dream or reality. The gentle quiet lulled me back to sleep.

The door slammed again after what seemed like a short time later, and I bolted upright in bed. Red digits of the alarm clock on the nightstand flashed 5:30. The sky was still black outside. Darkness was endless this time of the year.

Mike's side of the bed was empty. I yawned and rubbed my eyes. "Mike?"

"I'm here." His shadow was reflected by the fingernail of the moon that shone in through his bedroom window. Mike shut the bottom drawer of the dresser then straightened up and stripped his clothes off, laying them across a chair. He got into bed and wrapped his cool, strong arms around me.

"Where were you?"

His body tensed against mine. "Just taking Spike for another walk. Go back to sleep, baby." He kissed my hair, and I immediately obeyed, my head resting against his solid chest.

It was almost eleven o'clock before we actually rolled out of bed. I made scrambled eggs and toast, and then we went back to bed for another hour. Sunday was without a doubt our favorite—and most relaxing—day of the week.

"I love lazy days like this," I sighed.

"Time for a shower?" Mike kissed my ear and chuckled.

Grinning, I shook my head. "You need to behave. I'll go first. And alone. You can't get that bandage wet."

After I finished showering, Mike got in and proceeded to call several times for me to come back and join him. I laughed as

I tied my pink robe around me. I had started to blow-dry my hair when someone rapped on the front door. Puzzled, I padded barefoot out to the living room with Spike trailing after me.

Two uniformed policemen were standing at the door. My heart skipped a beat when I recognized one as Brian Jenkins. I'd first met Brian last September after my bakery had opened, and a former nemesis had dropped dead on my front porch. Brian had been the cop on duty that night. We'd become fast friends—and almost something else—as the investigation proceeded. Both he and Mike had asked me out for the same evening, and I'd been forced into a decision I hadn't wanted to make and also wasn't sure I was ready for. Now I knew for certain I had made the right one.

Brian hadn't been pleased when I'd turned him down and tried unsuccessfully to get me to change my mind. I'd only seen him once since then. He no longer frequented my bakery like he used to. Mike and I had been out to dinner at the Olive Garden a few weeks back when Brian and a leggy blonde were seated near us. He'd nodded politely, but the overall situation had been awkward. On the way home, Mike had grumbled that he'd caught Brian staring at me several times during our meal.

A look of surprise registered on Brian's face as I opened the door. It appeared that he hadn't planned on finding me here.

Brian's gaze fell to my robe, and his face reddened. "Hi, Sally."

"How are you?"

He cleared his throat. "I'm fine, thanks."

I couldn't help but admire how handsome he looked in the dark-blue uniform and matching jacket. Brian had thick dirty-blond hair and warm green eyes with flecks of gold in them. He also had a Greek godlike profile that could make any woman swoon.

Well, almost any woman. I belonged to someone else now.

He nodded to the dark-haired man with a moustache beside him. "You remember my partner? Adam Engster?"

Adam gave a small smile and tipped his hat. "Hi, Miss Muccio."

"Sorry if we're interrupting anything," Brian said.

"Would it be okay if we came in for a minute?"

"Of course." I stepped aside, allowing them entrance.

Brian's head turned in the direction of the bathroom where the shower could still be heard running. Then he glanced back at me while warmth heated my face. Heck, everyone in town knew Mike and I were a couple. Still, I couldn't help it. Embarrassment flooded through my entire body.

"Is Mike here?" Brian asked politely, although it was obvious he already knew the answer.

"Shower." I pointed toward the hallway. "Um, are you here about what happened last night? At the bar?"

I'd figured we'd both be questioned at some point today. Josie had texted earlier, relaying that a friend of Rob's who'd been at the bar said the police had shown up right after we'd left. They'd questioned several patrons about the incident. I knew it was only a matter of time until they found their way to us.

Brian looked uncomfortable. "Sort of. It's a little more complicated than that."

The shower stopped, and a minute later, Mike yelled out to me. "Where'd you go, baby? Come on back to bed. These stitches need more loving."

I winced in discomfort and stared at the floor.

When I didn't respond, he entered the living room with a towel wrapped around his waist—and nothing else. He was about to say something when his eyes came to rest on Brian.

It was moments like this when I wished the earth would swallow me up whole.

Mike managed a lopsided grin as he nodded to both of them. "Hi, Jenkins." He addressed Adam, "Officer. Something we can help you with?"

"We've come to talk to you both about Colin Brown." Brian stared at me. "Your ex-husband, correct?"

Mike drew his lips together and frowned. "What's that bastard done now?"

Brian cut his eyes back to Mike. "Colin hasn't done anything," he said quietly. "He's dead."

CHAPTER FOUR

———

The room swam out of focus for a minute. I inhaled sharply and stumbled back until I found the couch and sank into it. "No. He can't be."

"We found out where he was staying, so we went to his hotel room to question him early this morning." Brian was watching Mike's blank expression. "The door was slightly ajar, and Colin was lying on the bed. He'd been shot to death."

The horror of the situation started to sink in. Then I remembered Grandma Rosa's words from last night. *Colin and his threats will not amount to anything.* I clamped my hand over my mouth before a giggle could escape. Was I insane? A man was dead. My ex-husband, for crying out loud. I'd once loved this man. So why was I even thinking about laughing?

Maybe it was the thought of Grandma Rosa killing someone. That was truly insane. Or perhaps I was in shock. The panic rose inside me. Who hated Colin enough to kill him?

At that moment, the true reality of the situation hit me like a snowball to the face, leaving me breathless. "No."

Mike stood there silently, his gaze transfixed on me.

Brian gestured to the hallway. "Go put some clothes on. We need to talk."

Mike gave me one last look. His face gave away nothing as he turned and walked down the hallway without a single word.

I stared at Brian in confusion. "There's something you're not telling me. What exactly is going on here?"

Deep down, I already knew. I remembered the door slamming in the middle of the night and the truck roaring off. Mike hadn't taken Spike for another walk—he'd gone to visit someone about unfinished business. He also knew where Colin was staying, thanks to Luke volunteering that information earlier.

I looked up to see Mike standing in front of me, dressed in a gray Nike T-shirt, jeans, and sneakers. His eyes moved from me to both policemen, expressionless.

Brian's face was also unreadable as he shied away from me and reached down to his belt for a pair of handcuffs. "Turn around."

Mike did as he was told, still not saying anything.

Brian's voice remained calm as he snapped the cuffs on Mike's wrists. "You have the right to remain silent. Anything you say may be used—"

"No!" I screamed and bolted to my feet. Adam lunged forward and caught my arm before I could reach Brian. "He didn't do anything! Are you crazy?"

He ignored me and went on talking. "You have the right to an attorney. If you cannot afford one, one will be provided for you."

A sob escaped from my lips. "Please don't do this, Brian."

"Sal." Mike's tone was low. "Let the man do his job."

I stopped cold in my tracks and stared at my boyfriend. His entire face was devoid of emotion, almost as if it'd been set in stone. A chill encompassed me as I thought the entire situation through. Mike *had* disappeared last night. Could he possibly have killed Colin?

No. I would never believe that.

Brian finished reading Mike his rights. Adam grabbed Mike's jacket lying on the couch and escorted him outside to the waiting police car. I started to follow, but Brian grabbed me.

"Don't touch me!" I jerked my arm away. "You're going to arrest him for being in a bar fight? What the heck is the matter with you? Is this all because I chose Mike instead of you?"

I caught an intense look of hurt on his face. It was brief yet unmistakable. "Sally, you're dead wrong. I do happen to care about you, but that has nothing to do with the situation at hand. Not in the way you think." He stood at the screen door, watching Adam put Mike in the backseat of the patrol car. "I prayed you wouldn't be here today. I didn't want to do this."

I bit into my lower lip and tried to force back tears as I lightly touched his arm. "Then don't. Please. I'm begging you. Mike didn't do anything."

Brian stared at me for a long moment and reached over to tuck a stray curl behind my ear. "They found his fingerprints in Colin's hotel room. The readout came back a little while ago."

"No." I repeated stubbornly. "It's not possible. You don't know Mike like I do."

He put his hands on my shoulders. "I hope you're right. Really, I do. If the judge will grant bail, Mike might be out of jail tonight. Doesn't Gianna practice criminal law?"

"She isn't licensed yet." I knew nothing about the process myself.

"I'm sure she has a friend who can represent Mike. Call her. And call a bail bondsman. If bail is granted, it will be high because of the murder charge. My guess is around $200,000."

My heart stuttered inside my chest. "I don't have that kind of money! Where the heck would I—?"

He held up his hand. "You'd only have to put up a percentage of the bond, and if they can get the DA's office to recommend bail and the judge will grant it, Mike has a good chance of being released tonight." He looked at me soberly. "I've got to get going. There is one other thing that might help his case, and that's where you come in."

"What? I'll do anything."

He blushed. "If you can prove that you were with him last night—all night—that would help. It's always good to have a solid alibi." He stared at me again for a long moment, and I thought he was going to say something else. Instead, he gave me a small, sympathetic smile and let himself out the front door.

As the patrol car backed out of Mike's driveway, lights flashing, all I could do was stand there in shock, like someone had smacked me in the face and knocked the wind out of me. I couldn't breathe. I couldn't think. Some girlfriend. I couldn't even provide him with a solid alibi. Mike hadn't been with me all night. Plus, they had his fingerprints. I knew he hadn't killed Colin but had no idea how to prove his innocence.

I went into the bedroom to get changed. Before I did

anything else, I had to talk to Gianna. She would tell me everything I needed to know. Then I'd see if my grandmother might loan me some money. I had about five thousand dollars I could put toward the bail bondsman's fee. Maybe I could put the bakery up as collateral as well. I didn't know what might be required, and panic continued to rise within until it threatened to suffocate me.

As I stuffed my feet into my sheepskin boots, my eyes fell upon Mike's dresser, specifically the bottom drawer. It was the same drawer I'd heard shut when he'd returned home in the wee hours of the morning. I knelt down on the floor, blood pounding in my ears as I pulled the drawer open. I breathed an immediate sigh of relief. Socks and some CDs. An eight-by-ten framed photograph of us taken at a high school dance. Reassured, I lifted the picture out for a closer look. Then my blood ran cold.

Lying beneath the photo was a shiny black revolver.

No, I wouldn't touch it. In fact, I kept telling myself it wasn't really there because I'd imagined the whole thing. I replaced the picture and shut the drawer with a trembling hand. I remained sitting on the floor, immobilized. Spike toddled over to me, and I gathered him into my arms while I started to shake.

A gun. Fingerprints. No alibi. The truck roaring off in the middle of the night. Things were quickly adding up into a disastrous equation for my boyfriend.

* * *

"Don't worry, honey," my mother assured me. "Everything will be fine."

We were sitting around the dining room table in my parents' house after a long, stressful day. Grandma Rosa had loaned me the money, and Gianna's friend Jeff English had agreed to represent Mike. The arraignment had been over in a matter of minutes. Since Mike had no prior record, the DA recommended bail. I shivered as I remembered the look Mike had cast in my direction. He hadn't wanted me there.

After I posted bail, Mike was released and was now back at his house. Jeff had followed him over, and they were busy discussing details of what might happen if the case went to trail. Mike made it clear to me—in front of Jeff—that he'd like to speak to his attorney in private. Although hurt and taken aback, I'd left his house without another word.

I tried to understand this from Mike's perspective. He wanted to take care of me, not the other way around. I didn't know what sickened me more at this point, Mike's obvious anger or the thought he might soon be on trial for the murder of my ex-husband.

Gianna squeezed my hand. "Mom's right. We all know Mike didn't do this."

I tried to eat a bite of the braciole my grandmother had made especially for me. It was my favorite dish—thin slices of pan-fried meat filled with herbs and cheese and dipped in Grandma Rosa's rich homemade tomato sauce. Tonight it stuck in my throat like sawdust. "What will happen now?"

Gianna lifted her wine glass to her lips. "Since Mike waived his right to a preliminary hearing, the grand jury will meet and decide if there's enough evidence for the case to go to trial. The date is set for a week from Friday. Mike won't be present, but Jeff will be there, and he'll take care of everything. He's a fantastic defense attorney."

I gripped her hand tightly. "Do you think it will? Go to trial, I mean?"

Gianna sighed. "I don't know, honey. But it's never a good thing when they have fingerprints. Let's just hope they don't find anything else."

I thought of the gun, and fear gripped me again. If the police found the revolver then what would happen to Mike?

I kept checking my phone. I honestly didn't know how Mike would react when we had a chance to talk. My gut instinct told me he'd be angry at me for putting the money up. He'd told Jeff earlier to let him rot in jail.

My father grunted as he swiftly turned pages of the newspaper. "You've got your hands full this time, Sal. This town's going to eat him alive and spit him out when they're done. No one's going to hire your guy for another job."

"*Stupido,*" my grandmother yelled at him. "You keep your mouth shut."

My father's face took on a pained expression. "Dump him, Sal. You don't need that kind of grief. You've had enough, sweetheart."

"Mike didn't do this." I stared at my father in shock. "I think someone is setting him up to take the fall for Colin's death."

Grandma Rosa nodded in approval. "Mike is a good boy. We will find out the truth. It will all come out in time."

But would it be soon enough? When my phone pinged, I glanced down at a message from Mike. *Jeff and I are done. Going to bed. See you tomorrow.*

The words stung like a wasp. If he thought I would leave him alone tonight, he had another thing coming. I jumped to my feet then leaned down to give my father a kiss. "I'm going back to Mike's. Thanks for everything."

My father patted my arm and looked at me with a wistful expression. "I only want what's best for you, my *bella donna.*"

"I know." I blinked away tears as I placed my arms around his neck. "And Mike is what's best for me."

I grabbed my coat and headed for the door where my grandmother was waiting. I kissed and hugged her tightly. "Thank you so much, Grandma. Mike thanks you as well. I'll never forget this."

Her large brown eyes were solemn as they observed me. "Sally, my love, the days ahead will be hard for the both of you. Do not push him too hard right now. He is angry, and his pride has been wounded."

Tears streamed down my face. "I don't understand why he's being so cold to me."

She patted my cheek. "Mike feels it is his responsibility to take care of you, not the other way around. He has been kicked around so much that he does not know what it is like to be needed. But no matter what he says, he does need you. Give him time to come around, and make sure he knows you believe in him. Remember the words of the song."

"Song?" I asked.

My grandmother nodded. "Yes, the one the girl named Tammy sang many years ago. You know. *Stand On Your Man.*"

Despite the seriousness of the situation, I had to choke

back a laugh. "Grandma, it's called *Stand by Your Man*."

She nodded in approval. "That is good, too."

"I love you so much," I whispered into her hair.

"And I love you, sweetheart. Remember what I said. No matter what he says, do not let him go. He needs you as much as you need him. Maybe more. Never forget."

* * *

"Mike?" I called out as I walked through the tiny living room. No response. Spike came bounding out of the bedroom, wagging his tail in welcome. I reached down to pet him. "Hi, fella. Where's Daddy?"

He turned and tottered back toward the bedroom, and I followed, my heart pounding away inside my chest. I peeked around the corner. Mike was lying on the bed, fully clothed, hands behind his head. He was staring at the ceiling.

"Are you okay?" I asked.

He kept staring at the ceiling. "I told you not to come here."

I shivered. Mike's tone was colder than the temperature outside. His voice was low and not especially friendly. I walked over to the bed and sat down at his side. He kept staring at the ceiling.

I bit into my lower lip. "Would you please look at me?"

Mike swiveled his head in my direction, and I was taken aback by his expression. His mouth was hard and sullen, and the beautiful blue eyes I adored blazed with anger. I reached out to touch him, but he yanked his arm away.

My voice trembled. "Why are you acting like this?"

His eyes bore into mine. "You should have let me rot in there. I didn't want you asking your grandmother for money. I'm not a charity case, Sal!" He leaped to his feet and walked over to the window where he stared out into the night, hands perched on his hips.

Ugh. The pride thing again. My grandmother had hit the nail right on the head. I walked up behind him and put my arms around his waist. "I should have asked first. I'm sorry. But I knew you didn't belong there."

Mike was quiet for a few seconds. "I've got about ten grand in the bank. I'll write your grandmother a check. She can cash it tomorrow. I'll get her the rest as soon as I can. I'll sell my house if I have to."

I clearly wasn't getting through to him. "She isn't worried about the money. She's worried about *you.* And so am I."

He shook my hands off angrily. "I'm a lost cause. Isn't that what your father's been telling you? You can level with me. I know Domenic's never been a fan of mine."

My heart constricted inside my chest. "You've got it all wrong. My family knows you didn't do anything wrong. We're all on your side."

He was silent as he reached out to stroke my cheek with his fingers. "You deserve the best. And I just can't give it to you right now. I never could." Then he hesitated for a moment. "Don't you want to ask?"

I shook my head vehemently. "There's no need. I already have my answer."

Mike moved past me and strode out into the kitchen where he removed a beer from the fridge and took a long sip. "What would you do if I told you I did kill him?"

"Stop it." I grabbed the can out of his hand and threw it in the sink. "I *know* you didn't do it."

He folded his arms across his chest. "But I was *there*. At the hotel. You heard it yourself. I could have done it."

"Why did you go there? To threaten Colin and make sure he didn't come near me again?"

He didn't answer my question. Instead, he withdrew his cell phone from his jeans pocket and tossed it on the counter.

"What's going on?"

Mike pointed at the phone. "Go ahead and listen. Fifteen new messages since this morning. All job cancellations. Everything I had lined up for the next three months, including Embree." He forced a laugh out, but his tone was bitter and angry. "Good news always travels fast in this town."

"It'll blow over soon." I put my arms around his neck. "The truth will come out. And I'm making enough money right now. There's no need for you to worry. We—"

He gave me a surly look, and I wanted to bite my tongue off. I'd forgotten about the pride factor again. When would I learn to keep my mouth shut?

Mike blew out a sigh. "I love you, Sal, more than anything. But I'm no good for you. Years ago, when we first met, we had to deal with my drunken mother. I was embarrassed for you to see her like that. And now this. The demons don't go away for me. Please go home. I'm begging you."

I was dumbstruck for a moment. I had never known Mike to beg for anything in his entire life. The words bothered me to no end, but I stood my ground. "No. I'm not leaving you."

His shoulders sagged. "Fine. Stay. I don't care anymore." He turned and walked into the bedroom without a backward glance at me.

I thought about following him but decided to give him his space. A lump formed in my throat the size of a mountain. I thought of my grandmother's words again. No. I wouldn't give up on him no matter what he said. Unshed tears welled in my eyes.

"Sal?" Mike called out suddenly.

Hopeful, I walked into the bedroom. He was sitting on the edge of the bed. He looked up at me and forced a smile to his lips. "I haven't eaten since this morning, and I'm starving. Would you mind going out to grab me something?"

Relief washed over me. I bit into my lower lip to keep the tears from flowing again as I ran a finger across his lips. "Of course. What would you like?"

He got to his feet and put his arms around me. "I don't care. Anything sounds good at this point."

"Okay. I'll run over to Frank's and grab you a sandwich." Frank Taylor was Gianna's boyfriend. He owned a sub shop a couple of blocks away from the bakery.

"Do you need money?" he asked.

I shook my head. "I've got it covered."

"Okay." He smiled. "I think I'll take a shower while you're gone." He covered my mouth with his, and I responded ardently. When we finally broke apart, I was breathless.

Mike ran his fingers through my hair and kissed me on the forehead. "You mean the world to me. Don't ever forget that."

I whispered into his chest. "We'll get through this together. You'll see."

Feeling more hopeful than before, I grabbed my purse and coat from the living room and drove off into the night. Frank wasn't working, for which I was slightly relieved. I wasn't in the mood to chat about the arrest with anyone. I ordered Mike his favorite—roast beef with Russian dressing.

When I pulled into the driveway, I noticed Mike's truck was gone. Self-doubt quickly crept into my mind, and I tried to force it away. *No big deal. Maybe he drove over to the corner store. He probably wanted a newspaper. No, wait. That was his last beer I threw out. I bet he went to grab a six-pack.*

But deep down inside, I already knew.

I unlocked the front door and put the sandwich on the small dining room table. I walked down the hallway and turned into Mike's bedroom. On his nightstand sat a piece of paper propped up by the alarm clock. Next to it was a check for ten thousand dollars made out to my grandmother.

My breath caught in my throat as I grabbed the paper between my hands and read the message he'd printed in slanted letters.

Sal,

I'm sorry for everything. I love you and won't drag you down in this mess with me. I can't prove I didn't do this. I hope someday you'll forgive me.

P.S. Please take care of Spike for me.

It was simply signed, *M.*

I crumpled the note between my hands and sank to the floor. No. This couldn't be happening. In a span of twenty-four hours my life had gone from happy to horrific. My ex-husband was dead. If the police found Mike, he would probably stand trial for Colin's murder. I didn't know all the details but was pretty sure Mike would be in even more trouble if they'd discovered he'd left town. I had never felt so alone in my entire life. I covered my head with my arms and prayed for strength.

Something nudged my arm. I looked up to see Spike sitting there, wagging his tail at me expectantly. His beady, black eyes were full of hope as he leaned forward to lick my face. I picked him up in my arms and buried my face into his soft fur. Then the tears came.

CHAPTER FIVE

"You look like hell." Josie handed me a cup of coffee. "Did you get any sleep last night?"

I shook my head and took a sip of the steaming, hot liquid. It had been a long night of tossing and turning. I'd called Mike's cell at least twenty times, but it always went directly to voice mail. I'd texted him as well. *I love you. Come home. We'll get through this.* Still no response. It was as if someone had sucker punched me in the stomach, and I was still waiting to catch my breath.

I placed the coffee mug by the sink and grabbed some oven mitts to take a tray of Josie's coconut macaroons out of the oven. "You shouldn't even be here—it's your birthday. I thought Rob and the kids were going to make you breakfast."

She waved her hand impatiently. "Rob and I went to the movies last night. We'll celebrate next weekend. I wish you would have called and told me what had happened instead of my having to hear it from Gianna."

I transferred the cookies to a cooling rack. "She shouldn't have phoned you."

Josie tied an apron on. "Of course she should have. She knew you wouldn't do it yourself because you didn't want to ruin my plans."

I positioned my hands on the edge of the block table and blew out a long breath. "I need to get through this by myself."

She grabbed me by the arm and forced me to look at her. Her blue eyes swam with tears. "You're my best friend. And you're not alone. A lot of people happen to love you, including me. All we want is to help."

My lower lip trembled as I hugged her and then quickly

pulled away. "I can't give in to this now. I need to keep busy and keep my mind off—him." It hurt to even say his name.

"What about the contest?" Josie looked at me anxiously. "Do you want to back out?"

"No, I think we should still go. Maybe it'll be good for me to have a change of scenery for a couple of days."

"Have you heard anything about the funeral?" Josie scooped out rounded tablespoons of dough for sugar cookies and placed them on a tray.

"Colin's sister, Krista, left me a message earlier. She said the wake is tomorrow night, and the funeral is Wednesday morning. I'll have to let her know I can't make the funeral since our plane leaves early that day."

Josie pursed her lips. "How do you think that'll go over with Colin's mother?"

"I guess I'll find out tomorrow night." The worried look on my friend's face mirrored my own. "I don't want to go."

She placed a comforting arm around my shoulders. "You don't have to. You're not married to him anymore. Plus, he treated you like crap."

I shook my head. "I have to go. Krista asked me especially to be there. She said their mother is having a really tough time. She still refers to me as her daughter-in-law. It's like she tries to pretend the divorce never happened."

The bells over the door tinkled, and Josie glanced at her watch. "That must be Mitzi. I asked her to come in an hour before we opened so that I could show her around." She patted my arm. "Come on. We've finally got some extra help today. You should go upstairs and take a nap."

"No. I wouldn't be able to sleep anyway." I wiped my hands on a dish towel. "You go ahead and get her started. I'll grab the tax forms and meet you out front in a second."

Josie walked into the storefront to greet Mitzi while I opened the drawer of the block table and grabbed the forms I had printed off my computer for her to fill out. I still wasn't sure about this. There was something about the girl that bothered me. *Oh, forget it, Sal. You're not going to make sense out of anything today. We can always let her go if things don't work out.*

I felt a twinge of remorse as I remembered the phone call

I'd made to Sarah on Saturday, explaining we couldn't offer her the job. Her voice had cracked on the other end of the line as she'd told me she understood and wished us the best of luck with the bakery. I'd felt lower than pond scum as I'd thanked her and quickly disconnected the call. Another cloud that was currently hanging over my head.

Josie and Mitzi were standing by the window talking about different recipes. Mitzi stared at me in shock. "Oh wow, Sally, I didn't expect you'd be here."

I smiled politely. "I'm pretty much always here. It is my shop."

Her face reddened. "Er, I meant with your boyfriend being arrested for murder the other night and all that."

I exchanged glances with Josie. Good grief, why did everyone in this town have to know all the dirt about everyone? I counted to ten before I answered. "That's a personal subject I really don't want to discuss right now."

Mitzi's mouth fell open. "Oh, of course. I wasn't trying to pry. I mean—I'm sure he had his reasons and all."

"He didn't *do* anything," I snapped. Horrified at my behavior, I clamped a hand to my mouth. "I'm sorry. I didn't mean to bite your head off. Please excuse me for a moment."

I went into the back room and grabbed the sides of the table again, taking several deep, cleansing breaths. *Get it together, Sal. Don't lose it.*

Someone touched my arm, and I looked up to see Josie watching me with a worried expression. "Sal, I can handle things today. You should go rest."

"I'll be okay. Honest."

Josie looked doubtful. "Fine. I'm going to bring Mitzi back here and show her around. Is that okay with you?"

I nodded without another word and turned to take cookies out of the oven. Josie and Mitzi reappeared, and the girl was giggling away, saying something about how she loved the smell of sugar cookies.

Josie handed her an apron. "Your hair is pretty short, but we'll still need you to wear a hat or a hair net. Whatever you're most comfortable with." She motioned to the pink ball caps that were hanging on the wall next to Josie's and my coats. *Sally's*

Samples was written on them in black cursive lettering.

"Aren't these cute," Mitzi squealed as she donned a cap. "So what will my hours be?"

"They'll fluctuate for a couple of weeks," Josie said. "I know this is short notice, but Sal and I are going out of town on Wednesday until late Friday." Her face shone with pride. "We're contestants on Cookie Crusades."

Mitzi giggled. "I heard. Congratulations!"

Josie and I looked at each other, confused.

"How did you find out?" I asked. "We haven't made it public knowledge yet."

Mitzi blushed. "Well, I happened to see the announcement on their website. I guess I'm a bit of a stalker where that show is concerned. I want to be on it so bad." She turned pleading eyes on us.

I winced. Had Mitzi taken the job because she'd hoped we'd take her along? That was so not happening.

"Um, okay," Josie said. "So getting back to the tasks at hand—"

"Have you guys decided what you're going to make for the show?"

Josie started to say something, but I interrupted. "Um, not yet. We're still working out the details." Mitzi reminded me of a bloodhound sniffing around for valuable information. Perhaps I was overreacting. Maybe the real problem was with me. Was I too suspicious of everyone now? I'd had some trust issues in the past—especially with Colin—and now there was this whole thing with Mike, just when I thought I'd finally healed.

The fact remained that this girl was failing to win me over. I hoped I was wrong about her. We needed someone we could depend on for the coming week, and I hated to bother Gianna at such a crucial time. I also disliked the thought of closing the store down for three entire days.

"We'll need you to assist with the care of the shop while we're gone," I said. "I'm going to see if my grandmother will take charge. We'll shorten the hours each day, so that should help, too. Do you think you'll be up to the task?"

Mitzi grinned. "Bring it on. That sounds super fun."

I appreciated her enthusiasm, but given my lack of sleep and that nagging prickle of doubt, she was starting to get on my last nerve. I turned to Josie. "Why don't you work out front with Mitzi today after she fills out her paperwork? I think I'll stay in the back room, bake some cookies, and order supplies."

Josie winked but said nothing. She understood I wanted to be alone.

Despite the below-zero temperatures, we were busy all day. We had scaled back our hours on Mondays and Tuesdays and were now closing at six instead of seven. I couldn't help but remember what I had been doing a week ago at this time. Mike and I had gone out to dinner and then back to his house. We'd watched a movie and fallen asleep in each other's arms on the couch. A tear rolled down my check before I could stop it. I dried my eyes quickly and tried to concentrate on tallying up sales for the day.

Mitzi washed dishes in the back room while Josie sorted through some recipes at the table next to me in the storefront. "What do you think, Sal? How about the coconut macaroons for Round Two of Cookie Crusades?"

I nodded without looking up. "Sounds good."

She cleared her throat. "We have to pick two cookies for that round. And remember, during the third round, they can throw anything at us."

"The macaroons will be great," I said. "I think I left the recipe on the shelf next to the flour this morning. I was going to make some more but ran out of time. Besides, mine don't come out as well as yours."

Josie waved her hand dismissively. "I don't need the recipe. I could make those in my sleep." She made some notes on a memo pad. "We'll probably need one suitcase alone for all of our spices. They only provide basic ingredients. You know— flour, sugar. That kind of stuff."

"Yes, I looked at the guidelines before I emailed the contract back." I glanced at my watch. "I know it's ten minutes early, but I'm going to go ahead and lock the door. And I forgot to grab the paper earlier."

"Do you think Colin's obit is in there? What time is the service?"

I shook my head. "The service is from four to seven. And I don't think it'll be in till tomorrow. I'll check though."

I shivered as I grabbed the paper off the front porch, and a gust of cold air blew right through my thin T-shirt. The roads were clear, and it hadn't snowed today so all in all, a good day for the Buffalo region in the middle of winter.

I scurried back inside and shut the door firmly behind me, making sure to change the sign to *Closed*. Yes, a couple of days in Florida sounded very good right now. If only I knew where Mike had gone and that he was safe. I continued to feel like someone had dropped a giant boulder on my chest, and I could no longer draw a deep breath.

I sat back down at the table and took a sip from my fifth cup of coffee for the day while I thumbed the pages of the paper until I came to the obituaries. My heart skipped a beat as I focused on a picture of my ex-husband.

The picture was a close-up. He looked handsome and happy, not ragged and desperate like the night he'd died. I bit into my lower lip as I stared at his wavy hair, eyes dark as coffee beans, and the strong, defiant jaw. My stomach muscles tightened as recognition set in. Colin was wearing a tux. The picture was from our wedding day. Did they really have to use that one?

Colin David Brown, age 29. Beloved son of Elizabeth Brown and the late Arthur Brown. Brother of Krista Brown Eldridge and Kyle Brown. Husband of Sally Muccio Brown. Also survived by two nieces—

The room started to spin and I whimpered. "Josie?" I managed to squeak out.

Josie got up from her chair and hurried over to my side. Mitzi came running in from the back room. I guess my squeak was more of a scream.

Josie studied my face with concern. "Sal, what's wrong?"

I glanced at her then at Mitzi leaning against the counter as I kept the paper clutched to my chest. I could have sworn Mitzi was smirking. I looked away and tried to steady my voice. "Mitzi, I really need to talk to Josie alone. You can leave a few minutes early."

"No problem whatsoever." She went into the back room

to grab her stuff.

My best friend grabbed my arm. "What is it?"

I handed her the paper. She read the obituary silently to herself, lips moving, and I watched as her face paled.

"Oh my God, Sal. How could they do this to you?"

Before I could muster a reply, my phone buzzed from my jeans pocket. I glanced at the screen. "Hi, Mom."

"Sweetheart," she whined into the phone. "What have those people done to you? Is this some kind of terrible joke? We just looked at the paper. Your father is going bananas."

I slumped in my chair. "I know. I saw it, too."

"Why?" My mother wanted to know. "Why would they do this to you? Was it Elizabeth?"

"I'm not sure. Krista said she always talked about Colin and me like we were still a couple. She mentioned there were other things going on but wouldn't really elaborate on the phone when she called."

"Oh, honey," my mother moaned. "Don't worry about a thing. Your father and I will be there to protect you at the wake. Grandma and Gianna are coming, too."

I winced inwardly. I knew my mother meant well, but chances were that my entire family showing up at Colin's wake would not prove to be peaceful. They didn't do well at funeral services. I was thankful this was not the same funeral home that my father was currently driving for. "Mom, you don't have to do that."

"Wild horses wouldn't keep us away. I mean, the boy *was* our son-in-law. I'm sorry he's dead, but it doesn't excuse what he did to you. I feel so badly for his poor mother." Mom clucked her tongue. "Have you heard anything from Mike?"

Tears were welling in my eyes again. "Nothing."

"He'll be back," she assured me. "He loves you, honey. And I was just talking with your father. We want you to move back home for a while. You shouldn't be alone right now."

"I'm okay, Mom. I'm splitting time between his house and mine. I have to take care of Spike, remember? Oh, Grandma said I can bring him over to the house when we leave on Wednesday. Is that okay with your allergies and everything?"

She giggled, and I stared at the phone, mystified. "That

reminds me. Your father and I have a surprise for you. It's going to make you feel so much better about everything."

"What's that?" I asked.

Mom was silent for a moment then she giggled again. "No. I'm not going to tell you now. Then it will really be a surprise."

I rolled my eyes at the ceiling. God, I hated surprises.

"I want you to come for dinner tonight. You can bring Spike with you. Tomorrow's going to be a tough day, honey. You need your family around you."

"All right. I'll be there in an hour or so."

Josie was still standing at my side, her eyes shooting daggers at the paper. "I can't believe they would do this. You've been divorced for over four months. Just wait until I see the Brown family tomorrow night."

I removed the paper from her hands. "No. We're not going to say anything."

"Sal, how can you let them treat you like this?"

I pleaded with my best friend. "Maybe it was an accident. Maybe they meant to say former wife. All I know is Colin's wake is not the proper time to bring this up." We'll close up an hour early tomorrow and then go over."

"I could stay and close up for you," a voice said.

I whirled around. Mitzi was standing there in her wool coat and hat, watching us, a small smile perched on her lips.

I clamped my mouth shut in anger. How long had she been listening? "No thanks, Mitzi. Good night. See you in the morning."

"Oh, I forgot my gloves." She turned and walked into the back room again.

I waited till she had disappeared and lowered my voice to a whisper. "She was listening. Mitzi is really starting to bother me. There is something off about her."

Josie frowned. "I don't think so. And she was a huge help today. She freed me up so much that I was able to sort through a bunch of recipes for the contest and make some extra doughs for use while we're gone. Exactly what is your problem with her?"

"I don't trust her."

She waved her hand impatiently. "Oh, please. That's because of what you're going through with Mike. It's clouding your judgment about everything."

"And what is that supposed to mean?"

She put her hands on her hips. "It all relates to your divorce. You finally thought you found a man you could trust. And now you're afraid you might be wrong about him."

I clenched my fists at my sides. "That isn't true. He didn't kill Colin. I'd bet my life on it."

Josie sighed. "Look, Sal, we've been friends for a long time. I don't want to see you hurt again. Maybe you should forget about him. Especially if he *is* guilty."

My mouth dropped open in astonishment. "I can't believe you would say that. You *know* he didn't do this."

She thrust her hands forward. "Then he shouldn't have left town. It makes him look really bad. I was talking to Rob last night and—"

"Stop. Just stop." I whirled on my heel and started for the staircase. Mitzi was in the doorway, staring at me again with that smirk I longed to knock off her face. Instead, I pressed my lips together tightly, afraid something might leak out that I'd regret later.

"You can both let yourselves out. Josie, please lock the back door when you leave. I'll take care of everything else." I thumped my way loudly up the wooden staircase.

Josie called up to me. "Sal, wait. Please. I didn't mean anything by it."

I turned around and glared down the stairs at her. "I am so done talking to you."

I rushed up the last three steps and slammed the door to my apartment behind me. Within seconds, I'd raised the volume of the television as high as it would go. Then I ran into the bathroom and, for the second night in a row, promptly burst into tears.

CHAPTER SIX

———

The last time Josie and I had a fight was in the fifth grade. We were both eleven, and it had concerned a boy. Josie had a huge crush on Jimmy Caruthers and prayed he'd ask her to an upcoming dance. Instead, he'd invited me. Even though I'd refused, Josie was furious when she found out. We'd exchanged words, but our disagreement didn't last long. Not after my grandmother had brought us both together in the same room and demanded we apologize to one another.

That was over seventeen years ago. Josie and I didn't fight—it was as simple as that. We were always honest with each other about our feelings, which is why we were able to maintain such a strong friendship. We weren't afraid to tell each other the truth and never sugarcoated the situation. Josie had tried to be truthful with me, but I didn't want to hear it.

Anger formed in a ball at the pit of my stomach. Everyone seemed to think Mike was guilty. Maybe I was afraid I'd start to believe it myself.

I pulled into my parents' driveway and shut the engine off. As I glanced around into the black, miserable night, I felt as if I was sinking into my own endless well of depression with no way to climb out. I opened the rear door of my car, and Spike jumped into my arms. I hugged him against my chest and started toward the house, my boots crunching the snow.

I was slowly alienating people around me. True, I still had my parents and Gianna to lean on, but there was only one person who could help me out of the despair I was quickly sliding into. The same person who had been my rock for my entire life.

Grandma Rosa was waiting inside the front door. I set

Spike down on the rug and hugged her. She closed the door and patted my back reassuringly.

She whispered in my ear. "I know, cara mia. Things look very bleak now. But they will get better. I promise." She studied my face. "You have not eaten anything today, have you?"

I shook my head. "No appetite."

She patted my cheek. "Everyone is in the dining room finishing up. There is lasagna and a nice green salad, and I made your favorite for dessert." She wagged a finger. "But not until you finish everything on your plate first." At times Grandma Rosa still talked to both Gianna and me like we were children, but perhaps we always would be to her. On days like this, I found it comforting.

"You must keep your strength up," she said. "You will need it when the vultures descend upon you at the wake tomorrow."

Gee, what a cheerful thought. No doubt she was right though. The wake was being held in a neighboring town. Colin's parents had sold their house in Colwestern after Kyle had graduated from high school and moved into a smaller one about fifty miles away. I assumed several people would have heard about me and be foaming at the mouth. They were lying in wait for the black-hearted woman who had lied about her divorce and whose current boyfriend was rumored to have murdered her husband. It was almost like a bad soap opera.

For now, there were also people from my hometown who I would have to contend with.

Loud banging on the front door startled us both. Grandma Rosa looked through the peephole and sighed as she opened it.

In walked Mrs. Gavelli wagging her finger in my face. Like my grandmother, she was in her seventies. Her coarse gray hair was pulled back in a severe bun. She wore a long black coat that matched her recent mood. Her wrinkled face surveyed me with disgust.

"I knew you no nice girl," she spat out. "You live in sin with one man and look what happen. You make him kill your husband. Is all your fault."

"Nice to see you, too, Mrs. Gavelli." Somehow, I

managed a straight face.

She gave a loud harrumph. "You no funny. Why you lie about divorce? Is not right." She gestured at my grandmother. "You raise a harlot here."

My grandmother pointed toward the door. "Out, *pazza*. And my Sally did not lie. She and the boy were divorced months ago. You know this and also that he was unfaithful to her. The obituary got it all wrong."

"Yah, that what they all say." Mrs. Gavelli poked her finger into my grandmother's chest. "And why you call me crazy? You the one with the wacky family."

My grandmother pursed her lips together tightly and paused before answering. "I will count to three, and you had better be gone. And you stay away from that wake tomorrow night. We do not need you stirring up trouble. Sally will have enough problems."

Mrs. Gavelli puffed out her chest. "I guess I go where I want."

"Not if you want to live to see the light of day." Grandma Rosa reached for an umbrella in the stand by the door.

"You no scare me." Mrs. Gavelli frowned at me. "And you teach this girl some morals."

As she turned around and reached for the doorknob, Grandma Rosa whacked her in the behind with the umbrella.

"I get you for that!" Mrs. Gavelli shrieked then slammed the door behind her.

Grandma Rosa put her finger to the side of her head in a circular motion. "She has a few loose nails up there."

I laughed. "You mean screws."

She grunted. "Yes, that is what I said."

Gianna walked in from the dining room and glanced at both of us in confusion. "What the heck is going on out here? Was Mrs. Gavelli here again?"

I shrugged out of my coat. "She wanted to pay her respects to Colin's widow."

Grandma Rosa bent down to pick up Spike. She scratched him behind the ears and chuckled as he licked her face. "Come on, little one. I have something special for you in the kitchen."

My mother and father were sitting at the cherrywood dining room table. Dad had the paper opened to the obituaries in front of him, and I winced.

Gianna placed a piece of lasagna on my plate and whispered in my ear. "All we've been hearing about is Colin's obit. Dad's on his third glass of wine, so hopefully he's starting to settle down."

Dad held out his arms and motioned to me. "Come here, *bella donna*." The second I was in range, he hugged me tight and gave a loud hiccup. "No one treats my ba-baby girl like that."

My mother placed a bowl filled with salad in front of me. "Really, Domenic. You're as drunk as a skunk." She sighed as her gaze met mine. "He got fired today."

"Oh, Dad, I'm sorry." I sat in the chair to his left. My mother was at his right, and Gianna sat to my left. "What happened?"

He snorted into his wineglass. "They said I talked too much. That I was bothering the mornings—er, the mourners. Where'd they get an idea like that?"

"Gee, I wonder." Gianna kicked me under the table.

"Poor honey," my mother crooned. She got up and kissed the top of his head.

Grandma Rosa appeared from the kitchen and set a large glass of ice water in front of me. "Your father has a few loose nails, too."

My father pointed a wavering finger at me. "Those Browns will hear from me tomorrow night. Absolutely shameful the way they're treating you. They always were a bunch of lowlifes. I bet the kid doesn't even have a decent coffin. Probably nickel and dime stuff."

I almost choked on the lasagna I was chewing. "Dad, please don't say anything. His mother is suffering enough. We always got along well. Maybe she still saw me as her daughter-in-law. I don't think she meant any harm by it."

"My gal Sal, you're too nice for your own good." He got to his feet unsteadily then leaned over and kissed my cheek.

"I hope he's not going to burst into song," Gianna murmured.

My mother put her arm around him. "Come on, honey.

You should get some rest. It's been a rough day for you." She glanced over her shoulder at me. "Sweetie, please don't leave right after dinner. I want to have a girl talk and make sure you're okay."

Grandma Rosa stood in the doorway. She jerked her thumb upward. "I will take care of Sally. Put that clown husband of yours to bed, and let him sleep it off."

My mother blew me a kiss. They ascended the staircase, my father's shoes clumping loudly while he sang "(Don't Fear) The Reaper."

Gianna wrapped her warm hands around my cold one. "How are you doing? Did Mike call?"

I shook my head and stared down at my plate.

She squeezed my arm. "Hey, he's coming back. You guys will get through this."

"Here we are." Grandma Rosa placed a large piece of her famous cheesecake in front of me and kissed the top of my head.

I glanced at the cake then at Gianna and my grandmother and burst into tears.

Gianna threw her arms around me. "It's all going to be fine, honey. Mike's got one of the best criminal lawyers in the state. Jeff's been a huge help advising me, too."

I wiped my eyes. "You don't think Mike did this, do you?"

She looked at me in amazement. "Of course not. You know I don't."

"Gianna." My grandmother sat down in my father's chair. "Go and stack the dishes. I will talk to Sally."

"But Grandma—"

She grunted and pointed toward the kitchen. "You go. Now."

Gianna ruffled my hair but did as she was told. When she had left the room, Grandma Rosa took my hand between both of hers. "Look at me, Sally."

I raised my head, expecting to see my grandmother's warm smile reassuring me, but instead, her lips were clamped together. Her eyes were dark and determined as they searched mine. "You must stop this feeling sorry for yourself."

This was not what I'd expected to hear. "What are you

talking about?"

She cradled my face between her hands. "It is not good. You have to trust Mike to take care of himself. He will come home when he is ready."

"But, Grandma, if the police find out he's left town before his court date, he'll be in lots of trouble. Gianna said so."

"Bah. How will they find out? I am not going to tell anyone. He will come back. You need to focus your energy elsewhere."

I sighed as I stared at her luscious ricotta cheesecake. This had always been my favorite dessert, and I didn't even have an appetite for it now. Boy, I was a hot mess. "If you're talking about the contest, I couldn't care less anymore. I have half a mind not to go."

She grabbed my shoulders in a firm grip which startled me. "Now you listen to me. This contest is not just about you. Your best friend has her heart set upon it. She set everything up for the both of you. Have you forgotten that Josie has covered for you many times in the last few weeks so that you and Mike could spend some time together? Plus, she has a husband and four babies, too. Stop taking advantage of her."

"Grandma, I would never do that. You know I love Josie."

"Sì, but you are not thinking straight. Josie called here earlier. She told me you two had a fight. She was crying on the phone." Grandma Rosa clucked her tongue in disapproval. "Such good friends. Do not turn your back on her now. You need her. And you must stop this."

"She thinks Mike murdered Colin. I can't believe she would—"

Grandma Rosa looked at me soberly. "She does *not* think that. But maybe *you* are starting to believe it."

My breath caught in my throat. "No. I will *never* believe that. But I'm scared and don't know what to do."

"You must help him then."

"How can I help him when I don't even know where he is?"

"The killer is setting your man up for this horrible crime. Someone who may have been at the bar that night he and Colin fought. Does it not seem a little convenient to you that Colin died that very same evening?"

Goosebumps dotted my arms. "But Mike went to his hotel room. His fingerprints were found in the room."

She shrugged. "His going to Colin's room made things much worse, yes. Mike only helped the killer by doing that."

I sighed. "Everything looks so bad for him."

Grandma Rosa nodded. "Listen, my dear. Stop this moping around, and use your head. You need to find out who did this."

"But I don't know where to even begin."

My grandmother handed me a napkin so that I could dry my eyes. "You will talk to Krista at the wake tomorrow. She was always a very nice girl, and you two got along well. Do not forget you are leaving for Florida the next day. Maybe you could drive over to Tampa with Josie, and ask some questions. Perhaps Krista would know whom you should speak to."

I blew my nose. "Well, it's a start, I guess."

"But above all, you must stop feeling sorry for yourself. Mike feels like the whole world is against him right now. When he returns, you must be there for him."

"Then I definitely shouldn't go to Florida. I need to be here when he comes back. *If* he comes back."

My grandmother growled. "You are not listening to me. Mike will come back. I know this. Remember he is used to handling his own problems. He has been taking care of himself since he was a little boy. All he ever got from his parents were beatings. He is a survivor. And he will be all right."

"I just wish he'd answer and let me know he's okay," I whispered.

"He will, cara mia. Give him time. He has to figure out what to do first. But never doubt his love for you. And you must not doubt yours for him, either."

Gianna peered around the kitchen doorway. "Can I come back in now?"

My grandmother nodded. "Yes, dear heart. All is good."

"You okay?" My sister sat next to me.

I leaned over to hug her. "I've been so wrapped up in myself that I didn't even ask how you were doing. The test is next Monday, right?"

She clasped her hands together as if in prayer. "Both Monday and Tuesday. I can't wait to live again."

My grandmother waved a hand in the air. "You worry too much. You have been studying for months. You will place it."

"She means ace it," I said to Gianna.

Gianna sighed. "If I don't know the material by now, I never will. So I'm volunteering to help with the shop while you and Josie are away."

I was thunderstruck. "I can't ask you to do that. It's way too much."

She shook her head. "I think it will be good for me to keep busy. And Grandma has offered to help, too. When she's not babysitting Spike, that is."

Hearing his name, Spike bounded in from the kitchen, barking up a storm. We all laughed.

Grandma Rosa nodded in approval. "He is a good boy. We need a watch dog around here."

Some watch dog. I smiled as Spike got up on his hind legs to beg for a piece of lasagna from my grandmother. He knew he had already won her over.

My grandmother tossed a scrap in the air toward him. "If Mike returns home while you are in Florida, he will be sure to come here to get the puppy dog. I will have a talk with him, too—whether he likes it or not."

When Gianna nudged me, I grinned. Mike had always been a big fan of my grandmother. Then again, everyone was. If anyone could talk some sense into him, she could.

Grandma Rosa patted my knee and went into the kitchen to get me a coffee. I glanced down at my phone hopefully. No new messages. When I looked up again, a steaming mug was being placed in front of me.

I poured some cream into my mug. "I can't thank you both enough for the offer. It's too much to ask though. Maybe it would be better if Josie and I shut down the place for a couple of days."

"How's the new girl working out?" Gianna asked. "She can help. Then there wouldn't be as much for Grandma to do."

Grandma Rosa snorted. "I can handle that shop fine. I will run squares around you both on a bad day."

"Circles," Gianna muttered under her breath.

"What did you say?" Grandma Rosa asked.

"Nothing," she mumbled.

"I have my doubts about this new girl," I confessed. "I'm not entirely comfortable with her. And that's another reason Josie and I fought. She thinks that Mitzi is terrific, but there's something about her that bothers me."

Grandma Rosa nodded. "I will keep an eye on her. Do not worry."

Gianna's eyes bugged out of her head. "Wait a second. You and Josie had a fight? For real?"

The doorbell rang, and Grandma Rosa gestured to Gianna. "Go see who that is."

Gianna walked out of the room as I gave my grandmother another hug. "I don't know what I'd do without you. You've made me feel so much better."

She kissed my cheek. "What would I do without you and your sister, my sweet girl? Everything will look better tomorrow. I promise."

I reached for my phone. "I need to call Josie and apologize."

"That won't be necessary." A voice came from the doorway.

I whirled around to see Gianna and Josie watching me.

Grandma Rosa eased herself out of the chair. "I will bring more dessert. Gianna, come and help."

When they both left the room, I was alone with my best friend. I got to my feet and stared at her. A huge lump formed in my throat, and "I'm sorry" was all I could manage before the tears came.

Josie rushed forward and wrapped her arms around me. "I'm the one who's sorry. I never meant to imply anything. I know Mike didn't do this."

We stood together, sobbing into each other's shoulders, until Grandma Rosa came back in the room. "Okay. I am glad that this is all settled. Such good friends fighting makes me very upset. Now you two need to stop acting like a bunch of ninnies.

Go to Florida, and win that contest."

"Yes, ma'am," Josie grinned at her.

Grandma Rosa patted the seat of my father's chair. "Josie, sit down here, and have some cheesecake with Sally."

My appetite had returned, and I dug into my piece with a vengeance. "You told Josie to come over, didn't you?"

"Of course." Grandma Rosa looked pleased as she tapped the side of her white head with her finger. "I always know best."

Josie gave my grandmother a hug and a kiss and sat next to me. "Rosa, is it any wonder I adore you?"

Grandma Rosa folded her hands on the table and watched us devour the cheesecake. "I always said you were very smart, Josie."

After I had eaten my piece in record time, I pushed my chair back from the table. "I should take Spike outside for a few minutes. I'll be right back."

I picked the dog up in my arms and trudged through the snow to my parents' fenced-in backyard. My father had cleared a path for the tiny dog earlier, so I let Spike down for a few minutes to do his business as I stared out into the frosty night.

Several stars dotted the blackened sky. There was also a full moon, which gave me hope. Thanks to my grandmother, I was now slightly more optimistic about the future. As usual, she was right. I had to find a way to help Mike.

My phone pinged. When I saw Mike's name on the screen, my heart stopped beating for a few seconds. The message was only eight words long, but it made all the difference.

I'm okay. Need time to think. Love you.

A tear of relief leaked out of my left eye and fell onto the screen. My fingers flew to type out the words, *Please come home. Love you.* I waited a few minutes, staring at the screen, not daring to breathe, but no new message appeared.

In resignation, I returned the phone to my pocket, lifted Spike into my arms, and turned to go inside. A new determination had filled me. I was going to find out who had killed Colin and was trying to frame Mike. Nothing would stop me, even if I died trying.

Little did I know how likely that might be.

CHAPTER SEVEN

———

"Some employee," Josie mumbled as she scrubbed down the block table. "Works one day, and then she calls and asks for the next day off. Must be nice."

"You were the one who wanted to hire her," I teased as I washed the last few bowls in the sink.

Her face was somber as she glanced at mine. "I'll go put the *Closed* sign on the door. Do you want me to leave a little note saying the shop is closing early today due to a death in the family?" Josie's hands flew to her mouth. "Oh gosh, Sal. I don't know why I said that."

I blew out a sigh. "It's all right. I'll probably hear all kinds of things like that tonight."

The bells over the door announced we had another customer. Josie glanced at the clock. "We won't get there until after five at this rate. What time are your parents coming?"

"Four thirty." I dried my hands on a dishcloth. "And my father wasn't happy about it. He hates going to wakes late."

"Yoo-hoo," a voice called out as Josie and I both walked out to the storefront.

A man about my father's age stood in front of the counter, covered casserole dish in hand. I'd seen him in the shop before, but his name escaped me at the moment.

"Hey, Mr. Seymour," Josie said. "Sorry. We're getting ready to close."

Mr. Seymour nodded and placed the dish on the table nearest to him. He reached for my hand. "My wife and I were so sorry to hear about your loss. She made this for you. Her specialty. Chicken and broccoli casserole. May God be with you at this terrible time."

Josie and I exchanged horrified glances. We hadn't counted on this happening.

"Thank you very much," I stammered. "It really wasn't necessary. You see—"

He cut me off. "Funny, I didn't even know you were still married. I was going to fix you up with my son. He's a great catch. Well, maybe now, huh?"

"Mr. Seymour," Josie interrupted. "Sally is *not* married."

"Well, technically, no, she isn't anymore," Mr. Seymour agreed. "She's a widow." He stared at my jeans and woolen sweater in interest. "I guess modern-day widows don't do the mourning bit anymore, eh? Anyhow, when you're comfortable, we'd love to have Roger bring you over for dinner. After you and him go out a few times, of course."

I couldn't stand it anymore. "I was divorced from Colin. Months ago. The obituary got it all wrong."

He looked at me doubtfully. "Sure, honey. Whatever you say."

"Thanks for stopping by, Mr. Seymour." Despite the biting cold outside, Josie ran to the door and held it open for him.

Mr. Seymour grinned and took a step toward the door. "Good luck, dear. Remember, Roger's a great catch. And he won't last long on the market, either. I'm betting the ladies are all going to be lining up now that he got himself a job."

Josie rolled her eyes in my direction. "Isn't Roger almost forty, Mr. Seymour?"

He nodded eagerly. "Yeah, but it took him a while to find his calling. He's really liking the gig at the meat processing plant now."

Mr. Seymour smiled at Josie as he walked past her. From the look on her face, I was afraid she might push him into the nearest snowbank. The bells jingled merrily with his departure.

I let out a groan. "My God, I had no idea it was going to be this bad."

"We'll just explain things to people at the service tonight," Josie said. "Don't worry. It will be fine."

I threw up my arms in pantomime. "How is this going to

be fine? My parents will cause a scene. Everyone will be talking about me. *And* Mike." I slumped into a chair. "I don't know how I'm going to get through this. I wish he was here." Then I smacked my forehead with the back of my hand. "What am I saying? He couldn't go with me even if he was here. Colin's relatives would drag him outside and lynch him."

Josie sat across from me and patted my hand. "At least you know he's okay now. That's something, right? And your parents might be nuts, but they happen to love you very much. And so do I." She grinned. "No one's going to mess with you if I'm there."

I knew the evening would be a disaster from the word go, but managed to laugh at her last statement. "Thanks, Jos."

She examined her watch. "I'm going to run upstairs to freshen up. Or do you want to go first? I could stay down here and watch for your parents."

"You go ahead." My cell started ringing from my jeans pocket, and I grimaced as Josie started upstairs. "Please let it be a wrong number."

I stared at the screen. My former sister-in-law. I still had her contact information in my phone. This couldn't be good. "Krista?"

"Hey," she said quietly. "The wake has started, and I wanted to warn you. People are asking why you're not here. My mother is getting very upset."

My stomach churned. Because of nerves, I'd had no appetite and hadn't eaten all day. Instead, I'd consumed six cups of coffee today and was starting to think a nip of something stronger might help take the edge off. "I'm on my way. We'll be there by five thirty. I'm so sorry, Krista."

"Oh, I'm not blaming you." She paused and then exhaled a deep breath. I guessed she was outside the funeral home, inhaling a cigarette. I'd always been fond of her but hated the fact that she smoked around her kids. "Sal, I'm the one who's sorry. I had no idea my mother was going to list you in the obit. If I'd been there, I would have talked her out of it."

"She went by herself?" I couldn't believe that Elizabeth's children would have trusted her to make funeral arrangements alone when she was in such a fragile state.

Krista blew into the phone. I could mentally picture her sucking the life out of that cigarette. "Kyle was with her, but it's pretty much the same as if I'd let her go alone. He's another one who only cares about himself." She paused. "It'll be good to see you. Let me warn you though. People are not thinking kind thoughts about you. I've tried to explain, but no one wants to listen."

I looked up to see my mother, father, Gianna, and Grandma Rosa waiting at the front door. I walked over to unlock it and let them in. "Thanks for the tip. I'll see you soon." I disconnected.

My father pointed at the case. "We all need fortune cookies, Sal. Break them out."

I groaned. "Dad, if you want one, that's fine. But I have no desire to see what else is in store for me this evening. Krista just called. It seems people are lying in wait at the funeral home to crucify me."

"This is crazy," Gianna remarked. "Maybe you should bring your divorce decree with you and staple it to your forehead."

That brought a smile to my lips. "It's tempting, but I only want to get in and out of there. You know, pay my respects and then leave."

My mother's nostrils flared. "They'd better not start anything with you. I'll set them straight."

My father swatted her behind. "That's my girl."

"Good grief." Gianna glared at our parents and went behind the display case to grab a piece of waxed paper. She handed a fortune cookie to my father and opened another one for herself. My mother and Grandma Rosa declined.

"Come on, Grandma," Gianna said. "They're fun."

Grandma Rosa frowned. "They are not fun. Those cookies bother me."

I felt myself shiver inwardly. "What do you mean?"

As her gaze met mine, she smiled. "It is nothing. Sometimes they are a little rough on my stomach. That is all."

I wasn't so sure that was what she really meant but didn't press the issue. We could get into this later. "How's Spike? Do you want me to bring him back here tonight?"

Grandma Rosa shook her head. "He was napping when we left. Leave him at the house. It is silly for you to bring him back over so early tomorrow morning before the plane ride."

My mother smoothed the short leather coat she was wearing. It came down to about mid-thigh on her, and I could see no signs of a skirt underneath. I winced, wondering how short the outfit she had on really was. My mother had fabulous legs, and I couldn't blame her for wanting to show them off, but tonight was not the time. In addition, she wore black stockings and four-inch stiletto heels.

"Mom, aren't you freezing?" I asked. "Plus there's ice on the sidewalks outside."

She brushed my comments aside. "I'm fine, honey. I'm used to walking in heels in all kinds of weather."

My grandmother looked at her daughter in disdain. "You should have dressed more practically. There are going to be many people who have it in for Sally tonight because of that shameful obituary, and you are not helping."

My mother pulled a lipstick from her pocketbook. "Oh, pooh. They're not going to bother my baby. I won't let them."

Gianna broke her cookie open and read, "*Just breathe. You know more than you think.*" She put the slip in her coat pocket. "Well, this makes me feel a little better about the exam."

"You'll do great, honey." My father grinned as he read his. "Holy cow. I don't believe this."

My grandmother shook her head while I braced myself for my father's newest fortune. "What does it say, Dad?"

He nudged my mother, who leaned over his shoulder to read the strip. They looked at each other, and both laughed together at some private joke.

Gianna put her hands over her ears. "If it's sex related, I don't want to know."

Dad chuckled, and my mother smiled while he read the strip aloud. "It says, 'You deserve a break today.'"

I was confused. "Okay, that's nice."

"You're retired. Every day is a break for you," Gianna said.

He put the slip of paper in his pants pocket and put his arm around my mother. "We were going to wait until tomorrow to tell you, but now's as good a time as any." He nodded to Josie, who had reentered the room. "Your mother and I have decided we are coming with you tomorrow."

Josie gasped audibly behind me while I reached for the back of the chair to steady myself. "G-going where? You don't mean—"

My mother's face was glowing. "That's right, honey. I just booked us two tickets on a flight to Orlando. And we'll be staying at the same hotel as you and Josie. The flight you're on was booked, so we'll be there a couple of hours later. Won't this be fun?"

I counted to ten before I said anything. Everyone else in the room was silent. Gianna glanced at me with pity while Josie stared at the floor.

"That's really nice of you," I said, "but Josie and I will be fine."

My mother waved a hand dismissively. "We want to be there to lend our support. We're so proud of you both! And I even looked at Cookie Crusades' website. You're allowed to have two guests in the audience. Isn't that fabulous?"

"Um, I have to go change." I turned to walk up the wooden staircase, my legs similar to heavy blocks of cement. I loved my mother and father dearly, but this was not good news to hear. The last time my parents came to an important event of mine, it had been my wedding. My father had made a speech to the room about how no man would ever be good enough for me, gotten drunk, and passed out in the wedding cake before we had a chance to cut it. I should have known then that the marriage was doomed.

I changed into black slacks, low-heeled leather boots, and a black-and-white striped sweater. I had just finished styling my hair in the bathroom when I heard my front door open. I went out into the hallway and saw Grandma Rosa standing in my tiny kitchen.

"Why didn't you tell me about this last night?" I asked.

"You were upset about Mike, and I did not want to add to your misery." Grandma Rosa walked over to me. "It will not be so bad."

We looked at each other, sighed, and then laughed.

She kissed the top of my head. "Cara mia, if you can get through tonight, you can get through anything. You, like Mike, are a survivor."

I hugged her. "I'll be okay. As long as I have you."

The parking lot of Hainer's Funeral Parlor was packed, but we found a couple of spots on an adjacent side street. Grandma Rosa had ridden with Josie and me while Gianna had accompanied my parents.

Josie stopped her minivan in front of the entrance to the funeral home so that Grandma Rosa didn't have to walk far. She motioned to me. "You go with her. I'll catch up."

I knew better than to argue with my best friend, but I would have been happy to wait for her. All night if need be.

Grandma Rosa patted my arm. "Do not worry, dearest heart. I will protect you."

Although it was dark, the outside of the funeral home was flooded with enough lighting that mourners could see the gray, one-level brick building and salted sidewalks clearly. A couple of people stood on the large front porch talking while another man smoked a cigarette in the adjoining parking lot.

I glanced at my watch—5:45. The drive should have only been half an hour but had turned into forty-five minutes when we were stuck in a traffic accident on the thruway.

I held on to Grandma's hand tightly as we ascended the two stairs to the porch, and the front door opened. A man of about sixty in a gray suit nodded to us and stood aside to allow us entrance. When we stopped inside the door to sign our names in the guest book, I peered into the viewing room.

There were a couple of people in line waiting to speak to my former mother-in-law, who was flanked by Kyle on one side and Krista on the other. Several mourners were seated in the five rows of chairs placed in front of the casket. Before we entered the room, I stopped to examine the collage of pictures on the easel just outside the main doors.

The center photo, a large eight by ten, was Colin's high school graduation picture. He looked handsome and carefree while his large brown eyes shone with a glint of mischief.

Several of the pictures, much to my chagrin, included me. There was a photo of us in formal wear at a friend's wedding from early on in our marriage. Another one had been taken at the christening of our niece. We'd been asked to serve as her godparents. And, of course, there were wedding pictures.

No matter what happened, I would always remember the day well, but the pictures now served as a painful reminder. It had been a happy occasion at the time for me, followed by a wonderful night of passion in the hotel suite. But it hadn't taken long for things to go downhill, especially when I'd discovered Colin was fine with me supporting the both of us on my meager salary.

I had guessed there'd be at least one picture of our wedding, but I hadn't counted on seven. My stomach muscles constricted as I viewed them, and then my hands started to shake as I grabbed the piece of cardboard that surrounded the photos.

Grandma Rosa gently pried my fingers loose and held them between her hands. "It is time to go in."

"I want to go home," I said in my best little girl voice.

She patted my cheek. "Never fear, cara mia. I will not leave your side."

We walked into the room holding hands, and someone gasped. All eyes turned in my direction. People were nudging each other and whispering. Heat rose through my face. I couldn't actually hear what people were saying, but I knew. *Did you hear the latest about Sally Muccio? The cop who wanted to date her came to arrest her boyfriend for the murder of her ex-husband. But Colin's not really her ex-husband. Yeah, turns out they were still married. What a tramp.*

Grandma Rosa and I stopped in front of the casket and positioned ourselves on the kneeler. Although I had my back to the crowd, I was positive every set of eyes in the room was on me. The silence was so deafening that you could have heard a pin drop. I stared at Colin's face and whimpered. Grandma Rosa said nothing as she held tightly to my hand.

Colin looked so much better than he had the other day. The rage had disappeared from his face and had been replaced by a peaceful, sedate expression. For a moment I thought it must be a mistake—he's only sleeping. Colin wore a dark-blue suit, the same one he used to wear for job interviews. Back when he'd actually cared about having a job.

So many thoughts ran through my head that I found myself confused and disoriented by the rush of feelings I was experiencing. We had dated for five years and been married for another five before the divorce papers came through. Although I'd once loved him, I couldn't shed any tears now. I was sorry he was dead and tried to remember the good times we had shared, although, looking back, there weren't as many as I'd originally thought. Signs from the very beginning indicated our relationship might not survive—signs I'd chosen to ignore. It wasn't until I found him in bed with another woman that I'd experienced the necessary wake-up call.

I reached out and touched his hand, which was ice cold. The room was still silent behind me, and I sensed people were waiting to see if I would do something else. Maybe kiss him? No. I wasn't going to put on a show for them. The love between us had died a long time ago. Well, at least mine had. I wasn't so sure now that Colin had ever reciprocated my feelings. I pushed a strand of hair off his face, got to my feet, and stared down at him.

"Rest in peace," I whispered. "I will find out who did this to you."

I walked over to my ex-in-laws. Kyle nodded to me but made no effort to hug or touch me. He shook hands with Grandma Rosa and with Josie, who was now behind us, accompanied by my parents and Gianna.

Elizabeth Brown had aged considerably since I'd last seen her almost two years ago. She appeared even older than my grandmother. Her salt-and-pepper hair was short and a mass of tangled curls. The effect would have been cute if her face had been devoid of wrinkles and actually had some color to it. Dark eyes, like Colin's, were surrounded by heavy shadows and regarded me with irritation.

"How n-nice of you to show up, Sh-ally," she said, speech slightly slurred. "Why didn't you wait a l-little longer?"

Krista put a hand on her mother's shoulder. She was almost as tall as Kyle and slim to the point of borderline anorexic. Her light-brown hair fell below her shoulders, and there were visible bags underneath her dark eyes as well. "Hey, Mom. I think it was pretty nice of Sally to come. She didn't have to."

Elizabeth sniffed but nodded politely as my grandmother extended her hand. "Perhaps you were off screwing around with the man who shot my boy."

I bit into my lower lip. "I'm very sorry about Colin, Elizabeth."

"Now wait just a minute." My mother stepped between Elizabeth and me. I took in her outfit for the first time and thought I might pass out. She was dressed in a low-cut, strapless, tight black dress decorated with sequins. Perhaps she had thought we were attending a cocktail party? One never knew what my mother was thinking. All I wanted right now was to get out of here.

My mother spoke quietly. "Sally is *not* to blame for this. As a matter of fact, you should be apologizing to her. They were no longer married thanks to your son's indiscretions. It was tasteless to print her name in the obituary like that."

An audible murmur filled the room.

"You tell them, baby," Dad agreed. "And look at this coffin you've got him in, for crying out loud. Cheap, worthless pine. What a disgrace."

There was a gasp from the crowd.

I shut my eyes tight for a moment and wished this was all a bad dream. "Dad, please. You promised to behave."

Elizabeth looked at my father through slitted eyes. "Well, pa-perhaps if your daughter hadn't pissed away all the money I sent them the last few years, I could have bought my s-son something more f-fitting."

I stared at her in amazement. What was she talking about?

Elizabeth took an unsteady step toward me, and I winced. The stench of liquor coming from her mouth was overpowering. She might have been grieving, but it was now apparent that wasn't the total reason for her unsteadiness. Elizabeth was certifiably drunk.

"I warned m-my boy never to marry this tramp."

My mother, Gianna, and Josie all gasped simultaneously. I started to say something but then felt my grandmother's hand on my shoulder.

"That is enough," she said. "You should all be ashamed of yourselves. The boy is dead, and another innocent boy has been accused of his murder. You should be trying to find out who did this instead of fighting amongst yourselves."

"Rosa's right." Krista gripped her mother by the arm, probably afraid she might lunge at me, then gestured toward an older woman in the corner. Elizabeth's sister came forward after shooting several daggers at my family and me. "Aunt Susan, please take care of Mom for a minute. I need to speak with Sally alone."

"Not so fast," Kyle growled. "I need to talk to you first, sis."

"Fine. Whatever." Krista addressed me, "If you go back out to the entranceway, you'll see a hallway on the right with restrooms and another door marked *Private*. Kyle and I will be in there. Just give us five minutes."

I nodded as she followed Kyle to a door behind a display of flowers that was also marked *Private*.

There was no way I was waiting in the viewing room for them. I'd take Krista's suggestion and stay out in the hallway. I turned to make my way out of the room with my family surrounding me on both sides. Josie led the way while Grandma Rosa held one of my hands and Gianna held the other. My mother and father brought up the rear. Those milling in between the rows moved to let us pass.

"She's got a nerve," I heard one old lady say to another.

"Yeah. Trying to let everyone think she's so pure just because she's got the same name as a Peanuts character," the other woman grunted. "Charles Schultz must be rolling over in his grave."

"Ain't it the truth," the first woman said. "Pretending to be divorced and shacking up with the guy who murdered her husband. If Colin left her anything, I hope his family contests the will."

Josie whirled around in a fit of anger. "They were *divorced*, okay? And Sally has the papers to prove it. So back off."

"Stop it," I whispered. "There's been enough of a scene already."

We made our way out of the room and back to the entranceway which was deserted, except for the employee by the front door and a young couple signing the guest book.

"Let's get the heck out of here," my mother said to my father.

He snorted. "Well, I did want to talk to the owner and advise him that their setup is all wrong. Maybe—"

"Domenic," my mother interrupted. "You know I always indulge your hobbies, but I think we should go. Plus, we need to get up early." She giggled and leaned over to kiss me. "We'll see you in sunny Florida, honey. Don't forget to pack your bikini."

Bikinis and sunshine were the last things on my mind right now. All I wanted to do was talk to Krista and then get as far away as possible from the savages here who might soon be demanding my head on a platter.

Gianna embraced me. "Do you mind if I leave with them? I can't stand being here any longer. I was about ready to tell your former mother-in-law where she could go."

Josie leaned over to hug her. "My sentiments exactly. You go. I'll take Sal home."

Grandma Rosa gave Josie a peck on the cheek and reached over to envelop me in a warm hug. "Do not let these people bring you down. You know the truth, and that is all that matters."

I wiped away a tear. "I'll try to remember that."

She patted my hand. "It is good for you to go away tomorrow. There is too much ugliness and hate here. When Mike comes home, I will take care of him, cara mia. You can count on that."

CHAPTER EIGHT

———

After my family departed, Josie went to use the ladies room, and I was left standing in the hallway by myself when the front door opened and Luke appeared. He signed the register then glanced in my direction and smiled as he walked over to where I leaned against the wall for support.

"Hey, Sally." He stuffed his gloves into his overcoat pocket. "How are you?"

I wiggled my hand back and forth. "I've been better."

"I can imagine." His eyes were thoughtful. "They really gave it to you, huh?"

I sighed. "Let's just say I didn't get the warmest of welcomes."

Luke rested a hand against the wall, and I studied him for a moment. He was dressed in a black suit, his hazel eyes regarding me with warmth underneath long, thick lashes that any woman would kill for. I didn't know him well. Once in a while, he'd come back to the apartment to have a beer with Colin if they worked the same bartending shift or sometimes drop by on a Sunday to watch sporting events. If I'd been home, we'd make small talk, but that was pretty much the extent of our relationship.

Colin had said Luke was a good guy you could always count on if you were in a jam. He'd once mentioned that Luke had a girlfriend, but I'd never met her and didn't even know her name. After I'd left Florida, Luke had sent a card to my parents' house telling me how sorry he was to hear about the divorce and that Colin didn't deserve me.

"How are you?" I asked. "When are you going back to Florida?"

"Probably this weekend. I've got two weeks off, so

there's really no rush." He pursed his lips together. "I'm sorry about your boyfriend. How's he handling all this?"

A knot formed in the bottom of my stomach. I hated lying to people. "About as well as could be expected."

Luke frowned. "He didn't strike me as the type of guy who would kill someone. Colin once told me..." He stopped.

"Told you what?"

His cheeks reddened. "One time we were having a couple of beers at your apartment. I think you were working. I said something to him like he shouldn't be treating you like crap. That he should be out looking for a real job instead of having you support him. That really pissed me off."

"And?" I prodded.

Luke frowned. "He laughed and said it wasn't a big deal. Said you deserved to work like a dog after what you'd done to him. And I asked him what you'd done. He said you were still in love with your ex-boyfriend. That after all these years, you'd never stopped carrying a torch for him." He paused. "Colin said you were getting exactly what you deserved."

The words blew me away. Colin had never once indicated that he suspected I still had feelings for Mike. I found myself wondering if I'd done something to lead him to that belief. Maybe I'd talked in my sleep one night? I'd never know the answer now.

I narrowed my eyes at Luke. "Even if I did still have feelings for him, I never acted on them. I consider marriage to be sacred. Unlike other people."

"I feel the same way. Believe me." His face was somber. "I didn't know Colin was cheating on you until after you'd left him. He didn't deserve you."

"Thank you." I was touched and pleased by his statement. "I stopped loving him a long time ago, but I am sorry he's dead. No one deserves to die like that. And now I think someone's trying to frame Mike for his murder."

Luke's eyes grew wide. "Do you have any idea who it is?"

I shook my head. "None whatsoever. What about you?"

He sighed. "No, but I can tell you a lot of people wanted Colin to disappear forever."

I braced myself. "Was he involved in drugs?"

Luke snickered. "What wasn't Colin involved in? After you left him and he lost the apartment, I let him move in and sleep on my couch for a while. Rent free. I thought I was helping him, but it only made things worse."

I folded my arms across my stomach. "Didn't go so well, huh?"

"It was a disaster. I'd come home every day from work and find him with a new girl. In *my* bed, too. I couldn't stand it anymore, so I finally threw him out."

The bile rose in my throat, and I turned away for a minute, fearful I might be sick. I'd caught Colin cheating on me while we were married but had assumed at the time that she was the only one. Now I was starting to wonder how many women he might have been with *while* we were still together.

Luke touched my arm. "I'm sorry. Really, I am. For what it's worth, I thought you were the best thing that ever happened to him. I can't believe he threw you away without a second thought." He glanced toward the receiving room "I really should get in there and pay my respects. Are you available for lunch tomorrow after the funeral so that we can talk further?"

I shook my head. "I'm leaving for Florida first thing in the morning."

His face was startled. "Why are you going there? Are you looking into Colin's death?"

"Josie and I are in a baking competition. We won't be back until late Friday afternoon." I paused. "But if you have any ideas of who might have wanted Colin dead, I'd appreciate if you shared them with me. No way is Mike going to take the blame for this."

"Did someone mention me?" Josie came up behind us and slung a protective arm around my shoulders. "Is this another one of Colin's fabulous relatives?"

Luke held out his hand to her. "Hi, Josie. Luke Zibro. I saw you at the bar the other night. We went to high school together. Remember?"

Josie blinked twice. "Wow. I hardly recognized you. Nice to see you."

"Likewise." Luke addressed me, "Like I said, Sally,

Colin made a lot of enemies in Florida. He had a way of pissing everyone off. He took advantage of people and borrowed money with no intentions of paying it back. I don't know if you were aware, but he almost served time once, too."

Colin had always possessed somewhat of a hot temper. He'd never laid a hand on me during our marriage but I knew he'd been fired from a job once because of a fistfight. "Another bar room brawl?"

He shook his head. "It happened right after you left him. I helped him find another part-time job. One night he didn't cut a patron off. The guy was so drunk when he left that he could barely stand."

I shut my eyes. "Oh God. The man killed someone, didn't he?"

Luke grunted. "Well, not himself, of course. There was a couple in another car when the drunk crossed over into the opposite lane. The other driver was killed on impact. His girlfriend was in the passenger seat. She walked away with minor scratches."

I covered my face with my hands. "How come I never knew this?"

"Did they press charges?" Josie asked.

"Turns out they didn't stick," Luke said. "Colin's mom hired some hotshot attorney who got him off on a technicality. The drunk driver is currently serving a term of two to five years. Sickening, huh?"

Josie snorted. "That's putting it mildly."

"I really should get in there," Luke said. He took a business card out of his trousers pocket and handed it to me. "Let me know if you need anything."

"Thanks."

Luke was silent for a few seconds. "I'm not going to lie, Sally. I've walked away from him before, too, but when he got in trouble, he'd always still call me. I was the only friend he had. I thought I was helping, but maybe I made things worse. He could be pretty convincing."

"More like manipulative," I said.

"Yeah, that too." He smiled and held out his hand to Josie again. "Nice seeing you." Then he gazed into my eyes with a look I couldn't quite figure out. "Maybe we could get together for lunch or dinner before I go back to Florida? My treat."

I nodded. "Sure. Call me on Saturday. And thanks for being a friend to him."

"I wish I could have done more." He exhaled deeply. "I'll see you later. God, I really hate these things." With that, he turned and walked into the visitation room.

I glanced at my best friend who was grinning at me. "What's that look for?"

Her mouth fell open in surprise. "Oh, please. It was *so* obvious."

"Uh, no, not really." I drew my eyebrows together in confusion.

Josie's mouth curved upwards into a sly smile. "First off, might I say Luke Zibro has turned into one mighty fine specimen of a man. He looks nothing like he did in high school. All I remembered were those long, gangly legs of his."

"He ran track," I said.

"Yep, he's filled out nicely since then." Josie smacked her lips together. "And boy, has he got it bad for you."

I rolled my eyes at her. "Oh, give me a break."

"You are so blind, Sal," she said. "If Luke knew Mike was out of town, I bet he would have followed you home like a little puppy dog. So what does he do for a living anyway?"

I glanced at the card he'd handed me. "He's the manager of a nightclub. Hey, I know this place. Colin and I went there a couple of times. Luke must be making some pretty decent money."

"And he said nothing about having a girlfriend, either," Josie teased. "Sounds like a mighty fine catch."

"Okay, stop this. You know I'm with Mike. That's not going to change, no matter what."

An angry shout from beyond the *Private* door startled us both. We made our way down the hallway and pressed our ears up against it to listen.

"You're not giving it to her," Kyle yelled. "Let Mom have it to pay for his funeral. Why the hell should I cough up the money? I'm glad he's dead."

Josie and I exchanged horrified glances.

There was a pause, and then Krista's voice floated through the air. "You don't mean that."

"I do mean it," Kyle said. "For years, all I ever heard was Colin this and Colin that. He was too busy screwing other women all the time to make an honest living. Work? No, that was too good for Colin but fine for scum like me. No way in hell. Mom lost the house because of him and Sally. Get his grieving ex-widow to pay for the funeral with that fancy ring of hers. I'm done here."

There was a brief silence then the door opened, startling both Josie and myself. Kyle glared at me before he stomped past us down the hallway. The employee wearing the gray suit opened the front door for him, and Kyle disappeared into the night.

"What the hell was all that about?" Josie murmured.

Krista was standing next to me, her face worn and tired. "Sorry to keep you waiting. Come on in. Josie, you're welcome, too."

"I don't want to impose." Josie stepped back.

Krista gave a small sniff. "It's fine, really. I'm sure Sally will tell you everything later anyway. I know how close the two of you are." She smiled as she shut the door behind us. "I guess I'm jealous. I've never had a really close friendship like yours. I thought Bruce fit that category for a while, but—" She glanced down at her hand and twisted the gold band on her left finger. "We've been separated for a couple of months now."

"I'm so sorry." I was genuinely surprised to hear this. They always seemed to have a happy marriage, as well as two adorable little girls I'd been proud to call my nieces. "How are Callie and Emily taking it?"

She shrugged. "About as well as you'd expect. Bruce comes to see them on weekends. When he's not occupied with his new girlfriend, that is."

Ugh. I flinched. "That has to be rough on all of you."

She bit into her lower lip. "Sally, there are some things you should know."

My stomach twisted into a giant pretzel knot. I wasn't liking the sound of this. "What are you talking about?"

Krista sat down in one of the folding chairs that had

been placed there for family and motioned for Josie and me to join her. "Well, first off, as you could probably tell, my mother has turned into a full-fledged alcoholic."

My heart ached for her. "When did this happen?"

"About six months ago." She popped a piece of Nicotine gum into her mouth. "I don't know why I chew this. It doesn't help at all. Anyway, everything started when she lost the house last year. The one she kept remortgaging so that she could continue to lend Colin money. For the business he said you guys were starting."

Josie gasped out loud.

Why did Colin have to involve me in his lies? "Krista, that isn't true. I never saw a dime of your mother's money. I started my bakery last September, and that was with funds my grandmother gave me. Honest."

She nodded. "I believe you, but my mother doesn't. She seems to think that somehow you led Colin into this mess. The booze and the needles and everything else."

My initial fear about the drugs was confirmed. "So he was borrowing money from her to support his habit?"

"It looks that way. I'm not sure when he started, but he didn't really seem to go downhill until after you left him." She touched my arm. "And I'm not trying to imply that was your fault. He treated you like crap. I never told you this, but there were others. Kyle confirmed everything since Colin used to brag to him about his conquests all the time."

A surge of anger shot through me. "You or Kyle could have done me a huge favor if you would've let me know. I could have gotten out of that sham of a marriage much sooner. Were you aware he came to my shop the other day and threatened to take me to court over my business? Unless I gave him twenty grand, that is."

Krista's mouth hardened into a fine, thin line. "No, I wasn't. But I'm not surprised. My mother was on the phone with Colin a few weeks ago. I overheard her telling him your shop was doing well and that he should go get what was rightfully his. I had a sneaking suspicion he might pay you a visit."

Josie spoke up. "After everything Colin's done to Sally, it would have been nice if you'd shared this information with her.

We had no clue he would show up in town, especially since they were divorced before she even started the business."

"Colin ruined Mom's life," Krista said sadly. "You know he always was her favorite. For years she ignored me and Kyle yet made excuses for him. He was smarter. He was better looking. He could do anything." She sighed. "It never bothered me much, but as you heard, Kyle can't seem to forget it."

"Should I talk to Elizabeth?" I asked. "Explain to her that I knew nothing about the money?"

Krista shook her head. "It won't do any good. Mom always believes just what she wants to believe. And she's so loaded now, she won't even remember later on. I do the best I can. Kyle won't take her, so she's living with me. He kicks in for some of her expenses, but that's about it."

And I thought my family was dysfunctional. The Browns had always appeared to have their act together. Colin's father had died right before we were married. Maybe that was the start of the downfall for Elizabeth.

My voice trembled. "She always seemed to like me. Was that a lie, too?" I didn't know what to believe anymore.

Josie patted me on the shoulder, and Krista took my hand in hers. "No. She *did* like you. Then Colin started throwing you under the bus to save his own skin. 'Sally needs this for the business. Sally can't work because of the miscarriage. Sally—'"

"*What*?" I shrieked. The room seemed to turn upside down as I clutched the seat of the chair so tightly my fingers started to ache.

I heard Josie mutter a curse word under her breath.

Apparently confused, Krista stared at me. "I'm sorry. I shouldn't have brought it up. He told us never to mention it around you."

I put my head in my hands. "I can't believe this is happening. Krista, there was no miscarriage. Colin didn't even want children. I hoped he'd change his mind eventually, but I was never pregnant."

"That louse," Krista said in a tight voice. "If he was alive, I'd kill him again just to get even for everything he's done to all of us."

I got to my feet unsteadily. The room was warm and

close around me. I tried to wrap my head around all of these new tidbits of information. My ex-husband had been a drug addict. Colin had also lied to my mother-in-law about our needing money. He'd told them I'd once lost a baby. He knew how much I loved children and longed in vain for one. In my opinion, this was almost as bad as the infidelity. I was so angry I couldn't see straight. Had anything ever come out of his mouth that *wasn't* a lie? I had been deceived over and over again. How had I not seen through his act?

"I need to get some air," I said in a hoarse voice.

Josie put her arm around me. "I think I should take Sal home."

Krista's face was sympathetic. "I'm so sorry. Maybe this will help make things better." She reached into her purse and produced a little plastic bag with something glittery in it and handed it to me.

"What's this?" I asked, taking a closer look. A canary diamond, beautifully cut, that appeared to be about two carats in size. It was surrounded by a halo of tinier diamonds.

Krista drew her eyebrows together. "The police found it in Colin's wallet the night he died. Didn't you give it back to him after the divorce? I knew you wouldn't want to keep anything that he gave you, so I figured—"

I shook my head. "I've never seen it before."

I guessed my former sister-in-law had never paid much attention to my actual engagement ring. She was the type who wouldn't care if hers came out of a Cracker Jack box. The ring Colin had presented me with was comparable to one you'd find in a gumball machine. It was certainly nothing like this J. Lo-type jewelry.

Krista's brow furrowed. "I don't understand. If it's not yours, whom does it belong to? He wasn't dating anyone. Well, no one longer than the usual one-night stand bit. He enjoyed women he couldn't have on a permanent basis." She put her hand over her mouth. "I'm sorry, Sal. That was insensitive of me."

At this point, I was pretty much numb to the pain. "No worries."

I turned the ring over to examine the gold band. I had to squint to make out the inscription on the inside. *Love is a gift.* A beautiful sentiment and more than enough proof for me that Colin had not bought this ring.

"Will you be at the funeral tomorrow morning?" Krista asked.

I shook my head. "Josie and I are leaving for Florida first thing. We're in a baking competition and won't be back until late Friday. For what it's worth, please extend my sympathies to your mother."

There was no way I could face Elizabeth again. The woman seemed convinced I was a lying, money-grubbing slut. She was suffering enough already, and there was probably nothing I could say that would convince her of my innocence. Still, my heart ached when I thought of the few times we'd baked cookies together and the day she'd traveled almost an hour to bring me homemade chicken soup when I'd been laid up with the flu.

I handed the ring back to Krista. "I hope you find out whom this belongs to. Maybe it could help lead to who really killed Colin. And for the record, my boyfriend is not a murderer."

Krista's face turned crimson. "I believe you. I may be the only one, but—" A sudden gleam filled her eyes, and she handed me the ring again. "You take it for now. Perhaps when you get to Florida you can find out something. Maybe it's Amber's. She broke up with him not too long ago. But I don't know where he would have gotten the money to pay for this. It probably cost at least twenty grand, and as you know, he didn't have two nickels to rub together."

"Who's Amber?" I asked.

Krista took a small pad from her purse and began scribbling on it. "Amber Mills. Another woman he was fooling around with. A married woman to boot."

"Good God," Josie exploded. "He should have been castrated years ago."

Krista handed the slip of paper to me. "She lives near Clearwater Beach in Tampa. I don't have her address, but she shouldn't be too difficult to find. And this is the phone number for Colin's landlord. He listed me as a reference when he got the apartment a few months ago. The guy started pestering me last week when Colin left town, asking if I'd seen him. Apparently, he was late on his rent. *Again*."

"Why didn't he stay put in the apartment he had with Sal?" Josie asked.

Even though I already knew the answer—thanks to Luke—I let Krista respond. "He got evicted months ago when he couldn't pay the rent. He stayed with Luke until Luke got fed up with him. From what I know, Luke's a pretty easygoing guy, so that tells you Colin wore out his welcome everywhere. I think Luke also helped him find the current apartment."

"This doesn't make sense. How could he afford to buy a twenty-thousand-dollar ring for someone?" Josie asked.

I suspected I knew the answer to this as well. "Maybe he didn't buy it. Perhaps it's stolen. He might have been planning to support one of his habits with it."

Krista rubbed her eyes wearily. "Keep the ring for now. I trust you. You can bring it back when you come home. If you can't find the rightful owner, we'll use it to pay for his funeral. But I don't want to take it without first trying to find whom it might belong to. No matter what Kyle says."

Josie frowned. "Krista, we're not going to have much time when we're down there to play detective. The contest starts—"

"I'll do whatever I can," I broke in.

Josie looked at me in surprise. "But, Sal, how can—"

I shook my head. "I have to clear Mike's name. That's the most important thing to me right now."

CHAPTER NINE

―――――

"This is exactly what you need." Josie stretched in her seat as the plane took off down the runway. "A break from everything in good old New York State right now."

I closed my eyes for a minute and sighed. I hadn't slept well last night. Visions of Mike and Colin had flooded my dreams, and now I couldn't even remember what they were about.

"Just think, Sal. In two hours we'll be in sunny, warm Florida."

"Yes. With my ever embarrassing parents."

"At least you *have* parents who care about you," Josie said.

I stole a sideways glance at my best friend as she gazed out the window. I'd been so involved in my own drama the last few days that I hadn't stopped to think about everything she was going through. "It must have been tough saying good-bye to the kids this morning."

"It was. They kept asking me not to go, but when I promised to bring them back something, they stopped." She smiled. "What'd you do with the ring?"

I patted my handbag. "It's in here."

"Good. Keep it safe. We'll check in at the hotel and then go over to the television studio to get our instructions. That's all we have to do today, but tomorrow will be grueling. Nonstop from about eight o'clock in the morning till eight tomorrow night." She yawned. "I had hoped to sit by the pool today, but it seems you might have other things in store for us."

I shook my head. "This is my problem. I want you to enjoy yourself while you're here. You need this getaway as much as I do. Maybe more."

"Forget it," Josie said. "We're a team." She squeezed my hand. "Have you heard anything else from Mike?"

My throat tightened, and I stared down at my lap. "Nothing. I sent him a text earlier saying I would be in Florida till Friday, in case he forgot, but he didn't respond." Nor had he replied to the other ten thousand texts I'd sent. When I tried to call, it always went straight to his voice mail.

Josie's voice was gentle. "He'll be back. Mike needs time to figure things out. And we're the only ones who are trying to help him. Do you think someone followed Colin to New York so they could kill him? Or maybe it was an old friend from New York? Did he have any enemies while you were married?"

I shrugged. "No one in particular who I recall." Who knew? It had quickly become apparent that I hadn't known this man at all. How had I been so blind? Or had this all come about after our divorce? Maybe I had only seen what I wanted to before, until I was forced to confront the truth about him. "I still can't believe he's dead."

"I know it's hard," she said, "but you need to stop blaming yourself. You're not responsible for the mess his life became. Colin did that to himself. And he hurt you pretty bad in the process, too."

I knew she was right, but that still didn't make me feel any better about the situation.

A voice came over the loudspeaker, announcing that we could now unfasten our seat belts and move about the cabin.

Josie leaned her chair back. "So what's the game plan for this afternoon when we get things squared away for the competition?"

"Krista was going to call Colin's landlord and tell him we were coming. They can't get down here for a few weeks, so the landlord agreed to box up his clothes and such and put them in a storage unit."

"That was generous of him," Josie commented.

"Well, for a small fee, of course." I blew out a sigh. "I did tell Krista that if I saw anything of value, I'd bring it back with me, as long as it wasn't too large."

"Very nice on your part," she said. "You don't owe them

anything."

"Maybe not, but I feel terrible about this. He lied to his mother. She thought she was helping us during our marriage. I have to do something." Anything to help ease my conscience at this point was a bonus.

The plane touched down at Orlando International Airport shortly before eleven. We located our luggage and went to collect our rental car, a black Chevy Cruze. As I settled behind the wheel, I noticed I had a voice mail from my grandmother. Josie waited patiently while I listened to it and then started up the engine.

"Everything okay?" she asked.

I bit into my lower lip. "Grandma said that Mitzi didn't show up for work today. No call, nothing. As far as I'm concerned, she's fired."

Josie's cheeks reddened. "You were right about her, Sal. I'm sorry."

"No harm done." I waved my hand dismissively. "When we get back to town, I'll call Sarah. Maybe we can help her work something out."

We drove to the hotel and checked in, grabbed a quick lunch, and then headed over to the Wingding Television Studio on International Drive. We signed in at the front desk where the receptionist, Kay, gave us an envelope with a list of rules, name badges to wear during the competition, and a sign that said *Kitchen B* which was where we would be stationed.

"Congratulations on being featured in our Great Northern Episode," Kay said. "We have another team from New York, one from Jersey, and one from Vermont. We like to have a theme for each show." She beamed with pride.

"How original," Josie muttered.

"You can drop your ingredients off now if you like," Kay went on. "I'll place them in the kitchen for you."

When I handed her the suitcase, she informed us that we needed to be at the studio no later than seven the next morning. "Tomorrow is going to be a very long day. Get plenty of rest tonight. You'll need it. Do you have your recipes ready for Round Two?"

"Round Two?" I asked, confused.

She looked at me in surprise. "Round One is a standby favorite that the judges ask you to create. You know, sugar, chocolate chip, oatmeal raisin, et cetera—something like that. Round Two will feature two of your specialty cookies. We need to have the recipes ahead of time to make sure they're authentic. And Round Three will have a different theme for each contestant that must relate to the cookie you make. The judges will rate you on the originality and taste for that one. Rounds One and Two are worth 25 points apiece, and Round Three is worth 50 points. The team with the highest score overall wins."

Josie nodded in approval. "I know how it works and have the recipes with me." She reached into her purse and produced two index cards that she handed to Kay. "Coconut macaroons and jelly cookies."

"Oh, right. I knew what you meant." I chastised myself for having forgotten this part. Like Josie, I was familiar with the way the show worked. I had seen it live once, but as of late, my memory compared to a blank slate. All I could think about was Colin's death—and the fact that Mike might go to jail for something he didn't do.

Kay took the recipes without a glance and placed them into a manila folder labeled with my bakery's name, Sally's Samples. "If there's a problem, they'll let you know tomorrow. Good luck."

I longed to see the kitchen area where the taping and competition occurred, but Kay didn't offer. We mumbled a hasty good-bye and left.

"I really wanted to see the place," Josie said. "Get a feel for where everything is located, you know? Oh, well. Maybe they don't allow it beforehand. Anyhow, I've watched enough episodes on television that it should be easy enough to figure everything out."

I didn't say anything but wasn't so sure. My baking skills were okay, but I definitely wasn't in Josie's league. She could think up fantastic recipes with a minute's notice and bake and decorate with the best of them. Unlike me, Josie never burned cookies. They always came out perfect. I almost felt out of place in this competition. Josie would be the one barking orders tomorrow, and I'd be the one dutifully running back and forth.

Not that I minded, but it only served as further proof that my shop would be nothing without her.

Colin's apartment was located in Lakeland, between Orlando and Tampa. From the studio, I took I-4 to Highway 98. We got off at Exit 33 and had traveled past a strip mall when my GPS announced, "You have reached your destination."

We found ourselves in front of a three-level building complex with no elevator. The place was old but appeared clean for the most part. Some gray paint peeled from the sides, but it wasn't as bad as I'd expected. A couple of people sat on lawn chairs around the swimming pool, talking amongst themselves. A gated fence surrounded the entire building. We pulled it open and spotted a small office that branched off the building on the right-hand side.

A man sat behind a desk inside the office sifting through some paperwork. He was heavy set with rolls of fat slopping over the sides of the chair he was sitting in. He glanced up at us with a bored expression. His hair was a brilliant shade of red and his beard a spot-on match.

"Help you, ladies?" he asked.

"Hi," I said. "Are you the landlord?"

He snorted. "Well, I run this dump, if that's what you mean." He extended a hand. "Name's Charlie. We have a couple of vacancies in case you ladies are looking."

I shook his outstretched hand. "Um, no thanks. My name is Sally Muccio, and this is my friend Josie Sullivan. Krista Eldridge phoned you this morning about apartment 3D. She said you might be willing to let us in so that we could look around. I'm Colin's ex-wife."

He frowned. "Yeah, I guess so. Let me just say I ain't on board with this. That Brown fellow owed me two months back rent. And now I'm stuck with his stuff until the family gets down here. Being a landlord in this dump is for the birds."

"You do know he was murdered, right?" Josie asked. "The family didn't plan on this being an inconvenience to anyone."

"Whatever." Charlie eased his stout body frame off the padded office chair. "Follow me. You got one hour. And you tell the rest of his family they got thirty days to get the stuff out, or it goes to Goodwill."

We followed him out of the office and into the complex, up two flights of stairs with the smell of fried food and weed lingering through the air. Voices from the raised volume of a television drifted across the hallway from 3B.

Charlie inserted his master key into Colin's door and pushed it open. "This is the only efficiency on the floor. Kitchen, living room area, bathroom. That's all. Cheapest one in the building, and the loser still couldn't pay me. To top it off, now I've got to hire a cleaning crew to come in and take care of this pigsty."

I was rendered speechless by his attitude for a moment. True, Colin had done some horrible things, but the man was dead, after all.

"Thank you," I managed to say. "We won't be long."

He grunted in reply, and we watched his lumbering frame depart.

"Nice guy," Josie commented. "Really knows how to make you feel welcome."

The stench of spoiled food greeted our noses as soon as we entered the apartment. I glanced around the room. As I'd suspected, the place was a disaster. Dirty dishes filled the sink, flies buzzing around them. There was a mountain of clothes on the floor. A trash can that had overflowed with garbage in the kitchen managed to attract even more insects. I gagged for a second, afraid my stomach might explode.

I walked into the living room where an unmade sleeper sofa bed sat in the middle of the floor. A display of beer cans in the shape of a pyramid sat on top of the coffee table. There was a small television on a rickety stand and next to it, a recliner I recognized from our apartment. No other furniture.

Josie held a tissue over her nose. "I think I may be sick."

"I know. Let's hurry so that we can get out of here."

The place was deplorable and depressing. Colin had never been a neat freak, but he certainly hadn't been a slob, either. I wondered again what had happened to him in the last year. Was this all due to the alcohol and drugs? Since I had no experience with either, I wasn't positive, but I knew that at the young age of twenty-nine, his life was over. What had gone so horribly wrong? And what had my ex-husband done that would make someone kill him?

Josie waved a hand in front of my face. "Sal? Where'd you go?"

"Sorry." I forced my thoughts away. "I just don't understand how he turned his life upside down like this."

"Come on. I know you like a book. Stop blaming yourself. Now, let's get this search over with so that we can leave this putrid hole in the wall forever."

I walked into the kitchen and tried to ignore the flies buzzing around me. "It shouldn't take us long. God knows there doesn't seem to be much here, except for garbage."

Josie pressed her lips together. "Now that you mention it, I draw the line at going through his trash can. Just sayin'."

I stole a glance in the overhead kitchen cabinets that had no doors. Not much there. A few dishes and glasses. A couple of pots. Some staples such as peanut butter, a loaf of moldy bread, a box of cereal, and a bag of chips. I wasn't the world's best cook, but he definitely ate better when he had been married to me.

I pulled out the sliding drawer under the Formica countertop. Some overdue bills and a couple of photographs. There was a picture of Colin and Luke that I gathered had been taken when they worked together a few years ago. Another photo of Colin in swim trunks with a dark-haired beauty in a bikini. I turned the photo over and found an address on the back. In Colin's familiar chicken scrawl was written, *This one's a good time—55 Venice Place.*

Although I already suspected he'd been with numerous women—during our marriage as well—my stomach grew queasy as I read the words. Could this be Amber? Venice Place was in Tampa, near Clearwater Beach. This fit in with the area Krista had mentioned, so it seemed we might be on the right track.

"Sal." Josie sounded panicked as she went through another sliding drawer next to the refrigerator. She held up a small piece of paper that was clipped to a document.

Colin had written across the paper, *For Ramon.* That was all. The document was a photocopy of the real estate section from the *Colwestern Times* last month. At the top of it was my name, stating that I had bought property at Thirty-nine Elk

Street.

My blood ran cold. So this was how Colin had known I'd bought the building.

"What does this mean?" Josie asked. "Who's Ramon?"

I swallowed hard. "I'm guessing this was how Colin had hoped to get himself a nice little loan, by saying he owned part of my business. When we're done here, we have to try to find this Ramon guy to see if he knows anything that could help us."

"What a scumbag," Josie whispered. "And I'm betting Ramon is, too."

I walked into the bathroom. The tub was lined with so much dirt and grime that it looked like it hadn't been cleaned in months. The dingy shower curtain surrounding it was torn in several places. I opened the medicine cabinet and flinched when I found a syringe. There was nothing else out of the ordinary. A laundry basket filled with dirty clothes. The linen closet in the bathroom was being used for Colin's wardrobe, not for holding towels and washcloths. He probably didn't even own any. There were a couple of pairs of trousers, jeans, a few shirts, and some boxer briefs. One pair of sneakers.

I scanned the living room one last time. Nothing that caught my eye. On impulse, I ripped the soiled sheets off of the sleeper sofa and ran my fingers along the inside of the frame. My hand connected with something, and I pulled it out. It was another photograph. This time a close-up shot of Colin and a pretty woman with ocean-blue eyes and long blonde hair pulled back into a ponytail. They looked happy.

"Cripes," Josie mumbled. "He never got enough, did he?"

I placed the picture into my purse along with the other one then ran my fingers along the inside of the leather recliner, producing yet another photo. What an interesting and lazy way to store things. I gazed at the photo and sucked in a sharp breath. Our wedding day. Colin and I had made our way down the aisle at the church right after the priest had pronounced us husband and wife. Colin smiled and looked at me with adoration.

And my face had been blacked out with a felt-tip marker.

* * *

"Don't let it get to you," Josie said. "He probably did it after he found out you were running a successful bakery, and he was drowning in a cesspool of alcohol, drugs, and cheap tramps."

It was late afternoon, and we were lying on chaise lounges by the hotel pool. This was our one opportunity for a little relaxation before the competition tomorrow. I'd already told Josie that I wanted to try to find Amber tonight and possibly Ramon on Friday morning before our plane took off. We'd agreed to take this one afternoon to enjoy the sunshine and try to clear our heads before the competition. So far, it wasn't working for me.

Josie was probably right, but seeing those pictures made me realize I hadn't healed completely from all the betrayal. It wasn't so much about finding Colin in bed with another woman because that had been the actual wake-up call I needed to realize I'd been living a lie. It was more the fact that Colin had purposely done some malicious things to me, like attempting to steal away my bakery and lying to his family about my having a miscarriage. Although I hadn't suffered from physical blows at his hand, I was convinced in my heart that this was just as bad. During our divorce proceedings, Colin had said so many hurtful things to me that I was convinced I had in fact been a victim of abuse.

"It hurts," I confessed. "I didn't think it still would, but that picture made me realize Colin never loved me. Plus, he'd told me that the night he died. So why did he marry me?"

My best friend shrugged. "Maybe he thought your family had money. Maybe he did think he loved you at the time. Who knows? People change. It doesn't matter anymore. You've got Mike, and there's no doubt in my mind how much he loves you."

"Yet I don't even know where he is," I blurted out. "And to make matters worse, while you were changing clothes, I got a call from Brian Jenkins. He wanted to stop by and see me tonight."

Josie's mouth twitched into a smile. "Oh, really? Officer Hottie's moving in on Mike's territory already?"

"Very funny." I took a long sip of my piña colada. "When I explained I was out of town, Brian asked if Mike was with me. I said no, but I'm not sure he believed me. He said he'll stop over to see me when I get back. If Mike hasn't returned by then, and the police get wind of it, things are only going to get worse."

Josie rubbed suntan lotion on her legs. She looked terrific in the pink, two-piece suit she was wearing. I wore a black bikini with a bathing cover-up. The cheesecake dream had left me feeling a bit insecure these days.

"Look, you told Officer Hottie you'll be back on Friday?" Josie asked.

I nodded.

"Then don't worry. A lot can happen in a couple of days. Mike will be home by then."

"I hope you're right."

"Of course I am. Remember, the glass is half full, not half empty." She grinned and rose to her feet. "Which reminds me, my mai tai glass *is* empty. I'm going for another. Want one?"

I shook my head. "One drink is my limit if I'm driving later. Thanks though."

As she walked away, I glanced around the pool. Two guys, probably college age, lounged in chairs to my left. They watched Josie appreciatively.

"*Nice.*" The dark-haired, skinny guy next to me raised his sunglasses for a better look as she passed in front of him. When he and his companion noticed me watching, they both smiled in my direction.

The dark-haired guy winked. "How's it going?"

I smiled but didn't answer.

"Dude." The blond man grabbed his friend's arm. "Check it out."

A woman in a bright-red, skimpy bikini strolled down the patio, almost as if she owned the place. She settled herself in a lounge chair directly across the pool from us, her body tanned and legs perfect, long and lithe. The three-inch stilettos she wore were the same obnoxious color as the suit. She had donned sunglasses and a wide-brimmed beach hat. Every inch of her was flawless. As I watched her smooth suntan lotion on her legs, I realized I was not the only one watching. Every red-blooded male of assorted ages watched her, too.

"Damn, she's hot." The blond guy and his friend practically had their tongues hanging out of their mouths.

Ugh. Men.

"Uh-huh," said his friend. "Sexy as hell."

The woman removed her sunglasses and peered across the pool. When she spotted me observing her, she waved then blew me a kiss. I waved dutifully back.

"Wow." The dark-haired guy stared at me in admiration. "I'm impressed. You really know that hot babe?"

"Yeah." I nodded, praying this would be the end of the embarrassing subject.

The blond-haired guy turned in my direction. "Hey, no offense. You're not so bad yourself. But, like, she's got a body that totally rocks, ya know?"

I winced, but they didn't seem to notice. The topic of this conversation was really starting to bother me.

"Is she available?" The blond guy asked. "Can you introduce us?"

"No, on both accounts."

"Why not?"

I blew out a sigh. "Because that's my mother."

CHAPTER TEN

———

"So." My mother beamed at us from across the booth in the hotel restaurant. "What do you girls have planned for this evening?"

I glanced at my watch. Six thirty. "Uh, Josie and I might do some sightseeing. Tomorrow's a big day for us."

My father inhaled his second cheeseburger. "You should have brought some fortune cookies with you for luck. I hope we don't crash and burn on the flight back home."

Josie clamped her lips together while I tried not to groan out loud. My father, the voice of doom and gloom.

"What are you two doing this evening?" Josie asked.

My mother giggled as she downed the rest of her Bloody Mary and put an arm around my father's shoulders. "We'll probably turn in early. Right, honey?"

"Whatever you say, hot stuff." He reached over and bussed her cheek.

Okay, I loved my parents, but the public displays of affection were just downright uncomfortable to watch. After spotting my mother at the pool earlier, my father had joined her shortly afterward in Bermuda shorts, a tank top, white socks, and sandals. They'd cuddled together on the same chaise lounge for so long that I was afraid I might lose my lunch.

"What time should we be at the studio tomorrow?" my mother asked. "We don't want to miss anything."

My stomach muscles constricted. I prayed they wouldn't make a scene. How embarrassing would it be to get kicked out of a national baking competition because one's parents were groping each other in the audience?

"Um, I don't know," I lied. "I think you can show up

anytime. Maybe like three in the afternoon?"

My mother laughed. "Don't be silly, darling. We'll be there way before that. I can't wait to see my little girl bring home the grand prize."

When Josie exhaled sharply, I knew what she was thinking. As if we weren't nervous enough already, now we had this to deal with as well.

My father dipped a french fry in ketchup and pointed it as us. "You kids go have some fun. We'll take care of the bill." He blew me a kiss. "Stay out of trouble."

If he only knew. We waved good-bye and then went to retrieve our rental car in the parking lot. I entered the address I'd found earlier into the vehicle's GPS.

"Okay, it's kind of late in the evening to be making a social call, isn't it? We won't get there until almost seven thirty at this rate," Josie said.

"Well, we don't have a choice. We can't do it tomorrow, and Friday we're leaving early. It has to be tonight. Plus, if she works during the day, this will be the perfect time to catch her at home."

Josie frowned. "The address might not even belong to Amber. And the woman slept with your ex-husband. Do you really think she'll tell you anything? Are you going to ask her if the ring belongs to her?"

I paused to consider. "No, I'm not going to mention the ring. Let's see what direction the conversation takes first."

"Sounds like a plan." Josie settled back in her seat for the ride.

About forty minutes later, we found ourselves standing in front of a two-story stucco house painted a shade of light blue. We were only a few blocks from Clearwater Beach. Although darkness had already fallen, we were close enough to smell the salt water, which was one of the things I missed most about living in this area.

We stepped onto the small porch and, through a large bay window, I could see a television on with a small child sitting in front of it. *Great.*

I held my breath and rang the bell.

A dark-haired woman turned on the porch light and

opened the door a crack. She observed us with caution. "Yes?"

I stared with no doubt in my mind that this was the woman in the picture. Long dark hair, the same shade as mine, only hers fell down the small of her back in perfect waves. Her complexion was a tad lighter than my olive-toned one. She looked like a size zero and towered over my five-foot three-inch status in her high-heeled sandals.

"Are you Amber Mills?" Josie asked.

She wrinkled her nose. "Who wants to know?"

I cleared my throat. "We'd like to ask you a couple of questions about Colin Brown."

Her eyes widened in alarm. She glanced back inside the house in the direction of the child then shut the door behind her as she stepped onto the porch. "I haven't seen that lowlife in two months. What's he done now?"

"He's dead," I said.

To my astonishment, Amber merely shrugged. "I'm not surprised. So who are you? One of his relatives?"

I held out my hand to her. "I'm his ex-wife."

She looked me over then chuckled. "Get out. Sally, right? The Peanuts character? I was curious when Colin mentioned you. The way he described you though—I thought you were some fat, hideous creature. You're actually not half bad."

I blew out a breath. *Okay, you can do this, Sal.* "Colin was murdered. I was hoping you might be able to provide us with some information about who may have wanted him dead."

Amber reached into her blazer pocket for a cigarette. "Why do you care? He was your ex-husband."

I debated about how much to tell her. "Because someone close to me has been wrongfully accused of his murder."

"Ah." She lit her cigarette. "Well, I hate to burst your bubble, but I didn't kill him. I'm sure there are plenty of people who wouldn't have minded seeing that bastard turn up dead though."

"Why'd you stop dating him?" I asked. "Or did he break up with you?"

Amber narrowed her eyes at me. "I ended it when I found out he was seeing someone else. And then that slime had the nerve to threaten to tell my husband about us unless I gave him money to keep quiet."

I glanced at the hand wrapped around her cigarette. She wasn't wearing a ring. "Where's your husband now?"

"We're separated," she said.

"Did you give Colin money or something else to help him pay his debts?"

"I lent him some money," she said. "That was my second mistake after getting involved with him. I figured out a while back I'd never see the cash again. Colin Brown was nothing but a whore. Whoever killed him did the entire female population a favor. Especially you, honey."

Not quite. "You don't happen to know whom else he was seeing, do you?"

"Some little blonde," she said. "I don't know her name."

I reached into my purse and produced the picture I had found in Colin's couch. "Is this her?"

Amber's eyes blazed with anger underneath the porch light. "Yeah. That's the bimbo. I walked in on them one night. Do you know what that feels like? The betrayal?"

I sighed. "Uh, yeah, actually I do."

She frowned. "Sorry. But that makes me wonder if it was all some type of game to him. Did he want to see how much he could get away with? Did any woman ever mean anything?"

I thought about this for a moment. "Well, I can tell you *I* never meant anything to him, and we were married for five years. Colin shared that information with me shortly before he died."

Josie laid a hand on my arm.

"I'm okay." I turned back to Amber. "So you have no clue who this woman is?"

She hesitated. "Like I said, I don't know her name. I was giving a seminar on extreme couponing at the Hooper Inn on First Street about a month ago. I spotted little Miss Cutesy at the hotel that night. I'm not sure what she was doing there—she wasn't attending the seminar. I will tell you that when our eyes met, she scurried away like a rat."

Amber blew a perfect circle of smoke into the night as she continued. "Colin told me she didn't mean anything to him.

That she was engaged to someone else, and it was only a one-time fling. Nice, huh? He said he was using her. I mean, isn't that the best? Was there any woman he didn't use?"

Probably not. I'd once been convinced I'd known him so well. Sadly, I hadn't known him at all. Sure, we were no longer married, and I had Mike in my life, but the betrayal still hurt. I wondered if it always would.

I tried another tactic. "How about jewelry? Did you give him anything to hock?"

"Nothing," she said. "Only cash."

"Mommy." A little girl with dark hair like Amber's pressed her face up against the bay window and waved.

Amber bit into her lower lip. "I have to go. Whatever you're looking for from that bastard, I hope you find it." She put her hand on the doorknob and then turned back to us. "Did they have the funeral already?"

I nodded. "It was this morning."

Amber stared down at the concrete for a moment, not saying anything. When her gaze rose to meet mine again, cold gray eyes stared back at me filled with rage. "Good. I hope he rots in hell."

* * *

"Well, let's see," Josie said. "We're finding out a lot about your ex here. We don't know who killed him, but it's pretty obvious he didn't have many fans."

Our room was on the fifth floor. As we exited the elevator, we proceeded past a vending machine and couch. Two men were sitting on it. One was about fifty, bald with a protruding stomach. He tapped away on his phone. The other man appeared to be tall with jet-black hair and a matching mustache. Both wore expensive tailored suits, possibly Armani. They regarded Josie and me with curiosity as we walked past them to our room, which was the second one on the left side of the hall. I inserted the card into the lock. When it beeped, I lifted it back out. We shut and locked the door behind us.

Josie yawned. "I'm beat." She flopped onto one of the double beds and closed her eyes.

We heard a tap on the door, and she groaned. "God, I hope it's not your mother. I'm in no mood for a girl's night of gossip."

I went to the peephole and peered out. Fear swept over me as I took a step back and whispered. "It's the men who were on the couch when we got off the elevator."

Josie rose to her feet and stood beside me as she yelled through the door. "Can we help you?"

"Yeah," the tall man growled. "I'm here to see Sally."

Panic gripped me. "Do you think they have something to do with the contest?"

"Unless the chubby one is doing his best impression of the Pillsbury Doughboy, I highly doubt it." She yelled again. "What's this regarding?"

He grunted. "Look, just open the door. We ain't gonna hurt ya. I got some useful information for the lady about her husband, Mr. Brown."

Josie looked at me, alarm registering in her blue eyes.

I pulled my phone out of my purse and had 9-1-1 on standby if needed. "Okay, let them in."

Josie unlocked the door and undid the chain. The men entered the room and glared at both of us.

"Which one of you is Sally?" The tall man asked.

Josie pointed a finger at me.

He extended his hand and then shut the door behind him. "Ramon Ravole. And this is my pal, Punchy." He gestured at his pudgy friend.

Punchy gave us both a brief nod. His complexion was as white as sugar, and he had ears that rivaled Dumbo's. His lips curled back in a grin to reveal teeth well-stained with tobacco. *Ramon Ravole. Ramon...* Was this the Ramon Colin had known?

Josie gave a bark of laughter. "Ramon Ravole. Sounds like a rich Italian dish."

Ramon's gaze lingered on her face for a moment. "Ah, that's cute, honey. First time I ever heard that one. And what's your name?"

She narrowed her eyes at him. "Josie."

Ramon laughed then turned his attention back to me, eyes dark and menacing. "So does that make you one of the pussycats?"

Josie placed her hands on her hips and stuck her chin out. "Hilarious. Just when I was beginning to think you didn't have any original brain cells."

Uneasy, I nudged my friend, praying she'd be quiet. "Ah, what can I do for you, Mr. Ravole?" My stomach was queasy with uneasiness as I watched him and his mute friend.

Ramon stared at me like I had corn growing out of my ears. "I'm here for the money, of course."

Baffled, I stared back. "I don't know what you're talking about."

Punchy shook his head and frowned but still didn't say anything.

Ramon appeared bored. "Perhaps you don't understand whom you're dealing with here, sweetie pie. With interest, we're over ten grand now. It's pay up time. And I'm getting tired of waiting."

Stay calm, Sal. This is all a huge mistake. "You must have me confused with someone else. I don't even live in Florida. I'm only in town for a baking competition."

His smile was evil. "I know who you are and where you're from. You're Colin's wife, and your old man owes me money. Don't try to claim he never mentioned it to you."

My heart started beating so fast that I was afraid it might leap out of my chest at any moment. What exactly had Colin gotten himself into? More specifically, what had he gotten *me* into? "I'm Colin's *ex-wife*. We were divorced months ago."

"That ain't what the obit said." Ramon smiled. "And now that he's gone, the debt belongs to you."

"How did you even know we were here?" Josie asked.

"My patience is wearing thin, Red," Ramon said. "I got plenty of connections. Everywhere. And I know Mr. Brown skipped town last week. I can't believe you two were dumb enough to come here. Like flies trapped in a spider's web."

Holy crap. This guy reeked of a famous *M* word. Had Colin been borrowing money from the mob?

"Sicilian, right?" Ramon asked me.

I nodded. "One hundred percent."

That got a smile out him. "Ain't no other heritage as far

as I'm concerned, so I'm gonna give you a little break. You got till Friday morning to come up with the dough." His gaze traveled downward, taking in my white shorts and matching sandals. "It'd be a shame to have to break those pretty legs into pieces."

I opened my mouth to say something, but only air came out. The words stuck in my throat.

"Wait a minute," Josie said. "Sally isn't responsible. Like she said, they were divorced months ago."

"Not my problem," Ramon said. "Fact is, *someone's* gotta pay. So it might as well be you. Mr. Brown said his wife ran a successful bakery, and he owned half. He also said he had something he was gonna hock to get me my money. Since you're his next of kin, I'm guessing you know what that something is. Maybe it even belongs to you."

I thought of the ring in my purse. That must have been what Colin meant. No way was I giving it to Ramon since it was my sole lead right now. The only thing that might possibly help clear Mike.

"I guess you'd better take the money out of your business. Unless…" His gaze came to rest on my chest. "Maybe we could find another way to even the score."

Punchy licked his lips and moved toward Josie, but I stepped in front of her.

"I'd rather be shot out of a cannon," Josie muttered.

"Hmm." Ramon looked at her. "That's a new one, but hey, I'll try anything once."

Punchy started to giggle. It was a barely audible silly gurgle that reminded me of Scooby Doo.

Ramon gave a gallant bow then reached for the doorknob. "Remember, Mrs. Brown. If you don't pay up, you might just wind up like your old man."

CHAPTER ELEVEN

Josie handed me a paper cup of coffee. "Okay. We have to concentrate. One track minds here today. No thoughts of Colin or Mike. And no mention of potential mob guys. We have to focus all of our attention on this competition to have any chance of winning."

We stood in Kitchen B, waiting for the host and judges to arrive. The camera crew was setting up, the director shouting orders, and people were lined up outside waiting to fill the studio audience. I experienced a twinge of guilt that I hadn't given my parents a certain time to arrive by. If they were not here at nine when taping began, they would not be allowed in. At least that is what one of the employees told us when we'd arrived at seven. I'd tried to call my mother, but she wasn't answering the phone, and her voice mailbox was full. Typical. She always forgot to delete messages.

I nodded in reply to Josie's tense lecture. "Don't worry. I've got my head in the game."

She laughed. "No offense, Sal. I know you better than you know yourself. There's only one thing—or shall we say one person—that you're thinking about today. Now, it's your shop, and I respect that, but how do you feel about me telling you what to do? Just for today, I promise."

I grinned. "You *always* tell me what to do."

She shrugged. "True. But I thought I'd be polite for once and ask first."

I smiled at my best friend. "Don't worry. I have no problem following orders today. You are officially dubbed the boss."

Josie lifted her nose in the air. "I can live with that."

I'd had a terrible time sleeping last night and knew Josie had, too. I didn't want to wind up at the bottom of a river with my feet tied to cement blocks. Would Ramon really do something like that to me? My first impulse was to call Brian and see if he could help, but I didn't want to draw any more attention to Mike's disappearance. Instead, I tried to concentrate on the fact that in a little over twenty-four hours, I'd be heading home. This had not been the relaxing getaway Josie and I had hoped for. So far, all of the things I'd discovered about my ex-husband were ones I wished I'd never known about.

I was well aware how much this contest meant to Josie and thought of Grandma Rosa's reprimand the other day. If we won, the results for my business could be huge. The twenty grand alone was fantastic enough, but the prestige on top of it was more than enough reason to want to win. Josie was right. If I started thinking about Mike or Colin, it might ruin any chance we'd have today.

I leaned over the workstation and sipped my coffee as a man barked orders to the camera crew in the center of the floor, where the judges table was located. Four kitchens or workstations surrounded the table, set up in the shape of a square. Kitchen A was to our left, and directly across the room from us were C and D. On the other side of Kitchens A and C, the studio audience looked out at all of us. . Since there were no partitions separating each kitchen, we could see everything our competitors were doing and vice versa.

Every appliance, including the workstation I leaned on, was stainless steel. Behind Josie and myself was a thirty-six-foot cubic refrigerator we shared with Kitchen A. Each kitchen had its own two-bowl sink and a set of double Imperial convection ovens. Josie had practically foamed at the mouth when she saw them. Each oven held six grates and were the best for making cookies of this magnitude, she'd said.

A voice from an overhead speaker bellowed down at us. "Fifteen minutes till taping begins, contestants. Please get in your designated places."

"Sally Muccio?" A middle-aged, dark-haired woman in a black, tailored suit approached us. Her name tag read *Priscilla.* "Hi there. I've been reviewing all of the submissions for Round

Two, and it seems we've a little problem with one of your entries."

Josie's eyes went wide with alarm. "What kind of problem?"

Priscilla frowned. "Well, it looks like someone else is using the same exact coconut macaroon recipe as you." She clucked her tongue. "So it makes me wonder if this recipe was even yours to begin with. Perhaps a copycat."

"What?" Josie's nostrils flared. "Of course it's our recipe. I created it myself. Who else is using it?"

"Kitchen D submitted theirs first, so they get the rights to it. Sorry. You'll have to come up with something else and fast before we start taping, or you'll be disqualified." Pricilla turned on her heel and walked over to the judges' table to greet them upon their arrival.

Josie glared across the room at Kitchen D where a man and woman in their fifties chatted amongst themselves and seemed oblivious to the daggers she shot them. "Let me at those two. I'll drag the truth out of them."

I grabbed her arm. "Don't you dare. Then we *will* be disqualified. Okay, let's think. We need to come up with another recipe fast."

"Time to panic." Josie clutched her stomach. "What are we going to do?"

"Calm down. You have tons of great recipes. We're also doing the jelly cookies for Round Two as well, right?"

Josie nodded.

"Okay. How about we make sugar cookies? Yours are to die for."

"We can't," she moaned. "Remember, they might throw that at us during the first round. It's a standby, and they won't allow us to use them in another round." She glared at the couple as they laughed together at some private joke. "How the hell did they get our recipe? Who are they?"

"No idea. I'm dying to know too. But we have to wait until the taping starts, and they introduce the teams." I had a sudden thought. "Wait a minute. Another group is from New York. Do you think they came into the shop and had a lab analyze the ingredients?"

Josie paused a moment to consider. "I think that's pretty extreme. Plus, the website didn't even post the contestants until last Friday. That means they would've had to come into the shop on Saturday, but we didn't have many customers because of the storm." She stared at the woman from Team D. "There is something so familiar about her, but I can't put my finger on it."

I racked my brain. "Forget them for now. How about raspberry cheesecake cookies?"

She shook her head in dismay. "I overheard Kitchen C say they were making those when we checked in."

Okay, so maybe Josie was right. Now it was time to panic. "This is becoming a nightmare. How about the Italian butter cookies?" I asked.

Josie wiped at the sweat collecting on her forehead. "I didn't bring the recipe for them. I can't remember how much vanilla or baking powder to use. Oh my God, it's happening. I'm getting senile, and I'm not even thirty yet." She looked like she might cry. "We're going to be disqualified. All this work for nothing."

I grabbed my cell phone. "We are *not* going down without a fight."

"Whom are you calling?" she asked.

"The one person who always has the answers."

Gianna answered the phone at my shop. "Hey! Shouldn't you be at the competition about now?"

"We're here, and we've hit a major snag. Is Grandma with you?"

"She's putting some cookies in the oven," Gianna said. "I'll tell her you're on the phone." I heard her shout something, and my grandmother's voice mumbled a reply. "How's Florida?"

I thought of Amber Mills, Ramon Ravole, and his sidekick, Punchy. "Not exactly what I expected. Thanks so much for helping out. Did Mitzi ever call?"

"Nothing," Gianna said. "Kind of weird how she showed up for only one day, if you ask me."

"Never mind her. Have you seen Mike?"

There was silence on the other end for a few seconds. "No, honey, I'm sorry. And there's more. Brian Jenkins was in here yesterday afternoon. He asked if you were around. And then he wanted to know where Mike was working. I didn't tell him anything. I think the cops might be planning to search Mike's house."

I shut my eyes tight. One more day, and I'd be home. I could deal with this mess then. "Thanks. I appreciate it."

"Ten minutes," the cameraman yelled.

"Sal," Josie squeaked behind me.

Grandma Rosa's voice floated through the phone. "I am sorry, cara mia, we have not seen your young man. I drove past his house last night, and there was no sign of him. Poor little Spike—he misses him so. And you. But he is a good boy. I fed him lasagna again last night."

I smiled. "He probably doesn't miss us at all, thanks to your awesome cooking. Grandma, we need your help. We've got to have a new recipe to replace the macaroon cookies we were going to make. Someone else here is using it, and we only have a few minutes to come up with something."

"I had a bad feeling about this," Grandma Rosa said. "I bet someone stole it from your shop."

How was that even possible? "Can you help us? We can't use any of our shop specialties."

"What about the genettis?" Grandma Rosa asked.

"They take way too long to make."

She was silent for a few seconds. Next to me, Josie hopped back and forth on one foot and looked as if she might have a heart attack at any moment.

Grandma Rosa laughed. "Of course. The brownie biscotti."

I exhaled a long breath. "Oh, Grandma, you're a life saver. Those might be even better than the macaroons." I covered the phone with my hand and whispered to my best friend. "Brownie biscotti."

Josie grabbed an index card and started scribbling away.

"Of course they will be better," my grandmother announced with unmistakable pride in her voice. "Now put Josie on the phone, and I will go over the ingredients with her."

"Thanks so much. I love you."

"And I you, dear girl. Do not worry. Everything will be fine. How is your mama and papa?"

"They're fine. Lots of public displays of affection by the pool."

She sighed. "That is about what I would expect from those two."

I handed the phone to Josie who was writing furiously on the index card. Priscilla reappeared at our side with her arms folded, tapping her foot.

"Brownie biscotti," I said. "To go with the jelly cookies we're making."

Priscilla sniffed at the air. "You're in luck. No takers for that, but I need the recipe now."

Josie held up one finger, scribbled two more lines, thanked Grandma Rosa, and hung up. Beads of sweat were glistening on her forehead as she handed the recipe to Priscilla who ran off to make a photocopy of it and then returned to hand us the original.

"If you don't see me again, that means it's good to go. But I'll be keeping my eye on you two. Any more issues, and you'll be disqualified."

By the time she walked away, Josie looked as if she might collapse. "I need a drink."

"Okay." The director stood by the judges' table, addressing all of us. "We're going to start taping in a minute. Now, just act like the cameras aren't even here. Go about your business as usual. And remember, keep it real."

A moment later, the host, Danny Durango, was introduced and ran out in front of the judges' table. A sign flashed at the audience that read *Applause*, and everyone started stamping their feet and cheering.

Danny Durango had only started on the show a few months ago after the previous host graduated to the Cooking Elite Channel. Danny was not much taller than myself. This was a surprise to me. I knew television added ten pounds, but did it also add height? He appeared as a much larger presence on the boob tube.

Reddish-brown hair was combed back from a face that resembled that of a thirteen-year-old boy, complete with peach fuzz upon his upper lip. His medium-brown eyes were sharp and didn't seem to miss many details. The man couldn't have weighed more than a hundred pounds soaking wet. When he smiled, his over-bleached teeth almost blinded me.

He introduced the judges—Olivia Fabbeno, owner of the Cookie Boutique in New York City, and Pierre LeFountain, a pastry chef originally from Paris. They waved gaily from their seats and flaunted gleaming smiles. The applause sign flashed again.

"It feels so phony," Josie whispered. "Nothing like when I watch it from home."

"And now, let's meet our talented contestants," Danny said. The applause sign flashed again. "In Kitchen A, we have sisters Bunny and Biffy Snead from Trenton, New Jersey. They own a gluten-free cookie shop called The Cookie Terminator."

Biffy and Bunny were beefy-looking women who wore tight white T-shirts that read Terminator in large black letters. I stared in fascination at the rolls of fat on their bare arms. When the camera turned away, Bunny winked in our direction. "Go home, babies. This contest is for the big girls."

Josie muttered something under her breath seconds before the camera whirled back in our direction.

"Smile nice," I said.

Josie gave the cameraman a grin that rivaled the Cheshire cat. "I'm going to make mincemeat of those two Amazons."

"In Kitchen B," Danny boomed, "our contestants hail from Colwestern, New York. They've only been in business for five months, and their cookies are already the talk of the town. We have head baker Josie Sullivan and owner Sally Mooch from Sally's Samples."

My jaw dropped open. I held up my hand and waved it as if I was in third grade. "No, wait—"

"Cut!" someone yelled. A man with glasses and carrot-colored hair walked over to me. "Honey, no interrupting during the shooting." He yelled over his shoulder at someone. "Can we still use that piece, guys?"

"But he said my name wrong," I objected. "It's not Mooch. It's Muccio."

Bunny laughed. "Did you mooch your way here, honey?"

"See," Josie said. "They're all talk and no action, I bet."

Bunny narrowed her eyes at my friend. "Oh, I'll take you on anytime. Come on, princess, make my day."

The audience started cheering. "Cat fight! Cookie fight!"

"Keep it professional, ladies. Now let's move on," Carrot-top said.

Danny Durango shot me what I interpreted as a dirty look, but when the camera focused on him, the phony smile appeared again. "In Kitchen C, from Albany, New York, we have Glen and Barry Schwartz. They are the owners of the prestigious cookie shop 31 Flavor Favorites."

"Hmm. I'm sensing a lawsuit with a certain ice cream company here," Josie mumbled in my ear.

"And last but not least, from Bennington, Vermont, this couple runs an online bakery. Their specialty is vegan cookies. Please welcome George and Gina Graber."

Something niggled at my brain. What was it about that name? Where had I heard it before? Suddenly, I couldn't focus. I was too nervous about the competition to concentrate.

"Thieves," Josie hissed. "If it's the last thing I do, I'm going to find out how they got my recipe."

"Okay, contestants," Danny said. "There are three rounds of competition. In the first one, you'll be asked to make a classic staple cookie. How you decide to dress it up and for what occasion is entirely up to you. The second round will consist of your original recipes, two to be exact. And for the third round, we will give each one of you a word, and you'll make a cookie that relates to it. For example, audience, if I were to say *house*, what word would pop into your heads?"

Shouts of "gingerbread" filled the air.

"Excellent," Danny Durango said. A pretty blonde in tight jeans approached him with an index card, and I had to shield my eyes against the bright smile he cast at her. "Contestants, you have one hour to make a batch of cookies for our judges and hungry audience. Are you all ready?"

Josie gripped the sides of a mixing bowl between her hands while I got into racing position mode, ready to run in whatever direction she ordered.

"Sugar cookies!" Danny yelled. "Get set, go!"

"Vanilla!" Josie screeched. I ran into the pantry, but the other contestants were already there. Biffy and Glen almost came to blows over a bottle of extract, and the audience was loving it. I reached my hand around them and grabbed a smaller bottle then raced back to Josie.

"Set the oven to 350 degrees Fahrenheit," Josie said.

Wow, I was out of shape. We'd only started, and already I was out of breath.

Josie starting humming to herself. This was the method she used to maintain calmness. She mixed her dry ingredients together then placed the eggs and butter in a separate bowl. Within ten minutes, she had a tray ready to go into the oven. I ran to the convection masterpiece and popped the first tray in. I ran back for another. The cameraman followed me.

"Show me those pearly whites, honey," he coaxed.

What I really wanted to do was shove the camera back in his face. Instead, I smiled politely and pointed at the next tray of cookies as I placed them in the oven.

"This is fun," I lied.

"Way to keep it real, doll," he said and then switched over to Kitchen A.

"Get me confectioner's sugar. I'll need it for the frosting." Josie continued scooping a rounded tablespoonful of dough onto the cookie sheet.

I ran into the pantry for confectioner's sugar and then back to my best friend's side. She sniffed at the air then turned around and stared at our ovens. "What the—"

We both ran toward them together. Josie pulled out two trays of cookies that were already blackened around the edges.

"Sal!" she shrieked. "What did you do?"

The camera crew came running in our direction.

"Oooh, drama alert in Kitchen B!" Danny Durango yelled to the audience, who started cheering.

Confused, I looked at the oven dial. It had been turned up to broil. "Josie, I *know* I put it on 350. Honest."

We heard a low-pitched giggle coming from Kitchen A. Biffy and Bunny were trying hard to concentrate on their cookie trays, but wide smiles betrayed them.

"Sabotage!" Josie screamed and started toward them. I

grabbed her arm to hold her back as she struggled to free herself.

"Catfight!" people in the audience yelled and stamped their feet in unison.

"Stop it! We're wasting time." I glowered at the Terminator sisters. "We don't want to stoop to their level anyway."

"You wish you were at our level, honey," Biffy sneered.

"And the stakes have risen," Danny Durango said in a dramatic voice.

"Cripes," Josie muttered under her breath. "Could he please shut up?" She started scooping more dough and placing it onto a tray. I grabbed one, too.

"I made extra dough. Thank goodness you hadn't put any more trays in the oven yet." Josie shot a death glare at the Sneads who blew us a kiss in return. "I'll get even with them."

Before long, Danny Durango was announcing the countdown. Ten minutes, five, one minute, and *stop!* We had one hundred sugar cookies. Half were decorated with pink icing and half with blue. Our theme was baby shower.

"Aw," Danny crooned as he surveyed them.

Biffy and Bunny had formed their sugar cookies into motorcycles.

I was puzzled. "Can you buy cookie cutters in the shapes of motorcycles?"

Josie gave a toss of her head. "They're weirdos."

The audience was each given a cookie to munch on while the judges sampled one from every kitchen. They examined the texture and the frosting, talked amongst themselves, and then wrote their scores on paper.

"Okay, contestants," Danny Durango said. "The winner of the first round, with a perfect score of 25 points, is Kitchen B!"

We shrieked and hugged each other as the audience clapped and cheered.

"Okay, that's a rap," the director said. "You guys can relax for half an hour before we start Round Two."

Glen and Barry stopped to congratulate us. They appeared to be in their mid-twenties, both with multiple piercings in their lips, eyebrows, and noses. Hey, I was all for expressing yourself but still wasn't sure I'd want to eat anything they'd made.

I slung an arm around Josie's shoulders. "You are amazing."

She grinned. "They've got sandwiches in the back room for us. I'm starving. Let's go grab one before Bunny and Company eat them all."

"Yoo-hoo! Honey! Over here!" I heard someone call.

I turned in the direction of the voice and winced. There, in the front row of the studio audience, sat my mother and father. Mom wore a skintight, strapless, zebra-print minidress. My father was dressed in cargo shorts and a Red Sox T-shirt complemented with white socks and sandals again. Everyone else in the room, including Danny Durango, was staring at my mother. I wanted to hide under the workstation while she waved and blew kisses at me. Instead, I forced myself to wave back.

"Shoot me, please," Josie whispered, echoing my sentiments.

"They mean well."

She blew out a breath. "Jeez, couldn't you have given them the wrong address or something?"

I watched my parents heading toward the exit sign. "Bet Mom's going out to have a cigarette. She told me she quit, but I have my doubts."

Josie didn't answer. She stared at the studio audience then reached out to grab my arm in a deathlike grip.

"What's wrong?"

I followed the shaking finger that she pointed at the crowd. Then I froze, too.

Standing in one of the aisles, chatting gaily with the couple from Kitchen D, was our former employee.

Mitzi.

CHAPTER TWELVE

———

For a few seconds, we continued to stare. Everything had suddenly become quite clear. Mitzi knew we were going to be on the show—she had confessed that much to us. Her last name—Graber. *Head smack.* Of course. The Kitchen D contestants were her parents. On her one and only day of employment, she had stolen the macaroon recipe from my shop. After that, there'd been no need for her to report for further employment duties.

"I'll kill her," Josie whispered. "It's going to be slow and painful, and I think I'm going to enjoy it way too much."

As Mrs. Graber spoke to her daughter, Mitzi nodded her head, but her gaze remained fixated on us. There was no sign of remorse or fear. The blue of her irises was similar to steel—cold and emotionless.

For some odd reason, my stomach churned as I watched Mitzi, and I was angry at myself. Why should I be nervous about confronting her?

We walked over and stood next to her parents. My gaze never left Mitzi's face. The Grabers seemed genuinely surprised at our arrival but smiled and welcomed us.

"Nice win, girls," Mr. Graber said, extending his hand.

"Excuse me, Mr. and Mrs. Graber." I wondered if they were even aware of their daughter's scheme. "We're old friends of your daughter, Mitzi. Did you know that?"

Gina Graber's face gleamed. "Why, of course. I should have realized. Mitzi mentioned that she was in Colwestern the other day. I'll bet she was visiting you. Who would have known we'd be featured on the same show together? What a small world."

"Isn't it, though," Josie snorted.

Mitzi lowered her eyes to the floor. At least she had enough humility to look away.

"Would you mind if we spoke to Mitzi in private for a minute?" I asked.

"Of course not," Gina smiled as she addressed her daughter. "We're going to go grab something to eat, honey. We'll be back in a few minutes."

"Sure, Mom," Mitzi said, stealing a glance at the exit door.

When they walked away, Josie and I each grabbed ahold of one of Mitzi's arms.

"Let's go have a nice little chat in private," Josie hissed in her ear.

We went out into the hallway, past members of the studio audience who milled around. My mother waved, but I held up a finger to gesture that we'd be back in a few minutes. We found a ladies' room door that read *Employees Only* and ushered her inside.

Josie gritted her teeth. "You have some explaining to do."

Mitzi tossed her head in defiance like a teenager. "You can't prove a thing."

"You stole our recipe," I said. "You heard me say it was on the shelf in the back room that day. You knew we planned on using it for the competition. Why did you take it?"

Mitzi said nothing, but the color rose high in her cheeks.

"You had this planned all along, didn't you?" I asked. "I gave you a job you obviously didn't want. What I'd like to know is why."

"What do you have against us?" Josie asked.

Mitzi stared at Josie. "I don't have anything against you." Then her eyes met mine, and her face twisted into an ugly expression. "It's *you* I want to ruin."

I was thunderstruck as her eyes continued to shoot daggers at me. "What did I ever do to you?"

"You killed my boyfriend." Her eyes filled with unshed tears.

A sensation of dread swept over my body. Whom was

she talking about? There was only one person I could think of who might fit this description. "Oh God. Were you seeing Colin? My ex-husband?"

The tears streamed down Mitzi's face, but she still managed to laugh out loud. "I'd never date that scum of the earth. But he *is* responsible for ruining my life."

"Would you please care to explain?" I folded my arms over my chest.

Mitzi wiped at her eyes with the back of her hand. "He killed my boyfriend, Stan. Almost a year ago."

Okay, Colin was a lot of things. But a murderer? That was crazy. "There has to be some sort of mistake."

"There *is* no mistake." Her lower lip trembled as she thrust a finger into my face. "Stan was killed in a drunk driving accident. The other driver was totally wasted. And it's your fault because your husband didn't cut him off at the bar that night."

I thought I might be sick to my stomach as the realization dawned on me. This was the girl Luke had mentioned. Colin had almost gone to jail because of an inebriated man he let walk out of his bar who had, in turn, killed someone—Mitzi's boyfriend.

Josie's mouth fell open in horror. "Oh my God. That's terrible. But you can't blame Sally. She had nothing to do with it."

Mitzi's eyes blazed with venom. "Someone has to pay for this. The drunk driver is in prison, but I'll be waiting for him when he gets out. And I've been planning for exactly the right moment to get back at that SOB husband of yours."

"You do know that Colin died the other night, right?" Then I sucked in a sharp breath. "Oh. You were at the bar."

She smirked. "Yeah, I saw the whole thing. I also know your boyfriend's going on trial for his murder. But it's not enough that Colin's dead. I decided that you have to pay, too."

Despite the rotten thing she had done to us, I couldn't help but pity the girl. I reached out and placed my hand upon her shoulder. "I'm very sorry for your loss, but I didn't have anything to do with it. Colin and I were already separated when this happened."

She jerked away as if I'd burned her. "Don't touch me! I

need to get out of here. You'll never understand what I'm going through. Tell my parents I wasn't feeling well and had to go."

"Don't leave like this. You're not thinking straight," Josie said.

Mitzi reached for the door handle and then turned back to observe me. "We were in Florida for a vacation. That's where Stan proposed to me. We were supposed to be married at Christmas. Bet you didn't know that, huh? Instead, I had to plan his funeral. My entire life is ruined thanks to that lousy drunk and your scumbag of a husband."

I tried to reason with the girl. "Mitzi, Colin's dead. He's gotten his payback. I know it won't bring your fiancée back, but you can't let this hatred continue to destroy your entire life."

She snickered. "Yeah, wait and see if you sing that song when your boyfriend goes to jail for Colin's murder. As it should be."

Bile rose in the back of my throat. I glanced at Josie, alarmed, and guessed she was thinking the same thing. "Mitzi. You need to tell me the truth. Did you kill Colin and set my boyfriend up to take the fall?"

She gave a low laugh that sent a tremor of terror rippling through my body. "Guess you're going to have to figure that one out for yourself."

*   *   *

Having no choice, Josie and I went back to our workstation to prepare for Round Two. We had two hours to make the cookies but were both shaken by the recent confrontation with our former employee. I raced back and forth dutifully getting the ingredients Josie asked for, but Mitzi's words continued to haunt me.

I'd have to get in touch with Brian when we returned home and see if there had been any new developments. Mitzi's fingerprints would be in our shop. Maybe Brian could see if there was a match for them in the hotel room? Somehow?

My head was spinning, and when Josie reached out to grab the sugar from my hands, I jumped, sending half of it flying across the floor. A cameraman came running in our direction, his face glowing with excitement.

Josie held up a hand. "No drama here, mister. Only a simple accident. Try to control yourself."

While I grabbed a broom and swept up the mess, Josie clutched me by both shoulders. "Sal. You have to put it out of your mind for a little while, or we might as well pack up and go home. Get your head back in the game."

I blew out a breath. "You're right. Okay, let's do this."

"Fifty-five minutes left," Danny Durango shouted.

Josie put the biscotti into the oven while I concentrated on making the thumbprint jelly cookies. These were a huge favorite in my shop. People of all different ages raved about them. I grabbed the homemade strawberry jam Josie had prepared earlier in the week and placed a teaspoonful in the center of each cookie. This took some time, especially with my hand shaking. I glanced at the wall clock. Time was dwindling.

"Put in one tray at a time," Josie said. "Not every tray at once. We have to get some of these cooking."

I ran toward the ovens with one tray and barely managed to avoid Bunny as she ran past me with a piping bag full of frosting. Josie stuck her foot out, and Bunny and the piping bag went flying across the room. The camera crew raced over to the scene to snag a close-up of Bunny's face which was now streaked with frosting.

"Why you little—" Bunny glared at the camera, whose operator was hanging on her every word. "Witch."

Josie shot her a saccharin smile. "Sorry. I guess I slipped. Let's call it a knee-jerk reaction."

With only ten minutes left, I lifted the last tray of jelly cookies out of the oven and ran to insert them into the fridge to cool. The jelly portion was especially hot and would burn the judges' tongues at this stage. Josie made some intricate designs along the edges of some of the cookies and had cleverly inserted M&Ms into the mix for the brownie biscotti.

When Danny Durango finally yelled time, I was about ready to drop. "I don't know if I can survive a third round."

Josie's eyes gleamed. "If we win this round, we're guaranteed at least a tie for first place. If someone else wins the final round, then we'd have to go to a tiebreaker."

"No tiebreaker, please," I groaned. "I'm way too old for this."

She waved a hand. "Ah, I'm just getting my second wind."

We washed dishes and cleaned our prep area while the judges tasted the cookies and tallied their votes.

The halogen lights overhead reflected off Danny Durango's teeth. "And the winner of the second round is...Kitchen D!"

Josie and I both clenched our fists while the Grabers squealed and hugged each other.

Olivia beamed at the Grabers from her seat at the judges' table, macaroon in hand. "These have to be one of the most delicious cookies I've ever sampled. The coconut was so fresh and the recipe like no other I've tasted. Originality wins my vote every time. I can't stand it when people rely on boring old trends to help enliven cookies—such as M&Ms."

I thought I spotted actual steam pouring out of Josie's ears. I managed to pry her fingers loose from the countertop that she had a deathlike grip on. "We still have a chance. It's not over yet."

Her nostrils flared. "If that little twit hadn't stolen my recipe, we'd be in the lead." A tear streaked down her cheek. "I worked so hard to perfect that recipe."

"I know you did."

Josie sniffed. "This isn't about the money or prestige for me, Sal. All my life, I've never won anything. Whenever we had competitions at the culinary school, I'd place second. Someone was always better than me."

My heart ached for my best friend. Even if we did win this, I would be the one to be recognized, not Josie, simply because I was the owner of the shop. Josie didn't know yet, but if we did win, I planned on giving her half of the prize money. "You are second to *no one*. Without you I would not have a bakery, nor would it be the success it is. Just remember that. This contest doesn't mean anything. You're already number one in my book."

She wiped her eyes and hugged me. "Thanks. I needed to hear that."

I glanced at the clock. It was three thirty in the afternoon, and I already felt like we'd been here for days. By some miracle, adrenaline had finally started flowing through my veins. Now I wanted to win this competition more than ever. It was no longer about the money. This was for my best friend. It had become personal.

"As we enter the final round, let's take stock," Danny Durango bellowed. "Team B has 25 points. Team D has 25 points. The final category is worth 50 points, so it's still anybody's game!"

"That's why they break it down like that," Josie whispered. "It's impossible for anyone to win before the third round. The best you could do is tie for first place."

Danny gestured to the blonde model, Suzie, who approached Team A with a metal can. "Each contestant will draw a slip of paper out of the container. There will be one word written on it. You will read the word aloud, and then you have three hours to make three hundred cookies associated with this word. The winner of this round will also win the competition and receive a check this evening for twenty thousand dollars. The three losing teams will go home with a consolation prize of one thousand dollars each."

Josie was chanting to herself. "I can do this. I can do this."

We watched as Team A chose their slip, and Bunny grunted out loud. "Home."

Gee, I wondered what they would make with that one.

Team C chose their slip. "Cows."

"Oh, man." Josie clenched her teeth. "I could have made black-and-white cookies. Why is everyone else getting all the good slips?"

Team D chose theirs. "Water."

"I don't believe this," Josie sputtered. "Icebox cookies. We'll probably get the worst one. There's *always* a bad slip in there. We'll get one marked camel or something like that."

Grinning from ear to ear, Suzie walked over to us with the camera crew following behind her.

"This is it," Danny Durango shouted. "Can Team B take home the money? And what about Team D? Or could A or C have a sudden come-from-behind win?"

I was getting to the point where I wanted to stuff a tray of cookies down Danny Durango's throat. I reached into the container and then glanced at the strip of paper I'd selected.

I read the word aloud. "Chance."

Josie's face broke into a wide grin. "Oh, we've so got this."

"On your mark, get set, go," Danny shouted.

For the next three hours, I listened to Josie bark orders as I ran to and from the oven, making sure to keep a close eye that the dial hadn't been tampered with by our vengeful competitors. I also wrote out fortunes on three hundred strips of paper. Okay, so some of them were duplicates, but I didn't think anyone would notice. Now I understood why Josie complained she didn't have time to write them out for the ones in my bakery.

As I removed the fortune cookies from the oven, it was quite a challenge to place the strips in the center of the cookies and fold up the ends as fast as we could since they hardened within seconds. Sometimes we weren't quick enough, so Josie got creative and filled several cookies with a vanilla white chocolate ganache she'd whipped up. Then she tied the fortune strips around the outside of the cookies. For the cookies with the fortunes on the inside, we dipped them into a chocolate sauce. We used a melted toffee chocolate bar for several and chocolate hazelnut spread for others.

I noticed Josie's hands were shaking as we neared the end of the second hour, a visible sign of how tired she actually was. Her face gave away nothing though, and her mouth was set in a fine, determined line. I knew that expression well. Nothing was going to stop her now. Meanwhile, my legs ached so badly that I was afraid I might keel over.

"More sprinkles and nonpareils," Josie barked.

I raced into the pantry again then back to Josie. I hurried to the ovens to take out the next tray. During the competition, the audience was allowed to cheer us on whenever a sign was flashed. Several voices could be heard, but my parents' drifted above the rest.

"Come on, Sal," my mother yelled. "Work it baby, work it."

I shut my eyes and sighed. For a brief moment, I wondered if twenty grand was worth all the public humiliation we would endure when the show aired in a few weeks. And, of course, it would be worse if we didn't win.

"You stupid twit," Bunny yelled at Biffy as I ran by their workstation for more ingredients from the pantry. "The frosting is too thin. Here, let me have it."

"Whatever you say." Biffy took a wooden spoon, inserted it into the bowl, and then smeared it down the side of Bunny's head.

A loud gasp emitted from the audience as the crew came running. Biffy turned and charged the head cameraman like a bull then dumped the entire bowl of frosting onto his head. A security guard appeared and dragged Biffy away, leaving Bunny to finish the cookies by herself.

"I need a do-over!" Biffy screamed.

"The terminator got terminated," Josie laughed. "I love it."

We had our cookies completed with five minutes to spare. Danny started the ten second countdown, but everyone, with the exception of Bunny, was finished and standing around waiting for the judging to start. When the show actually aired, we knew it would be fixed to make it appear that we were all panicking at the last second. That was another way to build up the drama. I vowed at that moment that I would never watch another reality show again.

Finally, we heard Danny yell, "That's it! Your time is up!"

Josie turned and staggered toward me, throwing her arms around my neck. I hugged her tightly while trying to hold her up in the process. "You did it, kiddo."

She grinned. "No. *We* did it."

I had to go before the judges with the three other lead contestants and explain our reasoning for making the cookies. When it was my turn, I gave them my best sugary smile.

"To me, chance means luck. The main theme to my bakery back home is fortune cookies. With every purchase, customers get a free homemade fortune cookie created by my fabulous head baker, Josie Sullivan."

Josie blushed and stared at the floor.

Olivia examined her cookie. With the filling, it looked almost like a miniature cannolo.

"What a clever idea." Olivia sniffed at the cookie then unwrapped her fortune from the outside and laughed. "It says, 'Judge not, least ye be judged.'"

The audience howled at that one. Okay, so I had sort of planned that she'd get that particular fortune.

Olivia took a small bite then smiled at me. "These are the best fortune cookies I've ever tasted."

Pierre broke his cookie apart to examine it. "What is your personal take on fortune cookies? Do you believe there's any truth to the messages, Miss Mooch?"

I winced. "It's actually Muccio."

"Ah." He sniffed at his cookie. "Well, close enough."

I grinned in an effort to ignore his condescending attitude. "I don't believe there's any truth to the messages at all."

A shiver went down my spine.

I was dismissed and sent back to my workstation along with the other contestants. We were left to wait and speculate while the judges deliberated for a few minutes. Danny Durango chatted away with Suzie, and I wondered if he was asking her out. The cameraman returned with damp hair and all traces of frosting removed.

"Places everyone," the director yelled.

"Welcome back." Danny Durango's smile again filled the room. Had he ever been approached for Colgate commercials? "Our judges have made their unanimous decision. The winner of the Northern Cookie Crusades Episode is—"

Josie grabbed my hand in such a tight grip that I whimpered from the pain.

Danny grinned at the audience. "Okay, people, who do you think should win?"

"Team B," my father bellowed.

"Team A," another man shouted. "I liked it when she bitch-slapped the camera guy."

There were choruses of "Team D" and "Team B" until I thought my head might explode.

"For the love of God," Bunny screeched at Danny. "Just

read the damn name!"

"The winner is," Danny Durango announced, "Team B."

Josie screamed so loud I thought I might go deaf. We wrapped our arms around each other with her sobbing hysterically in my ear. People started running at us from all directions. The whole scene was similar to a stampede. An old man grabbed me in a tight hug and refused to let go until a security guard led him away. Team C and D ran over to hug and congratulate us. My mother and father flew out of the audience, and my father lifted me up in his arms to give me a bear hug.

Amidst all the hugging and congratulations, someone touched my arm. Danny Durango was standing there grinning as he pointed at my mother. "Is she your sister?"

Oh boy. I smiled and shook my head. "That's my mother."

His eyes lit up. "Is she available?"

CHAPTER THIRTEEN

———

After an hour of chatting with the media, smiling, and posing for pictures with Olivia, Pierre, and Danny Durango—till I thought my face might crack—we finally managed to break away. My parents wanted to take us out to dinner, but Josie and I begged off. Although I'd eaten nothing besides sampling the dough during the day, I still didn't have much of an appetite, and neither did Josie. We were both too exhausted. We went back to our hotel room and ordered room service, but I could only manage a couple of bites from my sandwich. I called Grandma Rosa to share the good news with her.

"I knew you would win." I caught the unmistakable note of pride in her voice while Gianna screamed in the background. "I am so proud of you, cara mia. Josie, too."

"I'm giving Josie half the prize money," I said, "but I want to repay at least some of what you lent me for Mike's bail."

She grunted on the other end of the line. "I will not take it. You keep the money and put it toward your business. I know you are thinking about expanding and every cent will help."

"Grandma, I would feel so much better if you would let me do this."

"No. I will *not* take it. Now, it is still early. Only ten o'clock. You and Josie go out and enjoy yourselves."

I glanced over at my best friend who was lying on her bed asleep, fully clothed, with a dusting of flour still in her hair. I smiled as I watched her. There would be no partying tonight. My mother and father had decided to go dancing, and I definitely did not want to be a witness to that.

"I will see you tomorrow. What time does your plane leave?"

"Two o'clock." I hesitated for a moment. "Grandma, have you seen—I mean, is—"

"No, my sweet girl," she said gently. "I have not seen him. But he will be back. I feel it in my heart."

Mine was heavy as I disconnected. I washed my face, brushed my teeth, and turned the television on low. I had no interest in watching anything but found the sound comforting. I changed into pajamas and spent a long time sitting on our private balcony, watching the fireworks coming from the vicinity of Disney World.

I knew I should be proud and happy of what we'd achieved today, but I ached for Mike. I wanted his strong arms around me, to feel loved and protected once again in his secure embrace. Despite Grandma Rosa's assurance, I worried he might never come back. I couldn't stand it any longer and sent him another text—only about the millionth one this week.

We won. Leaving for home in the a.m. Hope you'll be there waiting for me. I love you.

I sat there holding the phone between my hands. I waited and prayed but to no avail. My phone remained silent. A lone tear fell onto its screen. *He'll come home, and we'll work everything out. Have faith.*

That was all I had left now.

* * *

"We don't have to be at the airport until noon," Josie said. "So what's on the agenda for this morning?"

We were sharing the bathroom mirror. Josie was braiding her hair, and I was coating my mouth with lip gloss. "How do you feel about breakfast at the Hooper Inn?"

She looked at me quizzically, and then recognition dawned. "You want to ask about the blonde, don't you?"

"Amber said that's where she'd spotted her. Maybe she worked at the hotel or was a regular customer. It's not much, but we have to try something."

"Okay," Josie agreed. "Breakfast, and then we'll come back here to pack up."

Fifteen minutes later, we were inside the Hooper Inn's

no-frills restaurant adjacent to its lobby. Josie and I settled in a booth by the entrance. She ordered an omelet with bacon and toast while I settled on a Belgium waffle and coffee.

She stifled a yawn with her hand and grinned. "I slept like a baby last night."

I smiled. "You needed it."

Her concerned gaze rested on my face. "Did you sleep?"

"Not much," I confessed.

She reached across the table and squeezed my hand. "Our winning the contest is a good sign, Sal. Things are changing for the better, I'm sure of it. Mike will come home, and everything will get straightened out."

I wrapped my arms around my middle. "So far, I've done nothing to help him. We have suspects, yes, but no clue as to who could have done this."

Josie frowned. "Well, for starters, there's Amber. He did cheat on her with another woman. That's enough of a motive. And there's that Ramon character and his henchmen. Who's to say they didn't kill him because they were tired of waiting for their money?"

"But Ramon came to me looking for cash."

Josie waved her hand dismissively. "Don't you know anything about mob guys? They have no qualms about killing people. Then they just move on to the next person in the family to collect the debt. This way you know they mean business."

Although the thought was horrible, I admitted there was some truth to it. "Mitzi's a possibility. She didn't deny it when we asked her, either."

"I was just thinking about that lowlife. She's hell bent on getting revenge. I'm sorry for what she's been through with her boyfriend, but I wouldn't put anything past her. She's at the top of my list."

I sucked in some air. "And, of course, it's a huge coincidence that Mitzi showed up in town the night Colin died."

"Exactly my point." Josie cleared her throat. "She's wacko enough to commit the deed. But there are other people to consider as well."

I cocked an eyebrow. "Such as?"

"Kyle."

I thought about this for a moment and pitied Elizabeth. It was bad enough to have your child murdered. But to have your other son be a prime suspect? "No. I can't see it."

Josie pursed her lips together. "You have to admit it's possible. We overheard him telling Krista that he was glad Colin was dead. You told me yourself many times how they'd never gotten along. Kyle didn't even want to be in your wedding. Colin was always Elizabeth's favorite, and his brother resented him for that."

We fell silent as the waitress brought our food and waited until she departed before we continued with the conversation.

I sipped my coffee. "One thing's for sure. There were plenty of people who hated Colin." Goosebumps dotted my arms. How had I not seen his true colors? "Did he think I didn't love him and wanted to be with Mike instead?"

Josie gave me a sympathetic smile. "You did love him. You wouldn't have married him if you hadn't. The problem was that you never got over Mike, and Colin knew this. Plus, Colin was different when you first dated him. He was never one of my favorites and vice versa, but drugs and alcohol change people. I've seen it firsthand myself."

I looked down at my waffle decorated with strawberries and whipped cream. I still had no appetite but managed a few small bites. "If we can somehow find out who the blonde is and if the ring belongs to her, maybe that will tell us something. I have to call Brian when we get back to town, too. I need to pump him for some information."

"Ah," Josie said. "I'd almost forgotten about poor Officer Hottie. Just don't pump him too hard." She winked.

I almost choked on a piece of strawberry. "Josephine Sullivan!"

She grinned. "Brian still has the hots for you. I heard he broke up with that model he was dating. You've ruined him for all other women."

I rolled my eyes at her. "Oh, please. Nothing even happened between the two of us. And how the heck did you find that out? Why am I always the last person to know anything?"

Josie looked pleased with herself. "What can I say? The

customers love to gossip with me."

I drained my coffee cup and grabbed the bill. "Come on. Let's ask out at the front desk."

A man about our age was standing behind the front counter talking on the phone. His name tag read *Ben*. He smiled as we approached and held up a finger. A few seconds later, he thanked the caller and hung up. "How can I help you ladies?" he asked.

I showed him the picture of Colin and the blonde. "I was wondering if you've ever seen this woman before."

He studied the photo briefly. "Yes. I've seen her. Him too. They were together."

"Do you happen to know her name?" I asked.

"No idea. It's been a while since I saw them. The only reason I even remember is because one night they came in very late, and the guy could barely walk a straight line." Ben snorted. "Drunker than your average wino."

"Can you check your records?" I asked. "Is there any way we can find out who she is?"

Ben shook his head. "I don't remember exactly when they were in here. It'd be like looking for a needle in a haystack, so to speak. Unless you happen to know either one's name. We could try searching under that."

I gave him Colin's name, and he entered it into the computer system. He straightened up and shook his head at us again. "Nothing's coming up. They must have registered under the woman's name."

I sighed. We were so close to learning the truth but yet still so far away. "Thanks for your help."

As we walked back to the car, I realized I was officially out of ideas.

Josie clicked her seat belt into place. "Now what?"

I glanced at my watch. Ten thirty. "Pack up and head for the airport, I guess. I just don't feel like we got anything accomplished while we were down here."

"Ahem." Josie cleared her throat nosily.

I grinned. "Besides the competition, that is."

"Aren't you missing the boat on something here? Is it possible that Luke might know who this girl is? And who's to say she even had anything to do with the murder?"

I started the engine. "I guess I can ask him. He texted me yesterday and wanted to know how everything was going. Maybe I can arrange to meet up with him when we get back. I don't think he's returning to Florida for a few more days."

"I believe the answer to the murder is back in New York," Josie said. "And his name is Kyle."

It was too awful to even imagine. "I don't want to consider that right now."

"What about your parents?" Josie asked as we pulled up in front of the hotel. "Are they flying back with us? Please tell me no."

I laughed. "They're staying for a couple more days. Mom said they're on their second honeymoon."

Josie lifted her sunglasses off her face. "The way your parents behave makes me and Rob look like an eighty-year-old couple. And every day is a honeymoon for those two."

"You've got a point there. At least it will give Gianna a nice break. Especially with her exam coming up."

As we alighted from the elevator, I could see the door to our room standing open. Maybe the maid was in there cleaning? Then I caught sight of a mess on the floor and heard Josie's breath catch behind me. We both rushed inside.

Someone had been in our room, but it obviously hadn't been the maid. The person or persons had gone through our personal items—intent on finding something. Clothes had been lifted from suitcases, sheets torn off the beds, and my makeup carrier dumped on the floor along with all its contents. For good measure, they'd also thrown the television to the floor where it lay with a cracked front screen.

"Oh my God," Josie breathed.

It took me a moment to find my voice, which sounded strangely calm to my own ears. Maybe that was the result of too many bad things happening lately. "Call 9-1-1."

"What about the front desk?" Josie asked.

I put a hand over my chest, trying to slow my rapid heartbeat. "I'm sure they'll come up when the police do. There's no time to waste. If we don't leave soon, we'll miss our flight." More than anything, I wanted to go home now.

"Your parents," Josie said. "They could stay here and talk to the police for us."

I put a hand on the nightstand to steady myself. "Good idea. And for the record, I think you're wrong. I'm not so sure the answer to Colin's murder is in New York."

"To heck with that." Josie's eyes illuminated with fear as she held the phone to her ear. "There's more important things to worry about now. Like, what if you're next on the killer's list?"

CHAPTER FOURTEEN

———

I tried calling my mother's cell, but as usual, it kept going to voice mail. Neither of my parents answered the phone in their room. I was afraid they might be involved in extracurricular activities. In desperation, I called down to the front desk and asked if they could page them. Jackpot. They were finishing breakfast by the pool, and I was told they'd be right up.

They arrived in our room at the same time as the police. The hotel manager was there as well, offering his apologies. I tried to pay attention to the questions but kept stealing glances at my watch. No, I didn't think there was anything missing. No, I didn't know who had done this. Okay, that was a little white lie, but I was leaving town and doubted Ramon would follow me to New York.

At least, I hoped not.

I turned to the hotel manager. "I'm so sorry about the damages."

He waved a hand dismissively. "We're truly sorry that you had to endure such an inconvenience. We will be scanning the cameras placed out in the hall to see if we can catch the perpetrator."

My mother placed her hands on her hips. "This isn't a very safe hotel if anyone can break into your room—especially during the daytime hours. My daughter and her friend could have been harmed. How often do you change those access cards?"

"Yeah," my father growled. "I bet the maid did it. What if she had a friend in the contest yesterday, and they came to even the score?"

Okay, so I hadn't been thinking about Mitzi as a suspect

for breaking and entering before this moment. I guessed it was possible, but Mitzi's biggest concern wasn't about the contest. Mitzi wanted me six feet under like Colin.

Something told me Ramon might have ways to enter hotel rooms without an access card. Maybe I should have been forthcoming about my suspicions to the police, but I had to get home. To my business, to my life, and especially to Mike.

I managed a laugh. "I really have no idea who might have done this." I hoped they didn't notice I was crossing my fingers.

The policeman nodded to me. "You can start picking up your things. If we find out anything or need to ask you further questions, we have your number."

Josie and I flew around the room, throwing our items back into the suitcases while my mother and father continued to lecture the hotel manager.

I gave both of them a hug and a kiss. "When will you be back?"

My mother giggled. "Sometime on Sunday. We're both getting massages tomorrow. They're supposed to enhance your love life."

I winced, and Josie sucked in some air. The policeman stared down at the floor, and the hotel manager's face turned crimson. If there was one thing that did *not* need enhancing, it was my parents' love life.

"I'll call you when we land." I mumbled a hasty goodbye to everyone while Josie rang for the elevator. Fortunately, there was no one else at the front desk, so our checkout was quick and painless. We jumped into the car and sped off for the airport.

"I hope security won't take too long," Josie said.

"Security always takes forever at this airport." I glanced at my watch. Only forty-five minutes until our plane departed. We checked our bags, rushed through the airport, and found our way to security at the end of a long line. By some miracle, the plane had been delayed fifteen minutes. We were the last ones to board.

"Thank goodness," Josie breathed as we found two seats together near the rear of the plane. "We'll have to deal with a little extra turbulence, but I can live with that."

I clicked my seat belt into place. "I just want to go home."

She gave me a sympathetic smile. "It's going to be okay, Sal."

"It won't be okay until Mike is off the hook for this. Gianna told me that if the police find out he's left—and, God forbid, left the state—things are going to get worse. He'll go back to prison. And the grand jury is scheduled to meet in one week." My voice trembled. "He can't go to jail for something he didn't do. I have to find out who did this."

"Kyle or Ramon are my top picks," Josie said. "Ramon ransacked our room. And we know what he was looking for. What did you do with the ring, by the way?"

I patted my purse. "It's still in here. I'm going to return it to Krista on Sunday."

"It belongs to someone," Josie said. "That trinket had to cost at least twenty grand. I don't believe someone just happened to give it to Colin. I'm betting he stole it from one of his bimbo girlfriends."

I shrugged. "Well, we don't know who the blonde is, and it doesn't belong to Amber, so what else can I do? As far as I'm concerned, Colin's family can have it back and do with it as they please."

"What if Ramon sends someone after you?" Josie asked. "What will you do then?"

"I'll deal with it somehow. I have ten grand from the contest. Grandma's refused to take any money, so if I give it to Ramon, maybe he'll back off."

Josie's eyes went wide. "It's not your responsibility to pay Colin's debt back."

"Well, it's better than winding up dead. I can't help Mike that way."

She twisted her hands in her lap and stared down at the floor. "You can have my share, too."

I shook my head. "No way. You earned every penny of that money. Plus, you'll need it for the kids."

Josie's head shot up, and I saw that her eyes had filled with unshed tears. "I don't want a dead best friend, Sal."

I sighed. What a mess this was becoming. "We'll talk about it later. Is Rob meeting you at the airport?"

She nodded. "He can give you a ride back to the shop. Do you want me to come with you?"

"No. It'll be dinnertime by then. Go home and spend some time with the kids. I'll handle the shop."

*　*　*

"Well, look who's here." Gianna was standing at the wooden block table scrubbing it clean. She ran over and hugged me. "It's so good to have you back. And congrats. I knew you'd rock it at the competition."

I threw my arms around her. "I missed you. How's everything? And what about you? Feeling okay?"

"I'm great," Gianna grinned. "The house is so nice and quiet. And Grandma is a pro at this. She should have been running her own bakery years ago. It was a little slow today, so I went upstairs to your apartment and did some studying. Spike's up there now. I took him outside about an hour ago."

"Thanks so much for everything." I hesitated for a moment. "Have you seen anyone interesting lately?"

She shook her head. "I drove by his house this morning. It snowed last night, but I didn't see any tracks in the driveway." She bit into her lower lip. "Officer Jenkins was here about an hour ago, asking if you were back yet. He said it was important."

Oh boy. I'd wanted to phone Brian to tell him about the developments in Florida. Maybe he could help. But I still didn't think it was a good idea since he might figure out Mike had disappeared. "Okay, I'll call him."

She looked at me doubtfully. "Yeah, right."

I heard voices in Italian coming from the storefront. "Perfect timing. Sounds like Mrs. Gavelli is here."

Gianna nodded. "Yes, our favorite neighbor's been looking for you, too. Mrs. G and Grandma had a huge fight about you yesterday. Most of it was in Italian, but I caught something about you being one of Satan's followers."

"Just when you think life can't get any worse." I donned an apron, washed my hands, braced myself, and walked into the bakery.

Grandma Rosa was bent over, reaching into the case for a fortune cookie. Mrs. Gavelli was yelling something at her in Italian but stopped short when she saw me.

"You." She pointed her finger in my face. "I hear you go to be in beauty contest. Why you act like hussy?"

I laughed. "I went to be in a *baking* contest, Mrs. G. Not a beauty contest. And we won, too. Josie and I will be on television next month."

She snorted. "You see. Is all about the media for you. Young people today have no morals. And your boyfriend a murderer."

Heat crept up into my neck, and I counted to ten before I replied. "He's *not* a murderer, Mrs. G."

Mrs. Gavelli snorted. "Yah, that what they all say. I hope he look good in orange."

Grandma Rosa threw a fortune cookie at her. "Nicoletta, take your cookie and leave. You are a bad influenza on all."

Gianna was standing next to me. She leaned over and whispered into my grandmother's ear. "I think you mean bad influence. Influenza is a contagious viral infection."

Grandma Rosa nodded in approval. "That works, too."

Mrs. Gavelli shook her fist at us. "You all a bad lot. I no waste my time talking to you anymore." She glanced down at the cookie in her hand and broke it apart. She read the message silently and then let out a gasp. "'Kindness begins with you.' See, is fixed. Why I bother with you people." She threw the paper on the floor and walked toward the door then turned back to address my grandmother. "Poker tonight?"

Grandma Rosa nodded. "Sì. It is your turn to bring the anisette."

Mrs. Gavelli gave a loud harrumph. "Cheapskate." She pushed open the door, and the bells chimed in relief at her departure.

Grandma Rosa straightened the cookies in the display case. "When the good Lord passed out brains, that woman thought he said pains and said I want to be one—in the behind."

Gianna and I both laughed.

"Come," Grandma Rosa said, taking my hand and

leading me to a table. "Sit down and tell me. Did you find out anything to help your young man?"

I bit into my lower lip, afraid I might break down again. "Not really. The only thing we did discover was that Colin made a lot of enemies."

"I was afraid of that." Grandma Rosa lowered herself into the chair across from me. "That is what happens when you become friends with the drugs and alcohol."

I put my face into my hands. "Grandma, what am I going to do? It's so hard getting up every day and trying to pretend my life is normal." I stifled a sob. "I miss him so much."

Gianna's voice broke as she put her arms around me. "We're all here for you, honey."

Grandma Rosa pointed a finger at Gianna. "You go upstairs and visit Spike. Do some more studying. We will stay until closing with Sally."

Gianna nodded and gave me a brief hug before she ascended the stairs to my apartment.

I blew my nose. "That's not necessary. You've both already done more than enough."

"It *is* necessary." Grandma Rosa's large brown eyes bore into mine. "I will talk, and you will listen. Then you will go to Mike's house and bring back some toys for Spike. He tried to chew a hole in your father's recliner last night." Her mouth turned upward at the corners into a slight smile. "He is a good boy but gets bored easily. He misses Mike, too."

Tears fell from my eyes onto the tablecloth my grandmother had crocheted for me.

Grandma Rosa sighed. She stood and put her arms around me. "You must not give up hope, cara mia. He is coming home. Remember what I said to you the other day. About the Tammy song."

I forced a laugh. "I should stand on Mike?"

She grinned. "Ah, so you are a comedian now. Remember that sometimes love is not enough. There are other important things, too."

I drew my eyebrows together. "Such as?"

She patted my cheek. "Think about it for a minute. You will figure it out. And when you do, send him a note and tell him. Then Mike will come home, mark my words."

I exhaled sharply. "I hope you're right."

She nodded. "I always am." She pointed to the back door. "You go to his house now. I will take care of everything here until you get back."

I gave her a hug and a kiss, threw my coat on, and went out the back door to where my car was parked in the covered alley. I got behind the wheel and started the engine. Then I pulled my phone out of my pocket and studied the screen for a minute.

I had to try one last time to get Mike to come home. I hadn't heard from him since the text on Monday night which assured me he was okay. A lot could happen in four days. He might be anywhere by now. Another tear rolled down my cheek.

"Okay, enough," I muttered out loud. "Stop feeling sorry for yourself and think about how to help Mike."

What else could I say to make him come home? I thought about my conversation with Grandma Rosa the other night. She'd mentioned how Mike had been forced to rely on himself for most of his life. That all he wanted to do now was marry and take care of me. He knew I loved him, but maybe Grandma Rosa was right. There was something missing.

At that moment, it dawned on me. There were three words Mike longed to hear, but I'd been typing the wrong ones. With that realization, my fingers quickly flew across the screen.

I need you.

CHAPTER FIFTEEN

———

As I'd feared, and Gianna had already confirmed, there were no signs Mike had returned to his house. The mailbox was overstuffed with envelopes, and a package had been placed in a plastic bag and tied to the flag. I glanced at it briefly as I brought the items inside. The return address was from a kitchen supply store. Probably a faucet or something similar he'd ordered for Laura Embree's house.

I inserted my key into the lock, pushed the door open, and entered the code to disarm Mike's security system. I found myself hoping that I was somehow wrong, and he was in the house waiting for me. Yet only silence greeted me. Everything looked the same as it had on Tuesday night when I'd stopped over after Colin's wake.

My shoulders sagged as I retrieved another bag of dog food for Spike, some treats, and a few of the vast supply of toys Mike had bought for him. I placed everything in a plastic bag and headed for the front door then stopped myself. There was one other thing I needed to check on, and I wasn't looking forward to it.

I entered the bedroom and eyed the chest of drawers. I lowered myself to my knees and opened the bottom one. Holding my breath, I pushed aside the socks, removed the picture of us, and stared down.

The gun was gone.

I rose to my feet shakily and considered this new development. So Mike had taken the gun with him. Yes, it was good the weapon was gone in case police searched the house. But this was also bad. If Mike was stopped and the gun located, that could spell trouble, too. Plus, why had he never told me about it? I didn't even know if it was loaded.

A chill wafted through the air, and I wrapped my arms around me for warmth as I departed the room in a hurry.

I retrieved my bag and locked the front door behind me. It was six o'clock, and the sky had already darkened. More snow was predicted for tonight. Although I'd been anxious to return home, it had been nice to visit the Sunshine State for a couple of days. The weather here was dark and depressing, matching my current state of mind. I was angry about what had happened to Mike and myself.

I recalled our first date back in September. Mike had been sporting a large bandage on his foot and had some difficulty walking. He'd managed to fix dinner for me at his house, and we'd spent hours talking afterward. He'd kissed me and told me what I already knew—he'd never stopped loving me. When I told him I needed to take things slow, Mike said he understood. Then I'd departed for home but couldn't stay away, returning the next night to deliver some cookies from the bakery, or so I'd said. And I hadn't left until the following morning.

So much for taking it slow. I smiled and wiped my eyes at the memory.

When I returned to the shop, I persuaded Grandma Rosa and Gianna to go home. Flurries had already started to fall.

"I don't think we'll get many more customers," I said. "Plus, I can handle things. I'm closing up in a half hour anyway. You two must be exhausted. Order some takeout and relax in front of the television."

Grandma Rosa frowned. "I do *not* order takeout. There are stuffed shells waiting in the freezer. You will come, too?"

I shook my head. "I'm not hungry. Spike and I will watch some television and turn in early."

She gave me a sharp look but didn't argue. "Call if you need anything, cara mia." She kissed my cheek. "Stop worrying. It will all be fine."

Gianna dangled her car keys. "Get some rest, Sal. Hey, when are Mom and Dad coming home?'

"Sunday," I replied.

Her face brightened. "Looks like I got a vacation, too."

I shut and locked the back door behind them. I checked

the stock of frozen dough in the freezer and pulled out some for tomorrow morning. I probably should have made more sugar cookie dough, but I was too exhausted. I scribbled off a note for Josie, asking her to make more fortune cookies in the morning since our supply was low. Then I also gave myself a mental reminder to call Sarah and ask if she was still interested in the job.

At seven o'clock, I locked the front door and pulled the blinds down. I started up the staircase to my apartment when a loud banging on the front door startled me.

A flicker of hope ran through my body. *He got my text and came back. Grandma was right.*

I rushed back down the stairs and ran to unlock the front door. Brian stood there in his uniform looking very professional and handsome, Greek godlike face stern.

My excitement was quickly squelched, and disappointment flooded my body as I stared back at him. It shouldn't have come as a surprise—I knew he'd return. But what the heck was I going to say to him?

"Hi, Sally." His green eyes studied me carefully.

"Brian. What can I do for you?"

"Is there any chance we could talk for a few minutes?" He held out a bottle of wine. "I was hoping maybe we could have a drink together."

My mouth dropped open in surprise as I shut and locked the door behind him. "Aren't you on duty?"

"No, I'm finished for the night. Plus, I hate to go anywhere empty-handed." He smiled. "I thought you might want some company."

Was Brian aware Mike had disappeared and figured he'd take a chance on trying to win me over? Did he really think I was that vulnerable? I thought about refusing and ordering him to leave. But I was also afraid that if I annoyed him, Mike might be the one to suffer.

It was as if he'd guessed my thoughts. "I'd like it if we could be friends. That's all."

"Um, okay." Spike was barking from inside my apartment, and I gestured toward the stairs. "I'm not much of a drinker though."

He grinned. "Neither am I."

We climbed the staircase, and I opened the door. Spike came running over to us and wagged his tail at Brian.

"Hey there, little guy." He stooped down and reached out a hand to pet Spike. The dog immediately rolled over so that Brian could scratch his belly. "He's a cute one. Mike's dog, right?"

I swallowed hard. "Yes."

His eyes bore into mine. "So what's he doing here? Is Mike here, too?"

Oh boy. My chest constricted. "No. I think he's working late."

"Really? Whereabouts?"

He knows. I stared down at the floor. "Brian, he may be my boyfriend, but that doesn't mean I have to know where he is every minute of the day."

"Sally, I'm not trying to be difficult. I'm concerned about you."

I choked back a laugh. "Oh, please. You're so concerned about me that you couldn't wait to rush over and arrest my boyfriend?"

Brian righted himself. "I didn't enjoy that, honestly. But it's my job."

I snorted. "Maybe you felt it was payback since I wouldn't go out with you." My tone sounded acid-like, even to me.

His face fell, and I wanted to bite my tongue off. "I'm sorry. I don't know why I said that."

He didn't reply as he stooped down to pet Spike again. I crossed to the kitchen and brought out two wine glasses. Brian opened the bottle and poured a glass for each of us. We both sat down on my couch.

His voice was soft when he spoke again. "Like I said, I'm here as a friend. I care about you and always have. If Mike has left town, you'd better tell him to hightail it back here and fast. I promise not to say anything, but—"

"He didn't kill Colin."

Brian didn't answer while I took a long sip of my drink. I never drank much alcohol but secretly hoped it might somehow numb the pain I was experiencing. And Brian's failure to answer angered me.

I grabbed his arm. "Don't you understand? Someone wants Mike to take the rap for this. He threatened Colin. There were many people who witnessed their fight at Ralph's that night. Have you questioned everyone who was there? Did you find any other fingerprints at the hotel?"

He gave me an odd look. "Sally, by the time my partner and I got over to the bar, several patrons had already left, including you, Mike, Colin, and your friends. We questioned a few people about the brawl, but that was it. And, yes, we dusted the entire hotel room. Mike's prints came up a match because they were already on file."

I was aware of his knees touching mine, and embarrassment flooded my cheeks. "Mike's never been arrested before." At least I didn't think so.

He held up a hand in defense. "I didn't say he was. Seems he had to be fingerprinted for a job he was working on last year. Standard procedure for some high-tech security building. Mike installed carpeting for them. That's how the prints were already on file. When we dusted the room and put them through the system, he came up a match."

"Didn't you find anyone else's?" I asked.

"None that we could identify." He took a sip of his wine and put the glass down on my coffee table. "I also know that he owns a gun, Sally. He got permission to carry a while ago."

I was already angry that Mike had never mentioned the gun. Having to hear this tidbit of information from Brian only irritated me further, but I said nothing.

"Do you know where his gun is, Sally?" Brian asked. "I can get a search warrant easily enough."

My breath caught in my throat. "No."

There was a long pause. "You don't know where Mike is either, do you?"

I didn't answer. Instead, I pretended to be engrossed in watching Spike gnaw on a rawhide bone in the kitchen. My eyes filled with tears. When had I turned into such a crybaby?

Brian leaned over and placed my hand between his. I made no effort to move away. It was a comforting gesture. I was so lonely for Mike that my heart ached with pain.

When I'd first met Brian, he'd been kind and concerned about my getting involved in a murder investigation. We'd kissed a couple of times. Then he and Mike had both asked me to dinner on the same evening. I'd never regretted my decision. Now, as I stared at his handsome face and powerful muscular shoulders, I wondered briefly what it would have been like to have Brian as a boyfriend. There was no doubt in my mind that he was the type of man who would treat a woman like a queen. That was Mike's caliber, too.

I sighed. Why did there always seem to be no options for a good man or too many?

He ran his finger down my arm, and it heated from his touch. "I was really upset when you turned me down. I was crazy about you." He paused and brushed away the tears from my eyes with his thumb. "I still am."

I blinked, surprised. "Brian, you know I'm with Mike. Plus, you have a girlfriend. We saw you together a few weeks ago." Then I remembered Josie's gossip. "She was beautiful."

He placed his face next to mine, and I watched as it clouded over. "We're not seeing each other anymore. I broke it off."

"Why?" The small amount of wine I'd ingested was already making me sleepy.

He hesitated before answering, and I immediately regretted my question. Plus, it was none of my business.

"Honestly? Because I can't seem to forget about you."

My mouth dropped open in astonishment as I attempted to laugh off his reply. "Oh, you're kidding around."

His eyes shone as he gazed at me. "I'm dead serious."

I knew this conversation was headed for trouble. It probably would have been a good idea to ask him to leave. My mouth formed the words, but I couldn't quite force them out. I dropped my eyes toward the floor.

"I hate having to see you deal with this," Brian said. "If Mike goes to prison—"

My head shot up. "Don't say that!"

He rubbed my hand between his two strong ones, and a tingle ran through my body. "Sally, it is a possibility."

"No." Tears streamed down my face again. "Brian, he doesn't belong there. He's innocent."

Brian sighed. "Come here." He folded me into his arms while I sobbed against his massive chest. His strong arms held me tightly, and he whispered soothing words into my ear. It felt good to have someone hold me again. It also didn't hurt that he smelled wonderful—a woodsy type of cologne that reminded me of the great outdoors on a summer day.

He reached down and lifted my face between his hands. I saw the look in his eyes and realized what was coming next but didn't react soon enough. I should have moved away, but my entire body seemed to have gone numb. I was mesmerized as I stared into his brilliant green eyes. They were hypnotizing.

Brian pushed my hair back from my face and moved his finger lightly over my lips. Then he kissed me.

I closed my eyes. For a brief moment, I think I might have pretended that he was Mike. Maybe I imagined I was someone else, too. Was it like the dream with Bradley Cooper? I couldn't be sure. All I knew was that the pain was consuming, almost suffocating me, and I needed it to end.

The kiss deepened and became more urgent. Brian's hands splayed down my back as he lowered me onto the couch. His fingers reached underneath my shirt and brushed against my bare skin. Slowly, I staggered out of my mental stupor and tore my mouth loose from his. "I can't do this. I'm sorry."

Brian seemed not to hear me. His hands were at my waist, and he was preoccupied with kissing my neck. "You never even gave me a chance. He's going to break your heart again. Forget about Mike."

At the mention of his name, reality kicked in at full force. I pushed Brian backward and struggled to sit up. "I asked you to stop, and I meant it. Please."

Reluctantly, he released his hold on me. "I'm sorry. I didn't come here to take advantage of you. Do you want me to go?"

While my mind said yes, my mouth had trouble forcing it out. Brian was a nice guy, and I suspected he'd behave now. Plus, the idea of being alone depressed me to no end. If I was angry at someone, it was myself, not Brian, for giving in to a moment of weakness.

"No. You can stay if you promise to be good." I smiled and gestured toward the kitchen. "Would you like a sandwich or something?"

He shook his head. "I had a late lunch, so I'm fine. Thanks."

As his eyes studied my face, heat rose through my body. "Um, I did some snooping around when I was in Florida."

Brian yawned and settled back against the cushions of my couch. "Of course you did. That's your middle name." He eyed me suspiciously. "Did you find out anything about Colin's death that might help Mike?"

I told him about Amber Mills and the unknown blonde then relayed the information about Ramon and the break-in.

Brian's eyes widened. "You have been busy."

"I'm scared," I said honestly. "For myself and for Mike. What will I do if this Ramon character comes to New York to find me?"

"I can get you police protection," Brian said. "If you see any signs of him or his so-called associates, call me."

"Could you run his name through the system, and see if you come up with anything on him?"

He smiled. "My, you're quite the Nancy Drew now, aren't you?"

"I don't have time to waste. The grand jury is meeting in a week. I have to prove Mike is innocent."

Brian leaned forward to refill our glasses. "I'll do whatever I can to help him. We've been questioning Colin's family and his friend Luke whom he came to town with." He lifted his glass to his lips. "Luke said he was worried about you."

"I'll call him tomorrow. I want to ask him if he knows anything about the blonde Colin was seeing."

Brian narrowed his eyes. "I think that guy has a thing for you."

I let out a bark of laughter. "Oh, please. That's ridiculous."

His eyes traveled slowly down my body while I looked away in embarrassment. "No, it's definitely *not* ridiculous." He let out a huge sigh then focused his attention on the television.

"The Cavaliers and Celtics are playing tonight. How does that sound?"

I downed the rest of my drink in one gulp and yawned. "Sure. Go for it."

I'd never been a basketball fan. Even though I'd led cheer for games in high school, the sport had always bored me. So I let the wine take over. I remembered Brian talking about a penalty shot and then went out like a light.

When I awoke, the room was dark and quiet with the exception of one lamp on the end table casting a soft glow upon the room. The television was off. Brian's gun and cell phone lay on the coffee table in front of us, and he himself was sleeping next to me on the couch, snoring softly. One arm held me close against his bare chest. His shirt was lying on the table.

I was confused. How had we ended up like this? For a brief moment, a wave of panic engulfed me. Had I done something I'd regret? I glanced down. Nope—still fully clothed. This was a good thing. I squinted at my watch in the dim light. As comforting as it was to be nestled in Brian's arms, I had no desire to tempt fate once again. Gently, I lifted his arm while he opened his eyes and smiled at me.

"Hey." He yawned and stretched. "What time is it?"

"About three." I padded over to the window in my socks and peered out. The street light was dim, but I was able to detect snow coming down at a rapid, almost blinding rate.

Brian blinked and rubbed his eyes. "I should get going."

I hesitated. "You can't go out in this. It looks like a blizzard. You're welcome to spend the rest of the night here. I'm going to my bedroom."

His mouth turned up at the corners. "And where do I get to spend the night?"

"Right where you are."

He sighed. "Well, it was worth a try."

I grinned. "You don't give up, do you?" I grabbed the afghan from the back of the couch. My heart beat rapidly as his eyes watched my movements intently. With some difficulty, I tried not to stare at his smooth, muscular chest while I covered it. "Get some sleep. Good night."

Brian's eyes lingered on my face. "Good night,

beautiful."

I went to my bedroom and shut the door behind me. I thought about locking it then stopped myself. For goodness sake, he was a cop, after all. I felt safe and protected with him but also nervous as hell. I was also too tired to analyze the situation any further. Thanks to the wine, I fell into a deep, dreamless sleep.

The sun streaming through my window woke me. At least the snow had stopped. I glanced at the clock on my bedside table. Crap. It was eight thirty, and my shop opened in half an hour. When had I become such a slacker? I reached for my cell on the nightstand and dialed Josie's number. She answered on the first ring.

"I've done it again. I'm running a little late. I had an unexpected houseguest last evening."

"I'm already downstairs," Josie said. "I've been here since seven. Take your time. By the way, I noticed a squad car parked at the curb. That wouldn't happen to belong to Officer Hottie, would it?"

Ugh. "Well, yes, but it's not what you think."

"Look, honey, whatever gets you through the night is fine with me. I'm the last person to judge. You're not married, and you certainly aren't dead. Speaking of hot males, you had a visitor a few minutes ago."

My heart nearly leaped out of my chest as I scurried into the bathroom to brush my teeth with the phone still pressed to my ear. "Mike?"

"Calm down. Mike has a key, doesn't he? He would have gone right up. No, sweetie, I'm talking about another hot guy. You seem to be collecting them in droves these days."

I looked at myself in the bathroom mirror. My hair was standing up on end every which way and resembled something similar to a lion's mane. My eyes had bags underneath them, and my complexion was almost as white as powdered sugar.

"Yeah, well, I don't see anything in the mirror that looks appealing right now, so you're dead wrong on that account. Was it a good visitor or a bad visitor?"

"Like I said, he was cute," Josie teased. "But I'll let you determine the good or bad part. It was Colin's buddy, Luke."

Confused, I stared at the phone. "Did he say what he

wanted?"

"He said he wanted to make sure you were okay and asked if you'd call him later. Personally, I think it's baloney. He's got the hots for you."

"Okay, I so don't want to hear this right now. He's only a friend."

"Whatever. But the guy is gaga over you. You're putting together quite a list of admirers."

I blew out a sigh. "Some days I think life would be so much simpler if God had never created man."

Josie chortled. "Simpler, yes, but nowhere near as fun."

"Okay. I'm going to take a quick shower, and then I'll be down."

"Can I ask if you'll be the only one in the shower?"

"Oh, shut up. See you in a half an hour."

I disconnected and tiptoed out of the bathroom into the narrow hallway. The rest of my tiny apartment was in plain view, the small eat-in kitchen and the connected living room area. Plus, Brian's almost naked body sprawled across my couch. The afghan had fallen away, and he had stripped down to his boxers. Good grief. I was glad he'd decided to make himself comfortable.

A tingle ran through me, and I forced my eyes away from his taut body. What the heck was the matter with me? My boyfriend's gone for less than a week, and I can't control myself around other men? I returned to the bathroom, locking the door behind me.

I turned on the water as hot as I could stand it and let the spray envelop me. If only I could wash away my problems this easily. I shampooed and conditioned my hair, and then wrapped myself in a fluffy, pink towel that stopped midway down my thighs. I worked at my hair, blow-drying and styling until it was somewhat presentable. I reached for my robe on the hook of the door, but it wasn't there. Shoot. It was still in my suitcase. I'd just sneak across the hallway and grab it. Chances were that Brian was still sleeping.

I opened the door, stepped out into the hallway, and then let out a small squeak.

Brian was leaning against the wall. His arms were folded

across his bare, muscular chest. To my relief, he was wearing his uniform pants while he clutched his shirt in his left hand. His gaze dropped from my face to the towel I was tightly clutching around me.

"You scared me," I whispered.

He looked apologetic. "Sorry, Sally. I wanted to wait until you were finished so that I could say good-bye. My shift starts at ten, and I've only enough time to run home and grab a quick shower."

Brian's eyes focused on the towel again and then came to rest on my bare legs while my face warmed with embarrassment.

He winked. "Too bad I didn't wake up a few minutes sooner. Maybe we could have shared a shower."

My mouth opened in shock, yet somehow I managed to keep my voice steady. "That would *not* have happened. And I do think it would be best if you left now."

My cell started ringing from the bathroom. At the very same moment, Spike rushed to the front door and began barking in a frenzy. Then he stopped suddenly, wagged his tail, and whined. My heart stuttered inside my chest. There was only one person Spike acted like this around. I remained frozen in place as a key tumbled in my door.

Maybe it was Josie? No, she would have knocked first. Josie and Mike were the only ones who had keys to both the building and my apartment. I struggled for air as I watched the door open, and Mike's imposing figure filled the door frame. He reached down to scoop Spike into his arms.

"Hi, fella. I missed you." Mike glanced toward me then at Brian. I watched the color drain from his face and the wide smile change to a look of bewilderment. Even from across the room, I glimpsed a muscle tick in his jaw and a rage of storm clouds brewing behind his baby blues. He clutched Spike tightly in his arms and took a step backward. His eyes locked on to mine. In a brief moment, I detected hurt, confusion, and anger in his expression. *Lots* of anger.

"Sorry. Didn't mean to interrupt anything." He took another step backward then slammed the door behind him as he disappeared.

I was finally moved into action. "Oh my God. Mike,

wait!"

Brian grabbed me by the arm. "Sally, don't."

I shook his hands off furiously. "Let go of me!" Without thinking, I raced down the stairs, through the storefront, and to the glass door of my bakery. I was just in time to witness Mike's truck speed off. His tires, like his anger, were smoking. "Wait!"

It was freezing on the front porch in my bare feet. I turned around, defeated and sickened to my stomach. My heart was a dead weight in my chest. All I wanted to do was go upstairs and smack my head against a wall. Hard. Mike had finally returned home, and now he thought I was cheating on him. How could things possibly get any worse?

I stepped back inside the storefront and froze.

It was past nine o'clock, and we were open for business. At least five customers were standing in front of the display case. Six sets of eyes, including Josie's, were all staring at me. Me, the proprietor of Sally's Samples, dressed in nothing but a towel.

Josie clutched a bakery box in one hand. The other was clamped over her mouth in an expression of horror.

Ronald Feathers hobbled over to my side. He lived down the street from my parents. At eighty years old, he was bald, hard of hearing, and possessed no teeth. He was also Mrs. Gavelli's main squeeze. He chuckled and tapped me on the backside with his cane.

I seemed to have lost the feeling in my legs as I continued to stand there, grasping the towel with both hands.

Mr. Feathers winked. "Nice legs, honey. Nicoletta only comes over on Sundays, so I'm free tonight. From the looks of things, I'm guessing you are, too."

CHAPTER SIXTEEN

———

"Okay. What exactly just happened downstairs?" Josie stood in the doorway of my bedroom as I finished getting dressed.

She had dispersed the crowd in record time then ran upstairs after me to see what was going on. Her blue eyes were enormous in her face as she examined mine.

My voice shook as I pulled on my boots. "Mike walked in on me when I was wearing nothing but a towel. To make matters worse, Brian was leaning against the wall talking to me with no shirt on."

"Holy cow." Josie pursed her lips. "He thinks—"

I glanced around for my car keys. "Yeah, precisely. Did he say anything when he came into the shop?"

She shook her head. "I spotted him walking in the door. He nodded to me but headed right for the stairs. I called your cell phone. I *tried* to warn you."

I pulled on my jacket. "He finally comes home, and now he thinks I'm involved with another man." I glanced at her with hesitation. "I have to see if I can find him."

Josie gestured toward the door. "Go. I'll be fine."

"I owe you." I ran down the stairs, taking them two at a time. I flew out the back door, unlocked my car, and sped off toward Mike's house, wondering how my life had suddenly become such a train wreck.

There were fresh tracks in the driveway, but Mike's truck was gone. My heart sank. Could he have taken off again? Somehow I didn't think so. He knew I'd follow him here and apparently was in no mood to talk to me. Of all the lousy timing. Could there have been a worse moment for him to walk through my door? Well, if he'd caught us on the couch together last night, Brian might have been missing a few teeth by now. But why at that exact minute?

Then it dawned on me—the message I had texted last night. Maybe Mike had driven all night in the storm from wherever he was to get home to me. Deep down he had to know I wasn't cheating on him because why would I have sent him the text?

My brain was starting to hurt. I whipped out my cell and dialed his number. As usual, it went straight to voice mail.

"It's me," I whispered. "What you just saw—it's not what you think. Brian came by to ask me some questions about Colin and the murder last night. I had a glass of wine and fell asleep on the couch. I guess he did, too."

Okay, Sal, maybe you shouldn't have mentioned that part.

I choked back tears as I continued. "Please don't leave again. I've been miserable without you. Please don't jump to conclusions. I—"

The phone beeped, and I heard the message, "This mailbox is full."

"Damn it!" I sat in the car and wiped away tears of frustration with the back of my hand. I thought about what I had said. *Don't jump to conclusions.* Hadn't I jumped to conclusions ten years ago when I found Mike in a vehicle with another girl— Backseat Brenda, as she'd been dubbed because of her reputation—on prom night? I hadn't given him a chance to explain then. Instead, I'd promptly broken up with him.

You're such a hypocrite, Sal. Not knowing what else to do, I drove back to the bakery. I didn't have any other ideas of where to find Mike. Plus, I felt guilty leaving Josie to run the shop alone again. I hadn't been the most reliable owner as of late.

As I was alighting from the vehicle, my phone buzzed. I held my breath and prayed, but it wasn't Mike's number. "Hello?"

"Hey, Sal." Krista's voice greeted me. "Are you still in Florida?"

"No. I got back last night."

She hesitated for a moment. "Did you have any luck

finding the owner of the ring?"

"I spoke to Amber. I didn't volunteer any information, but I'm pretty sure the ring doesn't belong to her. She said that she and Colin broke up over a month ago. He was cheating on her with another woman—a blonde."

"Big surprise there," she said dryly. "Do you think it belongs to her then?"

Better to get this over with. "Did you know that Colin owed money to the mob?"

"What?" Krista squeaked.

As I'd suspected, my statement hadn't gone over very well. "Okay, maybe it's not the mob, but at the very least, the guy is a loan shark. He found out I was in Florida and told me he wanted the money Colin owes him. I'm wondering if he could be involved in Colin's murder."

Krista gasped on the other end of the line. "Did he threaten you?"

"Yes," I said, "and our hotel room was broken into. I think he may have been searching for the ring. He said Colin promised him something in exchange for paying off the debt. Don't worry. He didn't get the ring. I still have it safe in my purse."

She was quiet for a moment. "Sal, this isn't your problem. I'm sorry I ever involved you in this mess. You should have just given the ring to this creep."

"I'll stop by and return it to you," I said. "I had hoped it might somehow lead to freeing Mike from a possible murder conviction."

"Who is this guy? Do you think he killed Colin?" Krista asked.

"His name is Ramon Ravole. The Florida police should have been notified about him by now." I'd have to call Brian and check, but boy, how I was dreading that call. "And yes, I suppose it's possible, but for some reason, I don't believe Ramon killed Colin. Maybe it was someone at the bar that night. Or someone who knew Colin would be at the bar."

Silence greeted me from the other end of the line. "I know what you're thinking, Sally. You overheard the conversation at the funeral parlor that night."

"Krista," I began.

She started weeping. "Kyle owns a gun. And he visited Colin at his hotel room that night. Luke said he saw him there."

The double revelation stopped me cold. Kyle had immediately risen to the top of my suspect list. Good grief, was I the only person around here who *didn't* own a gun? "Is there any way you can get ahold of it?"

"What do you want me to do?" Krista shrieked. "Break into my own brother's house? Hand the gun over to the police so that they can check it against the one that was used that night?"

That was *exactly* what I was thinking, but I wisely kept the comment to myself. "I'm sorry, but Mike didn't do this. And he isn't going to prison for someone else's crime." I bit into my lower lip, hating myself for what I was about to say. "If you won't help me, Krista, I'll go ahead and give the police this information tomorrow."

She disconnected before I could say another word.

I unlocked the back door to my shop and walked into the kitchen. Josie's voice floated in from the storefront where she was animatedly chatting with someone. The inviting smell of her raspberry cheesecake cookies greeted me. I grabbed a mitt and opened the oven door, the aroma engulfing me in a moment of sheer bliss. That was the amazing thing about food. When the rest of the world seemed grim, I could retreat to my little shop and bury myself away in the happy land of cookies and icing. This was my safe haven.

I glanced at my watch—almost eleven. I thought about what I'd been doing one week ago at this exact same minute. Mike and I had both taken the morning off and spent most of it in bed. Then I'd awakened from a crazy dream of cheesecake, Bradley Cooper, and the Bahamas. Mike had asked me to marry him while I, in turn, had begged him to be patient. Now my ex-husband was dead and Mike the prime suspect in his murder. Within days, the grand jury would meet and see if there was enough evidence to send him to jail.

No. I wasn't about to let that happen.

I rubbed my eyes wearily. At least I had the power to make someone else's day better than my own. I grabbed my cell between my hands and scrolled through the contacts section. I pushed a button and waited.

"Hello?" a woman's soft voice asked.

"Hi, Sarah. Sally Muccio from Sally's Samples."

There was a long pause. "Hi, Sally. How are you?"

"Just great," I lied. "Listen, Sarah. I want to apologize. When you were in last week, I think I made a mistake in not hiring you. I was hoping you might still be interested in the job."

She gasped. "Are you serious?"

"Absolutely. Could you start on Monday?"

Sarah gave a little squeal. "I'd love to. By the way, one of my neighbors is willing to take Julie after school, so I can be a little more flexible now."

"That's wonderful. I'm so glad everything's working out. We're looking forward to having you here. I'll see you Monday at eight o'clock."

She sniffled on the other end, and a lump formed in my throat as I listened to her.

"Thank you so much, Sally." With that, Sarah disconnected.

I put the phone back in my pocket and smiled. It felt wonderful to do a good deed for someone else. I needed more of that in my life.

"Sal," Josie yelled. "Is that you?"

I tied on an apron. "Yeah, I'll be right out."

"I made more fortune cookies this morning. They're on the cooling trays back there. Can you bring some out with you? The case is almost empty."

"No problem." *Life goes on, Sal. Not everything is about you.* I grabbed a piece of waxed paper and transferred the cookies onto a plate. I reached for the last one and noticed it had broken. I couldn't serve it like that. I lifted it off the tray to throw in the garbage and caught the sight of the message that was staring me right in the face.

You will learn from your mistakes. You will learn a lot today.

Ugh. Mental head slap. Disgusted, I threw the strip into the garbage can. Too bad I hadn't opened this a few hours earlier, before my boyfriend had become convinced that I was sleeping with another man. Or maybe the fortune was referring to things yet to come?

Okay, stop this. It's a silly piece of paper. They don't mean anything.

I brought the platter of cookies out front and started arranging them on the bottom row of the case. I didn't even glance up to see whom Josie had been talking to.

"Hi, Sally," a deep male voice said.

I raised my head and discovered Luke peering through the glass at me.

"Hey. How are you?"

He grinned. "Better than you, it seems."

"Yeah, tell me about it."

Josie handed change to a young woman she was waiting on then turned to me. "This morning we received an order for a baby shower being held tomorrow. I'm going in the back room to work on it for a while." She whispered in my ear. "You should see if he knows anything that could help. Tell him about the pictures you found in Colin's apartment."

I nodded and then gestured toward one of the tables. The sun streamed cheerily in through my large front window. Without the blanket of whiteness outside, one might assume it was a glorious spring day. "Sit down, Luke. Would you like some coffee? Or maybe an espresso?"

"Coffee would be great. Dark roast if you have it."

I brought two paper cups over to the Keurig. Once they were filled, Luke leaped out of his seat to help me. I brought a pitcher of cream and sugar to the table.

"Thanks." Luke took a sip and then leaned his elbows on the table. "How was your trip? Did you find out anything useful?"

"Not as much as I'd hoped for." I narrowed my eyes. "And you forgot to tell me a few little things."

His expression was puzzled. "Such as?"

"Well, for starters, Colin owed money."

"I *did* tell you that."

"Well, it must be a pretty significant sum," I said, "because the loan shark threatened me unless I paid off the debt in its entirety."

"What? But you're not even married to him anymore,"

Luke objected.

I folded my arms across my chest. "Yeah, well, like everyone else, he caught the obituary in the paper and feels differently."

"Damn," Luke said. "I'm sorry about that. I had no idea Colin was in that deep."

The bells chimed over the door, and a middle-aged woman walked over to the counter. Before I could rise to my feet, Josie appeared and waved me off.

"I also met his ex-girlfriend, Amber Mills. She caught him cheating on her with another woman. A little blonde is how she put it. Said she thought she'd seen her a couple of times at the Hooper Inn over on First Street."

Luke's eyes widened. "Did she know who the blonde was?"

I shook my head. "I asked at the hotel. The man on duty remembered seeing her and Colin together one night because he had been drunk and almost caused a scene. I asked them to check their records, but since I didn't have exact dates, there wasn't much they could do."

Luke wrapped his hands around the cup. "So you have no idea who she was?"

"None at all. I was hoping you might."

He sighed. "Like I told you, he was bringing home a different girl every week. It was hard to keep up with him. I'm sure she was some tramp who didn't mean anything to him."

"Well, I found a picture of her at Colin's apartment."

"How'd you get the landlord to let you in? Colin owed him rent."

I sipped my coffee. "Krista arranged it for me. Like I said, I found some photos in there. The blonde pictured was the same girl he was with at the Hooper Inn. So I don't think it was a one-time thing. And I believe I might have something that belongs to her."

Luke leaned forward eagerly. "Like what?"

The bells over the door chimed again, and I glanced up. Three customers were now standing in front of the case, attempting to make their selections. Josie was behind the counter and glanced over in my direction, her expression pleading. I knew she didn't want to interrupt us, but she was on a deadline to finish the order.

I rose. "I'm sorry, but Josie needs me. Maybe we can talk again before you head back to Florida."

He stood as well. "No problem. Hey, what time does the shop close up tonight?"

"Seven." I grabbed the empty coffee cups and threw them into the trash.

Luke pulled on his jacket. "I'll do anything I can to help you, Sally. I don't want to see Mike go to jail for this."

"Thanks, I appreciate that."

He thought for a minute. "There's some other things about Colin you should know. Could we get together tonight after you close up the shop? Unless you have plans already."

"Sure," I said. "Why don't you meet me here about seven thirty."

Luke smiled. "How about I bring dinner? Nothing fancy. We could talk in your apartment while we eat. I'm heading back tomorrow, and after everything you've been through this week, I figure you could use a few hours off from cooking—or baking— for one evening."

I laughed, but something in his expression made me uncomfortable. I hoped Josie was wrong about him having feelings for me. I didn't want to have to deal with that on top of everything else right now. "That sounds—nice, but I'm due at my parents' house at nine for a birthday celebration."

He nodded. "No problem. We'll be finished before then. Whose birthday is it?"

"Gianna's." Okay, it was a little white lie, but I didn't want him to plan on getting too comfortable like Brian had last night. Plus, what if Mike returned while he was there? I thought about the fortune cookie message. Was I about to make another mistake?

"I'll see you then." Luke grinned. "Looking forward to it."

I ran into the back room to remove a tray of cookies from the oven. I was in the process of transferring them to cooling racks when Josie came back in.

"What was that all about?" she asked.

"He wants to meet me later and talk about Colin," I said. "He has some more information that might help. He's going to bring dinner, too."

Josie's eyes shone with merriment. "Wow, a different guy every night. You're going to get a reputation."

I groaned. "Oh, please. You know it's not like that."

"Maybe not, but I do suspect that Luke has it bad for you. What will you do if he tries to make a move?"

"Let's hope it doesn't come to that."

CHAPTER SEVENTEEN

———

A few minutes later, my phone buzzed. Hopeful, I glanced at the screen, but it was my parents' landline. Since they were still in Florida, I knew it was probably my grandmother. "Hello?"

"Sally, my love." Grandma Rosa's voice was gentle. "Your young man was here."

"What? Oh my God! I'll be right there."

"You do not listen," she said. "I said he *was* here. He has already left."

My heart sank into my stomach. I leaned forward on the block table where I had been icing sugar cookies. "What are you talking about? And where did he go? Why didn't you call me earlier so that I could come over?" My voice shook, and I thought I might collapse in tears.

"Cara mia, you need to relax," Grandma muttered. "Mike did not want you to know he was here. He was very upset at first, but I managed to calm him down. I made him some breakfast, and we had a very nice chat."

"Grandma, nothing happened. I swear. I know it looked bad, but—"

She clucked her tongue in disapproval. "You do not have to explain to me. I know that you did not do anything with the police officer. But it looked very bad to Mike's eyes. I told him appearances are not always as—what do they say?"

"They're not always as they seem," I said. "And Mike should know me better than that. I would never—"

Grandma Rosa interrupted. "Ah. Listen to yourself. I remember when you thought the worst of him too, ten years ago. And you never gave him a chance to explain."

I clutched the phone tightly to my ear. "Grandma, do you think he's willing to talk to me?"

"Mike loves you," she said gently. "You are the reason he came home. I told him to go to you, talk, and work everything out. He gave me his word that he would. He would never lie to me."

I slumped forward on the table. "I hope you're right."

Josie came in the room and looked at me curiously.

"He has a job today," Grandma Rosa announced. "He was going to his house to grab some tools, and then he was leaving for work. I told him he could leave Spike with me. Such a good puppy dog."

My mind raced. So he'd definitely be coming back—at least for Spike. "That was nice of you to take him, but watch out. He tore a hole in my couch last night. I'll need to have it repaired before it gets worse."

"I will come look at it on Monday," she said. "Place a piece of duct tape over it for now. That will protect the material."

I cleared my throat. "When is Mike coming back to see me, Grandma?"

"I think he is planning on tonight when his job is finished."

"Maybe he's just telling you that. He might never want to see me again. Maybe I'll go over to his place and wait until he comes home."

"No, cara mia," she replied gently. "Go about your business today. Learn to have faith. Mike will be there, but he thinks he might be late, so do not panic if you do not see him for a while. I told him he needs to stay here and fight. Then I mentioned how you went to Florida and were looking into Colin's death. He was not happy about that, but he knows you did it because you love him."

Tears rolled down my cheeks. "Thank you, Grandma."

Josie came over and put an arm around my shoulders. "Is he okay?"

I nodded and held a finger to my lips. "Grandma, what would I ever do without you?"

She chuckled on the other end. "You would be lost." And with that truthful statement, she disconnected.

I turned and buried my face into Josie's shoulder. "He went to see Grandma. He promised her he wouldn't leave town again. He's going to stop by and see me tonight."

"Oh, Sal." She hugged me tightly. When we separated, I noticed her eyes had filled as well. "I'm so glad."

I reached for a paper towel to dry my eyes and handed Josie one. "I won't screw this up again."

Josie's expression was thoughtful. "What about Luke? He's coming by tonight."

I drew my eyebrows together. "Grandma said Mike would be late. That might mean close to midnight. I told Luke I had another event at nine, so he should be gone way ahead of schedule. Mike won't even know he was there."

She blew out a breath. "Sal, you can't have a repeat of what happened this morning. Mike would go crazy."

"There won't be a repeat. And I won't be dressed in a towel, either. Luke's only coming over to talk about Colin, and he's bringing fast food with him." Gee whiz. If Mike thought I was entertaining a new guy every night, there really would be no hope for our relationship.

She gave me an encouraging smile. "You know you're never going to live that down. All of the customers will be talking about you."

"They're already talking about me, so what's the difference?"

Josie's mouth turned up at the corners. "By the way, you missed Mrs. Gavelli this morning."

"I can hardly wait to hear this. Did she call me a tramp again?"

She grinned. "No. She said you were trying to hit on Mr. Feathers and to knock it off."

I stared at my best friend for a moment and then did something I hadn't done in quite a while— laughed out loud. It felt good.

* * *

After Josie finished the baby shower order, she relieved me at the counter, and I went in the back room to make some more doughs. Afterward, I glanced over the shop's figures for the week. Despite everything, we'd actually made a profit. I had Grandma Rosa to thank for that.

At six, Josie came into the kitchen to help clean up. "I can't wait to get out of here. I'm beat."

"You can go early if you want," I said. "You've earned it—and more."

She yawned. "I think I may take you up on that. Rob and I are heading to the Sanders Mansion for a late dinner, and we're staying over since tomorrow's Sunday. His mom is babysitting. We need a little alone time. Plus, it's a late birthday celebration. He just surprised me with it this morning."

I smiled. "You guys deserve some fun. Enjoy it. I'm sorry our get-together got ruined last week."

"No worries." She glanced at me anxiously. "Sal, what if you can't help clear Mike? Then what?"

Before I could reply, we heard the bells jingle over the front door. "Hello? Sally?"

I knew that voice and winced inwardly. Brian.

Josie peered around the corner at him, waved, and then held up two fingers at me. "Boyfriend Contender Number Two. And Number Three is due shortly. All we need is for Mike to show up now."

"Would you quit?" I glanced out the doorway at Brian.

He held up a hand and waved. "Do you have a minute to talk?"

I clutched Josie's arm. "Come with me."

"Man," she breathed. "Three guys after you. It's times like this when I really miss the single life."

Brian nodded to Josie, but when his gaze met mine, I noticed a tint of red to his cheeks. I was confident mine were burning as well.

"Sally," he said, "I have some news."

I braced myself. "Did you find the person who killed Colin?"

He hesitated. "We don't know for sure yet. But the Florida police arrested Ramon Ravole for an unrelated incident this morning."

I put a hand over my chest in an attempt to steady my

uneven breathing. "Oh, thank God."

"And justice is served," Josie mumbled.

"What was he arrested for?" I asked.

"They have enough evidence to tie him to a murder that happened in Tampa last week," Brian said. "We think it was another situation similar to Colin's. You know, couldn't pay his bill on time."

I exhaled sharply. "Did they run his fingerprints? Were they found in Colin's hotel room?"

Brian shook his head. "I'm afraid not. If he was there, maybe he wore gloves. The police obtained a search warrant for his house today. He's been on their radar for quite a while now. Maybe something will show up there to link him to Colin's murder. If they find a gun, perhaps we'll come up with a match."

"I hope so." An uneasy chill ran through me, and I rubbed my arms for warmth. Something about this whole situation didn't make sense. I wanted to believe Ramon was the killer, but my gut instinct told me there was more to this scenario.

"What is it?" Brian asked. "You know something."

I sat down at a table, and he joined me while Josie remained standing. I pointed at the door. "Go home to Rob and the kids. I'm fine."

Josie glanced from me to Brian with apprehension. "Are you sure?"

Brian put his hands behind his back in a mocking gesture. "She'll be safe with me, I swear."

Josie frowned. "Oh yeah. You might be wearing a cop uniform, but she's about as safe with you as a guppy is with a shark."

"Go home," I hissed at her.

She leaned down to give me a hug. "Call if you need me." She turned and walked into the back room. A moment later, I heard the door to the alley shut.

Brian shifted in his seat. "Nice to know I have a fan club. Okay, spill it. What is it you're not telling me?"

I leaned forward and propped my head on my hands. "God, I hate that I'm saying this. Plus, I promised Krista I'd wait till tomorrow. But—I think there's a chance the killer might be in

New York."

He narrowed his eyes. "Do you mean Krista Eldridge, Colin's sister? What does she have to do with this?"

I shut my eyes for a second. "I'm not positive, but Kyle Brown might have something to do with the murder." I went on to tell him about the discussion we'd overheard at the funeral home. "There was an expensive diamond ring found on Colin, too."

"I know. It was in his pocket," Brian said. "When Krista came to collect his personal belongings, she said it was yours. That you returned it to him after the divorce."

"That wasn't my ring. Colin's family was hoping to sell it to pay for his funeral expenses."

His eyes blazed into mine. "You should have told me about this sooner."

"I hoped it might lead me to the killer. A crazy idea but all I had to go on." Then I told him about Mitzi and the baking competition.

Brian drew a small pad out of his pocket and made some notes. "Sounds like she needs to be brought in for questioning. Anyone else?"

I swallowed hard. "Level with me. Does the grand jury have enough evidence to charge Mike?"

He tapped his pen on the table thoughtfully. "I honestly don't know, Sally. If we can prove Ramon was in New York the night Colin was murdered, there's a good chance Mike will be cleared. I hate to speculate on anything though."

"What about security camera footage at Colin's hotel?" I asked.

"We've already checked into that. Hotel Six's camera was broken. We have no idea who was there that night—besides Mike."

Of all the worse luck. I sighed and leaned back in my chair, defeated. "Well, thanks for your help."

He got to his feet, and I stood as well. "What about that guy Colin came to New York with—Luke something—the one who has eyes for you. I questioned him at the bar after the fight. What do you know about him?"

"Luke went to high school with us, but he's a couple of

years older. I didn't know him at all until we moved to Florida. He's a good guy and probably Colin's only friend. He's heading back to Florida tomorrow."

Silence hung in the air between us as Brian put his hat back on. "I guess I should get going. I know it's none of my business, but did you straighten everything out with Mike?"

The truth of the matter was no, but Grandma Rosa's conversation with my boyfriend had left me a tad bit more hopeful. "There's nothing to straighten out. He trusts me, and I trust him. That's really all that matters."

Brian's gaze locked on mine. "He's a lucky guy. You deserve the best, Sally. I mean it."

He moved toward me, and for a moment, I was afraid he might try to kiss me again. Instead, Brian tucked a curl behind my left ear, gave me a wistful smile, and then disappeared into the night.

CHAPTER EIGHTEEN

———

I had finished the cleanup, locked the front door of my shop, and was starting up the stairs when a knock on the front door startled me. I glanced at my watch. It was only five minutes after seven. If that was Luke, he was early.

I rushed down the stairs to unlock the door and take some of the packages from his hands. He grinned sheepishly at me. "Sorry I'm early."

"That's okay." I sniffed the air. "Chinese?"

"Hope that's all right. I've got egg rolls, fried rice, sesame chicken, and wonton soup."

My stomach growled. Again, I had eaten nothing all day. At least it was paying off since I'd stepped on the scale this morning and discovered my weight was down by five pounds. This was also thanks in part to the difficult week I'd been having. "Sounds perfect. I'm starved."

I closed and locked the door behind him, and we carried the food upstairs.

Luke surveyed my apartment with interest. "This is nice. How long have you lived here?"

I set the bags down on the kitchen table and opened a cabinet in search of plates. "Since September. It does make it very convenient with the bakery right downstairs."

"I'll bet." He glanced at my couch and examined the spot near the bottom that Spike had enjoyed digging his nails into. "You should have this fixed before it gets worse."

"Oh, thanks for reminding me. I almost forgot." I opened the junk drawer under the counter and withdrew a roll of duct tape. "My grandmother told me to use this in the meantime."

Luke removed the tape from my hands. "Allow me."

"Thanks." I grabbed a bottled water out of the fridge. "What would you like to drink?"

"Water's fine for me, too." He waited a moment then smiled. "Uh, scissors?"

"Oh, duh. Of course." I reached into the drawer again and handed a pair to Luke. Within seconds, he had covered the hole. He left the tape and scissors on my coffee table and joined me in the kitchen.

I bit into an egg roll. "Mm, delish. Is this from that new place over on Perkins Street?"

Luke nodded as he spooned some fried rice onto his plate. "Yeah. I heard they were pretty good." He glanced at the plastic bag that held the condiments. "No way. They forgot our fortune cookies. What good is Chinese food without fortune cookies?"

I laughed. "I think I can handle that for you." I ran downstairs, switched on the light, grabbed a piece of waxed paper, and removed a fortune cookie from the display case. I thumped my way back up the stairs in my boots and handed the cookie to Luke. "Ask and you shall receive."

He laughed. "I forgot you had these. Awesome." He broke the cookie apart and frowned. Then he held the pieces up so that I could see that it was empty. "No fortune in here. Double cheated."

The hairs rose on the back of my neck. I didn't know much about fortune cookie lingo but was aware that an empty cookie supposedly meant death. Would Luke be the next one to die at the killer's hands? Or had that cookie been destined for me?

Okay, stop it Sal. This is ridiculous. These pieces of dough cannot predict the future.

Luke stared at me with a question in his eyes. "Everything okay? You look kind of pale."

I forced a mouthful of food down my throat and reached for my water bottle. "Fine. Sorry about the cookie. I can grab you another one."

Luke wiped his mouth with a napkin. "Don't worry about it. So how are things between you and Mike? I heard rumors that you guys weren't getting along so well."

I stared at him in surprise. "Where'd you hear that?"

"I was at the sub shop earlier," Luke said. "An old lady was in line in front of me. She mentioned you by name to the guy she was with. Must have been her husband. He looked about two hundred years old. Anyhow, she said you and Mike were broken up and that it was a good thing because she'd known you since you were a little girl. Something about what a shame for your grandmother and wacky family that you were running around with a murderer."

Ugh. Mrs. Gavelli strikes again. "I think I know whom you're talking about. That's my parents' next door neighbor. She tends to exaggerate a bit."

He gazed into my eyes and smiled. I wiped my sweaty palms on my jeans and looked away. He was a nice guy, and I liked him, but this made me uneasy. I sure hoped he wasn't reading anything more into this so-called dinner date.

Luke leaned forward on the table. "Did you tell Mike I was coming here? I wouldn't want to make him jealous."

"Well, he won't know, so don't worry." At least I hoped not. If he did get here early, which I doubted, at least I'd be wearing clothing this time. That in itself was a plus. I glanced at my watch. "So what did you want to talk to me about?"

Luke bit into an egg roll. "I can't believe I'm saying this, but I think Kyle may have something to do with the murder."

I froze, my fork in the air. "Why? What do you know? Level with me."

He shifted in his seat uncomfortably. "I should have told the police, but after I left the bar that night, I drove by Colin's hotel. I wanted to see if he'd made it back okay and then try to persuade him to go to the police. It was only a matter of time before they would have shown up to arrest him for stabbing Mike."

"And?" I prodded.

Luke sighed. "Kyle's car was there. I went inside and was about ready to knock on Colin's door when I heard them screaming at each other. Kyle told him he was a loser and to stop giving their mother heartache. He said everyone would be better off if Colin's drug dealer just offed him and ended everyone's misery."

A giant knot formed in the bottom of my stomach, and I put my fork down. My once ravenous appetite had disappeared again. "What did you do?"

"I got the hell out of there," he said. "Kyle's never been a fan of mine. You know what he said to me the other day? That I'd been enabling his brother. Isn't that rich? You try to help someone, and then you have to listen to that garbage."

I exhaled a long, careful breath. "You've got to tell the police, Luke."

He nodded. "I'll go first thing in the morning. But I have no proof he's the one who shot Colin, and I didn't want to cause any more trouble for the family, especially his mother. She's been through enough hell, you know?"

I pushed my plate forward on the table. "I do know, but this will help to clear Mike. There's also a chance the killer might not be Kyle." I relayed what I had discovered about Ramon's arrest.

Luke was silent for a moment. "Sally, it sounds like there's a good possibility Mike's case won't even go to trial. I'm no expert, but I'm betting they need to have something more concrete to convict him. It's another week before it goes before the grand jury, right?"

I twisted a napkin between my hands and sighed. "I want to believe that so much."

He reached a hand across the table to squeeze mine. I looked up. His hazel eyes were warm and soft. "He's so lucky he has you."

Uh oh. I smiled politely and withdrew my hand. "Thanks."

Luke seemed to get the message and finished his egg roll. "So where's that picture you found?"

I pushed back my chair and walked into the living room with Luke following. My purse was sitting on the coffee table. The envelope with the two photos was still inside.

Luke sat down on the couch, and I joined him. "I know this one is Amber but no idea about the blonde. Maybe I should give them to the police. They might be able to find out something."

"I doubt it." He examined the picture closely. "Like I

said before, she's probably just some lowlife whore." The lines around his mouth tightened.

My nerves tingled as I watched his expression. "Are you okay?"

Luke put the pictures down on the coffee table and smiled. "I'm fine. Sorry. I guess I'm caught up in my own private hell."

Puzzled, I drew my eyebrows together. "Talk to me. What happened with your girlfriend? Did you break up?"

He opened his mouth in surprise. "You knew about her?"

"Colin mentioned her once, right before I caught him cheating on me. He said you'd recently started seeing someone, and you were crazy about her. I'm guessing it's the same girl you broke up with?"

Luke leaned back against the pillows and closed his eyes. I glanced at my watch again. I wanted to be a friend and lend an ear to his troubles, but I was starting to panic at the thought of Mike finding him here. Plus, I didn't want to lead Luke on.

He glanced sideways at me. "Sorry. This really isn't your problem. You've got enough to deal with."

"Hey," I said. "We're friends, right? Tell me what happened."

He blew out a breath. "She was cheating on me, so I called it off."

I patted his hand for a brief second. "I'm so sorry. I understand how it feels, believe me."

He nodded. "I know you do. I felt awful about what Colin did to you, but I didn't realize how much it hurt until the same thing happened to me." His face took on a faraway expression. "Her name was Elise, and we'd just gotten engaged. I even had a ring designed for her. She was so beautiful."

"Her loss."

Luke smiled. "Thanks." He ran a hand through his hair in frustration. "How long before the pain goes away?"

I sighed. "I guess it's different for everybody. Colin hurt me pretty bad, but now that I have Mike, I try not to think about it anymore. I don't know if I'll ever forget though. When you find the right woman, it will help. Trust me."

"I needed to hear that, thanks." Luke stared at me so intently that I looked away in embarrassment. "Do you know what true love is, Sally? What it really means?"

I laughed uneasily. "Well, I hope so by now. It's taking care of each other and being true to one another for the rest of your lives. It's realizing that no one is perfect and accepting each other along with the flaws that you have."

He nodded in approval. "Exactly. It should never be taken for granted. Love is a gift."

I experienced a giant niggle at the back of my brain. Where had I heard that phrase used before recently?

Luke's eyes bore an odd expression, similar to Brian's the evening before. *Oh no. Why me?* I tried to move away but wasn't fast enough. He reached out and pulled me into his arms, pressing his mouth over mine.

Panicked, I pushed against his chest. "What do you think you're doing?"

"Don't play coy," he said. "You know I've always had a thing for you." His arms tightened around me again.

"Let go of me," I said. "I'm in love with Mike. If I gave you any other idea, I'm sorry. And I think it would be best if you left now."

I struggled to free myself, and he laughed. I managed a sharp kick to his knee with my boot, and Luke's right arm jerked out in surprise and collided with my coffee table. The table landed on its side, and everything on top went flying, including the duct tape, scissors, a magazine, and my purse. My bag turned upside down, and all of its contents spilled out onto the floor.

"Ouch." Luke gripped his knee between his hands.

I glared at him. "Get out of my apartment."

Luke raised a hand in defense. "Look. I'm sorry. I guess I went too far."

"You guessed right," I snapped.

"Let me help you clean up everything before I leave," Luke said. "It would make me feel better." Before I could protest, he'd righted the coffee table.

"It's not necessary." As I stooped down on the floor to clean up the mess, a light bulb clicked on in my head, and I remembered where I had heard that phrase.

Love is a gift.

A tremor of fear ran through my body. Of course. It was the inscription in the engagement ring that Colin had had on him when he died.

The same ring Luke was holding in his hand right now, waving at me.

"Nice," he said. "Where'd you get this?"

I studied his face. The color had disappeared, and his lips were compressed together in a thin, tight line. There was an expression in his eyes I'd seen before. Cold, calculating, and royally pissed—at me.

A killer's eyes.

Words stuck in my throat. I was afraid my expression—as always—might give me away, so I stared at the floor. I started stuffing the contents back into my purse and clutched my cell phone in my left hand, hoping he wouldn't notice. I tried to sound casual. "Oh, it belongs to a friend. I told her I'd have it resized for her."

He examined the ring more closely. "Someone went to a lot of trouble picking this baby out. They also paid a great deal of money. Don't lose it."

Fear and nausea consumed me at an alarming rate. Colin's killer had been right in front of me all along. His one and only friend. Why hadn't it dawned on me earlier? Everyone had their limits. And my ex-husband pushed people to their breaking point.

Colin's own brother hated him. He owed money to loan sharks. There was a young girl whose boyfriend had died because of his carelessness, who sought revenge on him.

During all of this, Luke had stood by his friend—until Colin betrayed him by sleeping with his fiancée.

I tried to keep my voice steady. "Excuse me. I need to use the bathroom for a second." I managed to throw a small smile in his direction before I headed down the hallway. I turned to go into the bathroom, my phone in hand. I was just about to shut the door when Luke's face appeared before me.

"What are you doing?" I attempted to slam the door on his hand, but he moved too quickly. Luke reached in and gripped me by the hair. I screamed in pain as he jerked me through the opened door and threw me onto the rug in the hallway. Startled, I lay there motionless while he came at me again. I raised my boots in the air and caught him square in the face with one. He groaned and fell backward against the bathroom door frame in obvious pain. I stuffed the phone in my pocket and scrambled to my feet, running as fast as I could for the apartment door.

My heart thudded against the wall of my chest, threatening to explode. All I needed was to get out of here and call Mike. Or 9-1-1. Anyone who could help me get away from this lunatic.

I breathed heavily as I unlocked the door. Before I could open it, Luke grabbed me from behind. I struggled, but he managed to lift me off the floor and into his arms. I flailed out, kicking at the air with my feet while trying to reach backward and claw Luke's face. He was much stronger, and I was clearly no match for him. He threw me against the side of the fridge where my head collided with a thud against the metal.

I crumpled to the floor, gasping for air. Stars danced before my eyes, and I caught a last glimpse of Luke standing over me, holding the ring between his fingers.

"I'm sorry, Sally," he said.

Then everything went black.

CHAPTER NINETEEN

———

A burning sensation around my wrists awakened me. I opened my eyes in confusion, not remembering where I was at first. Then recognition dawned that I was lying on my kitchen floor. I stared up at the ceiling. There was a mammoth-sized cobweb hanging over the fridge, mocking me. *Boy, I really need to dust.*

My head ached as the rest of the room swam into focus. I tried to stand, but my hands had been bound together behind my back with something, and my ankles were tied as well. The more I struggled to free myself, whatever it was that held them together only irritated my skin further.

Luke was sitting at my kitchen table, holding a frozen plastic bag of peas against the side of his face. He repositioned it, and our eyes met. He had a nice black-and-purple shiner, courtesy of my boots. *Good.*

He waved the duct tape at me. "Thanks. That worked well."

I didn't know what I was experiencing more—rage or terror. The listless expression in Luke's eyes made me inclined to go with the latter. "Untie me."

He threw the bag of peas down on the table. "I'm sorry, Sally. I wish it could have been different. But now that you know the truth, I don't have a choice."

"I don't know anything."

He laughed. "Please. Your face gave it away as soon as I mentioned the inscription. I don't want to hurt you, but there's no other option, I'm afraid."

"Josie knew you were coming here. Lots of other people knew too," I lied. "They'll figure out you killed me."

He smiled. "Doubt it. Oh, and I ran into Gianna at the sub shop earlier. I wished her happy birthday. Funny, she didn't seem to know what I was talking about. So I guess there's no fear of anyone looking for you tonight. Plus, the shop's closed tomorrow. I've heard rumors that Mike left town, so I'm guessing your boyfriend won't be stopping by for a lovefest, either."

Mike. I was relieved I hadn't shared the information with Luke that he was back in town. I stared at the wall clock hopefully. Nine o'clock. Was there a chance he would arrive soon? He was my only hope. My parents were still in Florida, and Gianna and my grandmother would be turning in for the night. Josie was out of town with Rob.

I thought about the text I'd sent Mike yesterday. *I need you.* The words had never seemed as crucial as they did right now.

Luke picked up one end of his broken fortune cookie and fingered it. "I've got plenty of time to get out of town tonight. Out of the country, actually. And enough money to tide me over for a while." He pulled the ring out of his pocket. "Thanks for this. I didn't think I'd ever see the little trinket again."

The more I struggled, the more the tape burned into my wrists. I managed to wriggle onto my side, but Luke reached down and prodded me with his foot, moving me onto my back again.

A lump of panic rose in my throat. "Where's Elise? Did you kill her, too?"

"No." Luke said. "She left town after I discovered her, shall we say, indiscretion. She had a friend who worked for the Hooper Inn. After I threw Colin out of my place, Elise offered to get him a room at the hotel pretty cheap until he found something else. Her friend even booked it in her own name. That must have been when they started hooking up. But after Colin started squelching on that bill, he had to leave. I helped him get another apartment, so he moved out of there."

Luke chuckled low in his throat as he continued. "God, he was pathetic. About a month ago, I had to go out of town overnight for a convention in Jacksonville. I'd been on the road for an hour or so when I got a call that the meeting had been cancelled because the main speaker was ill. I headed right for

Elise's. I planned to take her out to dinner and then make love to her all night long."

His eyes glittered at me as he said the words, and I swallowed hard in an effort to keep the bile in my throat down. With my hands and feet taped together, I was pretty much defenseless at this point. I prayed Luke was not nurturing any romantic ideas about me.

Luke tossed the broken cookie onto the table. "When I reached her apartment building, I noticed Colin's piece of crap car in the lot. It was hard to miss. That's when I finally put it all together. God, how they played me for a fool."

"But...but maybe he was there to see someone else." I had no doubt in my mind Luke was correct. It was obvious Colin had no morals, and there were no limits for him where sex was concerned.

Keep him talking. That was all I could do until someone—anyone—showed up to rescue me. *If* they showed up. What was Luke planning to do with me?

He stared down at me in amazement. "After what Colin did to you, how can you say such a thing? Besides," he added, "I heard them. I went inside the building and pressed my ear against her door." He shut his eyes tightly as if trying to block the episode out. "They sounded like animals in heat."

Was there anyone Colin *hadn't* been sleeping with? I wasn't sure anymore.

Luke observed me closely. "What did you do when you found Colin in bed with someone else?"

My head ached badly. Every time I spoke the pain was worse, but I was afraid I'd anger him more if I didn't respond. "I think I was in shock. I shut the door and got into my car without saying anything to them. Then I drove all night long."

"That son of a bitch," he said through clenched teeth.

"Why didn't you confront them?" I asked.

Luke's voice was bitter. "That would have been too easy. I wanted to make them pay in other ways. So I decided to put it to the real test. The next day, I called Elise up and told her I'd lost my job. That I could no longer afford to pay for her apartment. The big fancy wedding at the Country Club was off—we'd have to get married at town hall instead. But what did it matter since we loved each other so much, right?"

He laughed, the sound sending crystals of ice through my veins. "That whore was so damned predictable. She was quiet at first and then said she'd been wanting to talk to me about something. She wasn't ready to get married yet, so could we hold off on the wedding for a little while?"

"How honorable of her," I said.

Luke snorted. "She was in love, all right—with my money. So I told her, 'No problem,' and I'd take the ring back until she was ready. I'd had it personally designed for her. I've always felt love was a gift, you know? She started crying when I gave it to her. But not for the reasons I'd thought. She was greedy, same as your ex-husband." He repeated the words, "Love is a gift. Sounds nice, doesn't it?"

I tried to nod my head, which was about to explode. "That's a beautiful sentiment."

"It cost me over twenty grand," Luke sputtered. "That didn't bother me because I thought she was the one, and nothing was too good for her. When I asked for it back, she started crying and said she'd lost it. I figured she was lying so that she could keep the ring and hock it later. I never dreamed she'd give it to that loser."

"She might not have. Maybe he stole it from her."

Luke snorted. "True. Elise was always taking the ring off and forgetting where she'd left it. I loved her, but God that pissed me off. She lost a diamond bracelet I gave her once, too. She probably figured, 'Hey, no big deal. He'll just buy me another, right?' Yep, a regular gold digger. I went to her apartment the next day, but she'd already left. Cleaned out in a hurry. Her friend at the Hooper Inn wouldn't tell me anything, either."

"I'm sorry." I didn't know what else to say.

He laughed bitterly. "It had to hurt Elise. Now she actually has to work for a living. Unless she finds another sap like me. Yep, a gold digger, just like Colin. He didn't deserve to live after the way he ruined my life."

He picked up the knife I'd used for the sesame chicken. He started fingering its sharp edge, and a small gasp escaped from my mouth.

"But that wasn't the worst of it. I was Colin's only friend.

He alienated everyone else. I let him stay in my apartment—rent free. I tried to help him, and this was how he repaid me? By sleeping with my fiancée?" Luke rose from the table, picked up the chair he'd been sitting on, and flung it across the room in a sudden fit of rage. It landed against my living room wall, leaving a huge mark and breaking into several pieces.

A small whimper escaped from my mouth as I watched him. *He's going to kill me.* I wasn't sure how he planned to carry out the deed yet, but that much had become obvious.

"Seriously, what's wrong with women?" Luke asked. "I mean, I know he was a good looking guy, but were all of you really that stupid?"

"Gee, thanks, Luke." I attempted a laugh, but he clearly wasn't amused.

He picked up the knife again. "Hey, don't worry. I was stupid, too. I kept trying to help Colin. After I caught him with Elise, I bided my time. I knew he owed money and was in over his head. He was desperate to get out of town and begged to go along with me when I said I was leaving for New York." His eyes glittered. "What a schmuck."

A bead of sweat trickled down the small of my back. "So you planned to kill him all along?"

Luke's eyes bore into mine. "Like I said, he didn't deserve to live. And I had to even the score." He scratched his head thoughtfully as he studied me. "I'm sorry your boyfriend has to take the blame for it. But he might as well go to prison. The news of your death will send him right over the edge anyway. And then, when he dies, you two can finally be together forever."

I thought about the murder investigation at my bakery last September. I'd almost been a victim then, too. Ever since returning home after the divorce, I had managed to attract several crazy people into my life. How had I become such a magnet for lunatics?

"Please don't do this. You're not thinking straight. I promise I'll try to help you. Just untie me so that we can talk."

Luke sighed as his eyes lingered over me. "I'm sorry. Really I am. Damn, I had the biggest crush on you in high school."

I shivered. "Wow. That's very flattering."

He was busy cutting off a small piece of duct tape with the scissors. "Hmm. But you never noticed, did you? No, because you only had eyes for Donovan, even back then. Too bad. Your loss."

"Luke," I began.

"I'm not sorry I killed Colin. He had it coming. Today, when I asked you to meet, I had a feeling you might have found something to incriminate me. My gut instinct was right. Gee, this really sucks for you."

Panic gripped me tighter than the duct tape as he opened the oven door. *No. This can't be happening.* "Please, Luke. I'm begging you. Don't do this."

Luke reached behind my stove. "I'd probably use my gun if I hadn't already tossed it into the Niagara River. Quicker but messier. I don't like the thought of leaving you covered in blood. It would ruin my illusion of you. So I'm disconnecting the power to your gas stove. As a result, the electronic igniter won't work. Then I'll turn on the burner, and gas will fill the room. In about a half hour—maybe less—you won't be feeling any more pain. You'll slip into a nice deep sleep. Forever."

Tears filled my eyes. "No. Let's talk some more. Please."

"I'm done talking, Sally. And you should thank me. This is a pretty painless way to go. I mean, you bake all day, so this method is appropriate, right?"

I started to scream, and Luke leaned over to place the duct tape on my mouth. I tried to bite his finger, but he was too quick for me. "Good-bye, Sally."

Luke turned on the burner, gave me one last sympathetic look, and shut the door of my apartment noiselessly. I heard him run down the stairs, and the bells jingled on the front door, announcing his departure.

Tears streamed down my cheeks. I managed to wriggle onto my side again, the tape further irritating my wrists and ankles. I groaned as I inched my way across the floor into the living room. It took forever. Had Luke left my phone somewhere? Maybe I could tip the coffee table over and sever the tape on my wrists with its sharp corners. The gas smell was already starting to sicken me. How long before I passed out?

Could the building possibly explode?

I tried to think straight but wasn't sure how much time I might have left. If I could reach up and somehow unlock the door with my feet, what would I do then? Roll down the stairs? That might kill me, too. My brain was becoming a confused jumble, and my headache worsened as gas continued to fill my tiny apartment.

I was never going to see my family again. Or Mike. We'd never have our happily ever after that we'd fought so hard for. I finally reached the carpeted flooring and the coffee table. As I was trying to knock it over, a key turned in my door. I looked up to see Mike staring down at me.

For a second, he just stood there, his face registered with disbelief and confusion. The expression immediately changed to one of horror as he rushed to my side and tore the tape off my mouth. I groaned from the pain.

"Baby, who did this to you?"

"Turn off the burner," I croaked. Mike sniffed at the air and ran into the kitchen. He rushed through my apartment, opened every window, and then raced back to my side. He lifted me effortlessly into his arms and gripped me tightly as we made our way down the stairs and into the cold black night.

Mike laid me down on the backseat of his truck and then reached for his cell phone to dial 9-1-1.

"My girlfriend's been attacked," he said to the operator. "Thirty-nine Elk Street." Mike produced a pocketknife from his key ring that he used to free my wrists and feet while he continued talking into the phone. I whimpered when he removed the tape.

His eyes blazed with anger as he looked at me. "Who did this to you?"

"Luke Zibro." I was afraid I might pass out again. "He k-killed Colin."

Mike spoke to the operator. "The guy's name is Luke Zibro. He shot a man named Colin Brown to death last week." He reached over and massaged my wrists. They were painful with large red welts. He brought one to his lips as he continued talking. "I don't know his address. He tied her up and tried to kill her. No, she seems to be all right. Just hurry. Please."

Mike left me for a moment to start the engine. He cracked open the driver's side window and then came back with a blanket to cover me. He slid onto the seat next to me and gathered me in his arms.

"Sal, I'm so sorry. This is all my fault."

"No." My throat was dry, and I wanted to nap. "Not your fault."

His lips were in my hair. "Don't go to sleep, okay, baby? Open your eyes and look at me."

I did as he asked and stared into the deep-blue, mesmerizing eyes I adored so much. They were filled with unshed tears as he crushed me to him. "I don't know what I'd do if I ever lost you."

I managed a smile. "You're never going to lose me. You're stuck with me."

"Thank God." I felt him tremble against me. "I shouldn't have left you. I thought it was better that way. I didn't want you involved in this mess. But I only made things worse." He buried his face in my hair.

"Stop saying that." The fresh air was helping my alertness, and now I was shivering from the cold. "Don't ever talk like that again. Don't you understand how much I love you?"

He brushed a kiss across my lips. "I missed you so much."

"I need you," I said. "Always."

CHAPTER TWENTY

———

The next hour passed in a blur. Police arrived on the scene, along with the fire department and paramedics. They administered oxygen, and then I was brought to a local hospital where my head was checked, and the doctor ran several tests. He said that I was very lucky Mike had found me when he did. I had a minor concussion and was ordered to rest tomorrow. The doctor said someone should stay with me for the next twenty-four hours.

Mike clutched my hand tightly as he spoke to the doctor. "I won't leave her for a second. I promise."

Gianna and Grandma Rosa had also arrived at the hospital after Mike called them from the ambulance. He'd telephoned Josie as well who immediately wanted to make the trip back. Mike assured her I was fine, and he would take care of everything. I'd spoken with her briefly and begged her to stay put. I didn't want to ruin her birthday celebration again. Plus, I had Mike.

That was all I needed right now.

After being assured I was okay, Gianna and Grandma Rosa got ready to depart.

Gianna kissed me. "Sal, I don't know how you always manage to find yourself in these predicaments." She gave Mike a hug. "See that she stays out of trouble."

He grinned. "I'll take care of her. Don't worry."

Grandma Rosa patted my cheek. "You are a tough girl, and everything will be fine now. Your young man is back, and all is as it should be."

Mike gave her a peck on the cheek. "This is all thanks to you. If you hadn't convinced me to come here tonight—" His voice filled with raw emotion. "I can't even bear to think about it. I never should have left town."

Grandma Rosa smiled at him. "You were there when Sally needed you the most. That is what counts."

I hugged her tightly. "*Grazie mille*, Grandma."

For a split second, I thought I saw her eyes cloud over. "*Prego*. You both will come for dinner tomorrow night. I will make Mike's favorite."

His mouth opened in surprise. "Oh, wow. Do you mean *pasta e fagioli?*"

She nodded. "Sì. With a nice green salad and homemade garlic bread. Maybe some tiramisu, too."

"Damn." Mike winked at me. "There are so many advantages to saving your life."

We all laughed, and then Gianna and my grandmother departed. They hadn't been gone five minutes when Brian poked his head into my room. Mike's face turned crimson at the first glimpse of him.

Brian was dressed in uniform. "Is it okay if I come in?"

Mike shrugged and gripped my hand tighter.

I was afraid World War III might commence. "Sure, Brian."

He strolled into the room, hat in hand. "I heard about what happened. Are you okay, Sally?"

"I am, thanks. Mike rescued me in time." I squeezed his hand reassuringly.

Brian cleared his throat and looked uncomfortable. "I'm glad. I wanted to give you an update. We were able to locate the rental car Luke Zibro was driving. We caught him heading for the Canadian border. Several squad cars were pursuing him when it became apparent he wasn't stopping. I was one of the cars involved in the chase. I think Luke made up his mind that he wasn't coming back. He drove his car straight into the river."

My breath caught in my throat. "Where is he now?"

"I was there when they fished him out of the water. Another officer managed to get a confession out of him." He paused and locked eyes with me. "He died on the way to the hospital. I think it was from internal bleeding."

Mike and I were silent for several seconds while he

stroked my hand gently with his fingertips. "It's all over now, baby. He'll never hurt you again."

I closed my eyes for a moment. "The ring belonged to Luke, Brian. His fiancée was sleeping with Colin. I think Colin might have stolen it from her."

"We didn't find the ring on him," Brian said. "It's probably sitting at the bottom of the river by now. I'm glad you're okay and that you guys can finally put this mess behind you."

He smiled at me and then extended his hand for Mike to shake. After a brief hesitation, Mike brushed his fingers against Brian's. "Thanks for coming by."

Brian nodded. "No problem." He gave me one long, last look and left the room.

Mike sat on the edge of the bed and wrapped his arms around me. "Ready to go home, princess?"

"I thought they said I couldn't go back to my place tonight. The building needs to be aired out."

"I meant my house. Our home as far as I'm concerned."

He gazed into my eyes and gently covered my mouth with his. I ached with longing for him. After we broke apart, tears streamed down my cheeks. "I missed you so much."

Mike sighed and brushed my tears away with his fingers. "I can't live without you, Sal."

I couldn't stand it anymore. "Tell me what happened that night."

He tensed against me. "I only meant to warn him. Honest. I never would have killed him, I swear it."

"I know that. Tell me what happened when you arrived at the hotel."

A muscle ticked in his jaw. "I never told you, but I got a license to carry a while back, after my house got broken into. Even though I'd installed an alarm system, I didn't feel it was enough. A little extra protection never hurts."

I wiped my eyes with the back of my hand. "I found the gun after you got arrested. I know you brought it with you that night when you went to see Colin. I saw you place something in the bottom drawer when you returned home from visiting him."

Mike lowered his eyes to the floor. "I'm sorry I didn't tell you about it sooner. Maybe I was afraid you'd freak out if you knew. I'm not sure why I brought it with me that night. God, I was so angry at him. Not for cutting me but hurting you. He'd already done so much—I couldn't stand the thought of him inflicting any more pain on the woman I loved. So I was only going to scare him off."

"What happened when you got there?" I asked again.

"I went to his room," Mike said. "I was standing there, getting ready to knock, and noticed the door wasn't shut all the way. So I went inside. Big mistake, right? Colin was lying on the bed in some kind of drunken stupor. Or he might have been high. Who knows? I tried to wake him, but he was out cold. So I left." He shook his head. "I never should have gone. It only made things worse. Who would have thought someone would kill him that night? And that they'd find my fingerprints in there?"

"Luke," I said. "He tried to make me believe Kyle was there when he arrived, but I'm betting he was watching and saw you go into the room. After the fight and the threat, it was a perfect time to kill Colin and implicate you in the murder."

"I thought I'd gotten rid of all the anger inside me. But when I saw him hurt you—well, I guess I exploded. If he ever laid a hand on you again, who knows what I would have done to him."

I put a finger to his lips. "You were just trying to protect me. It's all over now. You've been cleared. That's what really counts."

He smiled. "I'm no longer a man on the run. And I have you to boot. What more could a guy ask for?"

He kissed me again, and I forgot about everything else for a while.

We arrived home after two in the morning. Mike was diligent about waking me up every hour, although I wasn't particularly happy about it. I didn't think he'd slept at all. At about seven o'clock, after he woke me once again, I gave up on sleep.

"Let's do something," I winked.

He grinned. "Are you sure you're feeling up to it?"

I wrapped my arms around his neck. "Oh, most definitely."

It was late morning before I finally rolled out of bed to take a shower. Mike made me breakfast, and for the first time in days, my appetite was back in full force.

Mike pulled out my chair for me. There were pancakes, sausages, and a steaming mug of coffee waiting at my place.

"You're spoiling me," I said.

"Nothing's too good for my princess." He kissed the top of my head.

I took a long sip from my mug. "So how about telling me where you were for the past five days?"

Mike's face clouded over as he reached for his mug. "I went to Canada. To see my grandmother."

My mouth opened in amazement. I'd never heard him speak of any relatives before and had assumed they were all dead. "Why didn't you tell me?"

He shrugged. "Jenny's not my real grandmother. They're both dead. She's more of an adopted one. She was a good friend of my mother's and tried to help her kick the habit, even though we both knew deep down it was useless. After she died, Jenny helped me with the funeral arrangements and said if I ever needed anything, let her know. And I told her likewise."

I reached out my hand to him. Mike brought it to his lips before he continued. "A few weeks ago, she sent me a letter. Said she needed some repairs done on her house and if I ever got to Canada, please stop by. When all of this went down, I figured it was as good a time as any. I stayed at her house while I completed the work. Jenny cooked my meals, and I didn't charge her anything for the work. I figured I owed it to her."

"She sounds like a wonderful person. I hope I get to meet her sometime."

He nodded. "You will. I told her all about you. How much I love you, what happened in the past to us, and how we'd been given a second chance. And that I still wasn't good enough for you and had screwed up everything." His beautiful eyes filled with pain. "Again."

A lump formed in my throat. "Stop saying that. It's not true. What did she tell you?"

Mike smiled. "She's a lot like your grandmother. She told me that I was only hurting you by staying away. That it sounded like you needed me too, and I should go back and fight this. Then when I got your text, I couldn't stay away any longer."

"It was awful not knowing where you were."

"Leaving you was the hardest thing I ever had to do." He narrowed his eyes. "But when I walked in on you with Jenkins—"

Mental head slap. "I know. That must have looked awful. I swear, nothing happened. He came over the night before to ask about your whereabouts. To his credit, I think he knew you were gone, but he never told anyone. I had a glass of wine and fell asleep on the couch. I guess he did, too. When I woke up, it was the middle of the night, and the snow was coming down heavy. I didn't have the heart to ask him to leave then. So I went to my room, and he slept on the couch."

Mike nodded. "I know the storm was bad. I drove in it all night because I couldn't wait to see you again."

I bit into my lower lip, afraid I might cry suddenly. "I'm sorry. He was waiting for me when I came out of the shower that morning. He was saying good-bye when you showed up."

His eyes were soft. "I believe you. Looks can be deceiving, right? I guess we're even now, huh?"

I thought about the incident ten years ago when I'd found Mike in Backseat Brenda's car and nodded. Never assume, my grandmother had told me at the time. If only I had listened to her.

"I'm glad you had Jenny looking out for you and relieved you went to see my grandmother instead of leaving town again." I toyed with my spoon. "I decided something this morning. About Colin."

He leaned forward on his elbows. "What's that?"

"The prize money from the contest. I want to give five thousand of my share to Colin's family for the funeral expenses."

Mike's jaw dropped. "That's your money, Sal. You don't owe them anything. All they've done is cause you pain."

I had already filled Mike in on the lies Colin told his family about me. "I know I don't, but it would make me feel better about the entire situation."

He reached for my hand. "It's your decision, and I'll support whatever you decide to do. But I thought you wanted to use that money to expand the shop?"

I winked. "I happen to know an excellent builder. I think there's even a good chance he'll give me a discount."

Mike laughed. "Hmm. Anything's possible. Speaking of which, guess what? I had several calls this morning. My jobs are all back on—starting tomorrow."

"That's so awesome." I hesitated. "Wait—even Laura Embree?"

"Especially Laura." He grinned, and I stuck my tongue out at him.

He gestured at my plate and gave me a devilish smile. "So, Miss Muccio, you'd better keep your strength up. Start eating. We need to make the most of our free time today."

* * *

It was late Sunday afternoon, and we were back at my apartment. The place was freezing but considered safe for us to enter. We'd closed the windows, and I'd turned the heat up. Everything downstairs in the bakery had remained undisturbed, much to my relief.

Mike had gone upstairs to see about repairing the ding in my wall while I checked on some inventory in the freezer. My cell buzzed, and I studied the screen. My parents' landline. "Hello?"

My grandmother's voice greeted me. "How are you feeling, my dear?"

"I'm fine, thanks."

"That is good news. Your mama and papa are home. I told them that all was well, and they were very much relieved. But your papa—he would like you to bring some fortune cookies over tonight." She clucked her tongue. "I do not know what the matter is with that man. He is such a crack."

I smiled. "You mean a quack?"

"That is what I said," she said. "How are you and your young man? Did you have a nice chat? Everything is good now?"

"Everything is great. You've been such a big help. I don't know what I'd ever do without you."

"I am glad, cara mia," Grandma said. "You are seeing things more clearly now, no?"

"What do you mean?"

My grandmother chuckled. "You will figure it all out in due time. I will see you at six o'clock."

Grandma Rosa disconnected, and I grabbed a piece of waxed paper while mulling over what she'd said. I placed some Italian butter cookies—my father's favorite—inside one of my little pink boxes and then reached down for some fortune cookies. I hoped my father wouldn't insist I open one this time. Ugh. After Luke's fortune yesterday—or lack thereof—I was seriously starting to wonder about these cookies.

Might as well give him half a dozen. As I picked up the last one, it fell apart in my hands. Josie must have been in a hurry and hadn't folded it properly.

I looked down at the message staring me in the face and sighed in resignation. "Okay, let's have it."

The greatest risk is not taking one.

That was all. There was no ominous message announcing I was going to die tonight or to stay in the house with the sheets pulled up over my head. But these words definitely left me thinking.

There was a risk in my life I was afraid to take. Even though Colin was gone and my divorce behind me, I was afraid to try again. I yearned for a happy life with a husband who wouldn't betray me and a house full of children. I knew Mike was also anxious to settle down and start a family. We'd been discussing the topic since we were teenagers. Plus, Mike was nothing like Colin, so there was nothing to fear there. So why was I still afraid?

After the divorce from Colin, I hadn't wanted to get involved with another man. Mike had promised to give me space, but once we had started dating again, we'd been drawn to each other like magnets. Heck, we had a lot of making up to do for ten years apart.

A week ago, I had been convinced I was not ready to cohabitate and definitely not ready for marriage. But a great deal had happened in the past seven days. The unthinkable had almost occurred. We'd come close to losing each other. If anything, this week had taught me how precious life was and that nothing should ever be taken for granted.

I thought about Gianna, pouring hundreds of hours into the exam she would finally take tomorrow. I knew in my heart that she'd ace it and couldn't wait to celebrate with her afterward. This was her lifelong dream, as mine had been the bakery, a husband, and children. It was a huge risk, but Gianna was diligently following through.

Then there were my parents and their screwball antics—my father driving a hearse and my mother dressing up like a Barbie doll to show someone a house. Entering a Hotties Over Fifty pageant. We all took risks every day. It was part of life.

I thought about Mike, growing up without anyone to love him. He'd been forced to rely on himself at an early age. He was always helping someone else, like the situation with Jenny. All he wanted was to be with me and have a family someday.

As I held the little strip of paper between my hands, I knew the time had come. I smiled to myself as I imagined Gianna's face—how happy she'd be to get away from my parents. She'd land a terrific position as an attorney soon, and the low rent would be easy for her to maintain. It felt good to do something for my baby sister. Jeez, after the experience with Luke last night, it felt good to live. My life was everything I wanted it to be now. Yet there was still something missing.

After one last proud look around my shop, I tucked the paper into the pocket of my jeans and slowly climbed the stairs.

Mike was buffing out the living room wall and winked at me. "Good as new."

I stared at him, unable to say anything, and he frowned. "Baby, what's wrong? Is your head worse?"

Despite a slight headache, I'd never felt better. I could finally see everything clearly. In the past, I'd always been terrible at making decisions about my life. But I knew the one I'd just made in my mind and in my heart was—without a doubt—the right one.

"I'm fine. And thanks for fixing the wall. That will make Gianna very happy."

Mike immediately latched on to the hidden meaning in my words and strode across the room to where I was standing.

He lowered me into a sitting position on the couch and put his arms around me. His eyes shone as they gazed into mine. "Does this mean what I think it does? You're ready to move in with me?"

I looked at him, at this man whom I'd loved since I was a teenager—the one person I could no longer bear to be away from anymore. He'd saved my life and given it meaning, too.

My voice trembled. "No. That's *not* what I meant."

Mike's face registered disappointment, but he tried to make light of the situation. "Oh. Well, that's okay. I promised I wouldn't rush you and meant it. We'll just keep going back and forth to each other's places—like we have been."

I cradled his face between my hands. "You're not listening to me. And, no, we're not going to keep doing this."

He frowned, and a panicked look came into his eyes. "Sal, I don't understand. What are you trying to say? Just tell me what you want, sweetheart."

I grinned. "I want you to marry me."

Spice Cookies with Pumpkin Frosting

¾ cup softened margarine
1 cup sugar
1 egg
¼ cup molasses
2 cups flour
2 teaspoons baking soda
1 teaspoon ground cinnamon
½ teaspoon ground ginger
½ teaspoon ground cloves
½ teaspoon salt

Frosting ingredients:
8 ounces cream cheese, softened
18-ounce can pumpkin puree
2 cups confectioner's sugar
½ tsp ground cinnamon
¼ tsp ground ginger

In a mixing bowl, cream margarine and sugar. Add egg and beat well. Add molasses, and mix thoroughly. Combine flour, soda, salt, and spices in a bowl. Add to creamed mixture, and mix well. Chill overnight in airtight container. Shape into ½-inch balls. Place 2 inches apart on parchment-lined baking sheets. Bake at 375° Fahrenheit for 6 minutes. Cookies will be very flat. Cool for 2 minutes, and then place on a wire rack and frost. Makes about 4 dozen cookies.

For frosting: Beat cream cheese in a bowl until smooth. Add pumpkin puree and mix well. Add sugar, cinnamon, and ginger. Beat until smooth. Be sure to refrigerate the cookies until ready to serve. Store leftover frosting in the refrigerator.

Josie's Jelly Cookies

1 ½ cups (3 sticks) of butter, softened
1 cup of sugar
3 egg yolks
1 teaspoon vanilla
4 cups of flour
Jam—Strawberry, Raspberry, Grape, your choice. (Can be seeded or unseeded.)

Preheat oven to 350° Fahrenheit. Cream butter, sugar, yolks, and vanilla together. Sift flour, and mix ingredients into wet mixture. Shape cookies in hand to make a ball about the size of a tablespoon, and press thumb firmly into the center. Fill imprint with favorite jam. Bake on parchment-lined cookie sheet for about 10 minutes or until edges start to brown. Let cool—the jelly especially will be very hot! Makes about two dozen cookies.

Brownie Biscotti

⅔ cup sugar
⅓ cup butter, softened
2 eggs
1¾ cups all-purpose flour
2 teaspoons baking powder
¼ teaspoon baking soda
1 teaspoon vanilla extract
⅓ cup unsweetened cocoa powder
¼ cup chopped walnuts, if desired
½ cup mini chocolate chips

Preheat oven to 375° Fahrenheit. Cream sugar, baking powder, baking soda, and butter in large mixing bowl until light and fluffy. Add eggs and vanilla, and beat well. Beat in cocoa and flour. Stir in chocolate chips and nuts. Divide and shape dough into (2) 9x2x1-inch loaves. Place loaves about 4 inches apart on a parchment-lined cookie sheet. Bake for about 25 minutes, remove from oven, and then let cool.

Cut loaves into slices (diagonal) about ½-inch thick. Flip the slices on their sides on the cookie sheet. Bake at 325° Fahrenheit until brown. Turn slices over, and bake the other side in the same manner. Be sure to keep an eye on the chocolate while it's baking. Transfer cookies to wire racks, and cool completely. Makes between two and three dozen, depending on the thickness. Texture should be on the soft side.

Coconut Macaroons

14-ounce package of sweetened shredded coconut
⅔ cup of flour
¼ teaspoon of salt
1⅓ cup of condensed milk (from a 14-ounce can)
2 teaspoons vanilla
1 teaspoon almond extract

Preheat oven to 250° Fahrenheit (not 350). Combine coconut, flour, and salt. Stir in condensed milk and extracts. Drop by tablespoonful onto greased cookie sheets. (Cooking spray works the best.) The cookie dough will change shape such that it will collapse and expand during the baking, therefore requiring at least two inches between the cookies. Bake for 35 minutes. Cool. Can store in plastic bag to soften if desired. Makes about four dozen cookies.

ABOUT THE AUTHOR

Catherine lives in Upstate New York with a male dominated household that consists of her very patient husband, three sons, two cats and dogs. She has wanted to be a writer since the age of eight when she wrote her own version of Cinderella (and fortunately Disney never sued). Catherine holds a B.A. and dual major in English and Performing Arts. She has worn several different hats over the years, including that of secretary, press release writer, newspaper reporter, real estate agent, and most recently auditor. In her spare time she enjoys traveling, shopping, and of course, a good book.

To learn more about Catherine, visit her online at
www.catherinebruns.net

Enjoyed this book? Check out these other novels available in print now from Gemma Halliday Publishing:

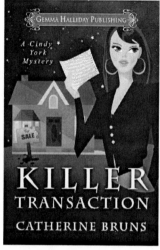

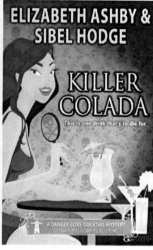

www.GemmaHallidayPublishing.com

CPSIA information can be obtained at www.ICGtesting.com
Printed in the USA
LVOW11s1903080616

491761LV00001B/126/P